Beneath

THE

GRANDSTAND

Beneath

THE

GRANDSTAND

Amy-Alex Campbell

AAC Publishing Australia

Cover design by germancreative
Sketch by Conrad Ruiz

Printed in Australia
First Printing October 27, 2020

ISBN 978-0-6486992-4-8
AAC Publishing Australia
Sydney, Australia

Amy-Alex.Campbell@outlook.com

A catalogue record for this
book is available from the
National Library of Australia

For Ja.
My own personal security guard.
Thanks for putting up with the countless questions,
brainstorming, and rambling.
Love you.

Part One

May 3rd, 2019

1

The stench of BO and stale sweat hung in the air, thicker than the throng of people packed into the vestibule of the train. As the doors opened at Redfern Station, the passengers took a collective gasp and squeezed in tighter together, as more people forced their way into the overcrowded space. Someone elbowed Cameron in his back, and shoved him nose-first into another man's armpit; on his other side, he could feel someone's dick grinding into his hip. Cameron grimaced and managed to turn his face away from the armpit. *The day these people spend $3.95 on some deodorant, I'll have a bloody stroke,* he thought irritably.

With a jerk, the train started rolling slowly towards Central Station. Peak hour on any Sydney train was a nightmare, especially on one of the older trains that were overheated and stunk like dirty leather. Cameron berated himself for taking the 07:00 shift; it was Friday and supposed to be his day off. His last shift had finished at midnight, and with over an hour travel each way, he had been lucky to get three hours sleep.

The train pulled in at the station with a screech and another jerk. Cameron patted his arm to ensure his security license was still firmly in its pouch on his arm, then braced himself. As soon as the doors opened, he was swept with the crowd of commuters onto the platform, and into the tunnel towards the concourse.

Once he reached the concourse, the crowd thinned, and he was able to walk at his own pace again. There was a slight chill in the air; winter was just a few weeks away, and soon that chill would turn into an icy frost. Cameron shivered and walked faster towards the main exit.

He knew better than to even try to catch the light rail that early in the morning. He tapped his Opal card at the barriers, and cut through the park next to the station. It would be much faster to walk the distance than try to squeeze onto another overheated sweatbox.

The park was full of brightly coloured tents, the only shelter that the homeless people had. Cameron felt bad for them; he himself was a bee's dick away from being homeless, and the thought of living on the streets terrified him. With a lurch, he pushed the thoughts from his mind, and picked up his pace.

By the time he got to work, he was flushed from his walk. He desperately needed a coffee, but there was no time. With a miserable sigh, he waited for the large roller doors to grind open.

"Morning. Oh, you're not our regular guard," the duty manager said, beckoning him in.

"Sanjeep's sick, apparently," he replied. "I'm Cameron."

"I'm Lisa. Head over to the service desk, the sign-in and logbooks are over there."

"Thanks," he said, stifling a yawn.

It's only a nine hour shift, he told himself. *At least I can go home afterwards and catch up on some sleep.*

The thought of home made his gut lurch again. He had one week left to find a place to live, or he, too, would be out on the streets. He had enough money saved for a deposit for a cheap place, but the problem with living in Sydney was that cheap just didn't exist.

By the time 11:30 came around, Cameron was busting for a piss and desperate for a coffee. He caught Lisa's eye from across the registers, and pointed towards the back of the store. She nodded, and he made his way to the lunchroom.

He was grateful that most supermarkets had coffee available for staff, and usually didn't mind if the security guards had one during their break. No sooner had he relieved himself and sat down, and his phone rang.

"Hi, Graham, what's up?"

"Hi, mate. We have a problem," his boss replied.

"What now?" Cameron groaned. He knew what was coming.

"We've just had a priority job come up that we have to take," he replied. "It's at minimum a two week job, but could be extended. We need our best on this one, and that means you."

"Where and when?" Cameron asked.

"Stanmore Private Hospital," Graham said. "They had a fire take out a section next to one of the loading docks. They need it guarded so that junkies can't sneak in and steal anything. The tradies will be there rebuilding through the day until around 22:00."

"What time do you need me there?"

"Start at 18:00 tonight, Sarah will relieve you at 06:00."

"Fucking hell. I've had three hours sleep in the last twenty-four hours. I'm on another site already until 16:30, I can't just go home and sleep then come back."

"I know mate, but we need you," Graham pleaded. "You can always come back to the office, have a nap, then head to work from there. I have a replacement on the way already."

Cameron buried his face in his hand for a moment. Not a week went by where he wasn't dicked around mid-shift and asked to save the company's arse.

"You fucking owe me," he sighed. "How soon until my replacement gets here?"

"Asiff is on his way, should be there in thirty," Graham replied. "See you soon."

* * *

The hospital was a hive of activity when Cameron arrived at 17:30. The fire had left a large gaping hole in the side of the building, and from the road he could see Sarah leaning against the wall, bored shitless. She was short and chubby, but strong, and could certainly handle herself against men. Her blonde hair was cut short, making her look butch. Cameron waved and walked over to her.

"Hi, Cam," she yawned. "I see they're screwing you around too."

"Don't even get me started," Cameron grumbled. "If I didn't need the money, I'd tell them to stick it up their arses."

"I know what you mean," she said.

"What am I looking at here?" Cameron nodded towards the burnt-out building.

"Through the day it's not so bad," she replied. "A few people have warned me that this is a bad area at night, though. That shitty building over there is a backpacker hostel, and can get rowdy, so don't let your guard down."

"That's why we've been sent here." Cameron snorted. "You and I are two of the few in this company who don't sleep on the job or steal shit."

"I know, hon. You look like shit by the way."

"I had a nap back at the office. I'll be fine." Cameron shrugged. "Is there anywhere to get coffee around here?"

Sarah pointed down the road.

"There's a 7–Eleven just down there. If you need the loo, call this number for hospital security and ask them to cover you." She handed him a card and yawned again. "At

4

least we get twelve hours between shifts. I can't wait to get home and climb into my nice warm bed."

"Yeah." Cameron felt his stress levels fly through the roof; still no call from the real estate agent.

"You ok, Cam?" Sarah asked.

"What? Oh, no I'm fine," he mumbled. "Just tired."

"If you say so." She looked at him with a raised eyebrow. "I'm here for another ten minutes if you want to go and get your coffee."

"Alright, thanks."

Cameron turned and walked towards the 7–11. The neighbourhood didn't look too bad in the fading light; most of the houses looked respectable. A few homeless people had gathered in an empty carpark for the night, and sat huddled with blankets around their shoulders. They shot him a suspicious look as he passed, and he nodded politely to show that he meant them no harm.

Armed with a jumbo coffee, a donut, and a pack of ham and cheese sandwiches, Cameron headed back to the hospital. Sarah had her car keys in her hand already, eager to fly.

"I guess I'll see you in the morning, then," Cameron said.

"I'll be here," she smiled. "See you then."

He watched as she climbed into her car and drove off with a honk of her horn.

It didn't take long for Cameron to grow bored, but as always, he remained alert and didn't allow himself to become complacent. It was just after midnight when he heard a soft sneeze; he froze, and looked around to find where the sneeze had come from. His eyes fell on a lone figure seated in the small overgrown garden adjoining the hostel. Although the garden was hidden in shadows, a single security light in the shop next door dimly outlined the person. Cameron kept a watchful eye on them, but wasn't too concerned. He remembered the words from his trainer, *"If you leave them alone, they'll leave you alone. Most of the time, that is."* He knew how to spot an unfriendly lurker, and the figure was the least of his worries. Around 05:00, Cameron looked up and noticed they were gone.

Sarah arrived at 05:45 well rested and ready to rock.

"Anything exciting happen?" she asked as she joined him.

"Nothing," Cameron yawned. "Except for knocking off that is."

"Don't you live over at Marrickville?" she asked as he pulled on his backpack.

"Nah, other side of Parramatta." He shrugged. "I'll see you tonight, mate."

* * *

It was 07:30 by the time Cameron made it 'home'. The house looked the same as it always had in the nine years that he'd lived there. What had once been his refuge and happy place was now the last place on Earth that he wanted to be.

He unlocked the front door as quietly as he could, and tiptoed to his room. He could hear Paul in the shower, and breathed a sigh of relief. He locked the bedroom door and climbed out of his uniform.

Cameron looked around what was once the spare room; a single mattress with his blanket and pillow were shoved into the corner, and his suitcase lay open on the floor with his neatly folded clothes. A fresh uniform was hung neatly on a hanger ready for his next shift, and the rest of the room was taken up by stacked boxes full of Paul's shit.

Cameron crawled into bed and set his alarm for 15:00. Seven hours of sleep was a luxury he didn't always get. With a yawn, he settled down and was already drifting off to sleep when another man's voice jolted him awake.

"Thanks for the night, sexy."

"You were wonderful," Paul gushed. "I get off at 5:30 tonight if you want to go out for drinks again."

"How about we skip the drinks and come straight back here?"

"Sounds perfect." The sounds of kissing made Cameron's stomach turn.

"Are you sure *he* won't be here?"

"Like I told you, he works more than he's home. He has until next Saturday to get his worthless arse out of this house." Paul almost spat the words.

"Alright, I just don't want him to walk in and ruin the night."

"Don't worry about it, Josh. I need to get moving, I have to leave in half an hour."

"Alright sexy, I'll see you tonight."

The sound of more kissing, followed by the front door opening and closing, made Cameron's insides turn to lead. He hadn't even moved out yet, and Paul was already fucking someone else. It was little wonder; he was handsome and had some charm about him. Behind closed doors, though, he was nasty and abusive. Cameron had suspected he'd been cheating on him for a while; they hadn't been intimate for longer than he could remember.

"You are nothing without me. If it weren't for me, you would be homeless," Paul had sneered. *"No one will ever love you like I did. You're not even attractive, so it's not like you'll ever find someone else."*

Cameron soon fell asleep with the taunting words of his childhood sweetheart going around and around in his mind.

* * *

Paul was gone by the time Cameron dragged his arse out of bed. He threw his uniform into the machine and forced himself into the shower for a quick wash and shave. As he stared at his reflection in the small mirror, he felt a wave of hopelessness wash over him. He was almost twenty-eight, and had nothing to show for it except for baggy eyes and stress lines. No home, no boyfriend, and almost no belongings. Paul was right. He was a failure.

Cameron looked closer at his face in the mirror. His eyes were puffy and grey from not enough sleep, and his skin looked paler than usual. His light brown hair was a little longer than he liked, but he had no time for a haircut. *"Look at you, you're a mess. You can't even take time out to get your hair done. When are you ever going to grow up, Cameron?"* Paul's words stung as much then as they did when he'd yelled them a year ago.

Cameron sighed and got out of the shower. Once he was dry, he headed back to his room to get ready for work. As he closed the door, the face of his phone lit up with a missed call. He disconnected it from the charger and checked the number; it was the real estate.

"Fuck," he mumbled, and quickly hit redial.

"First House Real Estate, this is Kristy speaking."

"Hi, Kristy, it's Cameron Greenwood. I just missed a call from this number."

"Oh hi, Cameron. I'm just following up to see if you are still looking for a place to rent?"

"Yeah," Cameron said, a little too enthusiastically.

"I still don't have anything available in your price range," she said. "But..."

"But what?" Cameron asked, holding his breath.

"I just finished inspecting an apartment, and the tenants have caused a lot of damage. I've spoken to the landlord and he wants them evicted. So, I *might* be able to offer it to you, but there could be a month's wait."

"I'm going to be homeless as of Saturday," Cameron said, as a wave of anxiety washed over him. "I literally have nowhere to go. What am I going to do for a month?"

"I'm sorry Cameron, it's all I have. It's $235 a week, in Western Sydney, not far from Marsden Park. It's close to the station so it won't be too hard for you to get to work. You know yourself that the average rent is $400 a week anywhere else."

Cameron stood mulling over what she had said. He had tried other agents all around Sydney and none of them had been able to help.

"You know, there's one option you have, if you can afford it, I mean," she said gently, breaking the awkward silence. "I've heard that some of the backpacker hostels offer ridiculously cheap rates. Maybe you could look into staying in a hostel until the apartment is available?"

"Um. How much am I going to have to pay up front to get this place?" he asked.

"Four weeks rent as bond, plus two weeks up front," she replied. "So that's around $1410 if the landlord doesn't increase the rent."

"Ok, put me down as a definite yes," Cameron sighed.

"Done. I'll email you the address. In the meantime, if something else comes up, I'll give you a call."

"Thanks, mate. Bye."

Cameron tossed his phone onto the mattress and quickly got himself dressed. He hadn't ironed his shirt, but he doubted that he'd need to take off his work jumper or jacket at night. He quickly took his freshly washed clothes from the machine and hung them up in his room to dry, helped himself to a glass of water from the tap, and rushed out the door to catch his bus.

The train ride that afternoon was much less crowded than in the mornings. Cameron was lucky enough to get a seat, and spent his time looking for cheap places to stay. He looked at one in Leichardt close to the office, but they wanted $84 per night. He shook his head and kept scrolling.

The hostel opposite the hospital flashed up; $30 for

a double room, or $20 for a shared room of eight. He could afford $140 a week until he was able to move; all he had was a suitcase of clothes to bring, so he didn't need to worry about storing any belongings. Before he could change his mind, he hit the 'Book Now' button and filled in his details.

Welcome to rock bottom, he thought to himself. *Thank god I still have my job.*

* * *

Cameron rolled out of bed at 14:00 on Monday and stumbled into the shower. The stress and anxiety of his predicament had made it hard to fall asleep, despite the fatigue that was always lingering from his deepening depression. He stood under the shower that had been a part of his life for so long, for one final time. *"Your parents didn't want you. I don't want you. Nobody will ever want you. You're a pathetic failure."* Paul's words punched him in the gut. *"This is all your fault. Everything that has ever gone wrong with us was because of you. You brought all of this upon yourself, not me."*

Cameron broke down into tears, and stood sobbing his heart out, with his forehead resting against the tiled wall. The pain of the drawn-out decline of their relationship formed a tight knot in his stomach, and for a moment he felt like giving up.

What have I got to live for? No one would miss me if I were gone. His sobs intensified, until his usual inner-voice of reason kicked in.

If I give up, I'm just proving to him that I am indeed a failure. I can't give him that satisfaction. I need to keep going, to take one breath after another and continue to function. Come on Cameron, there are people out there with much bigger problems than you. You have a job, and in a month, a home. Pull yourself together, man.

It took him a while to get his emotions under control, and rebottle them tightly. He turned off the tap and dried himself off. As though he was in a trance, Cameron wrapped his towel around his waist, then gathered up his shaver, toothbrush, toothpaste, and comb. His mind was made up; it was time to go.

Cameron dressed slowly, then packed away all of his clothes and items in his suitcase and zipped it up. He folded up the blanket and sat it neatly in the middle of the mattress, and sat the pillow on top with a letter.

Dear Paul,
You're right. I am a pathetic failure.
I'm sorry I made your life so miserable. You'll be pleased to know that I am gone from your life forever as of now. I hope your new guy will at least bring you some happiness.
-Cameron.

With an overwhelming feeling of anguish, he sat his house key on top of the letter, and wheeled his case towards the front door. He had thought about taking one last look around the house that he had lived in for a third of his life, but the sick knot in his stomach tightened, threatening to move into his throat. With a deep breath, he stepped outside and closed the door for the last time, and headed for the bus stop.

2

♫ *Hello – Adele* ♪

Armed with a coffee and pie from the station in one hand, and pulling his suitcase along in the other, Cameron made it to work with five minutes to spare. He saw Sarah sitting to the side of the dock on a park bench that wasn't there the previous shift.

"Going on a holiday, huh?" Sarah asked, eyeing his case.

"Having a break, huh?" he shot back, eyeing the seat.

"One of the supervisors told the tradies to sit it out here for us." She shrugged. "They're really impressed by our work."

"Everyone's impressed by our work," Cameron pointed out. "Isn't that why we get so many shifts these days?"

"I know, hon. Are you sure you're alright?" she asked, studying his face again.

"I just have some shit going on at the moment." He shrugged. "Nothing major."

"Cam, I've worked with you for six years now," she said pointedly. "I've never seen you looking this miserable before. What's going on?"

Cameron felt himself tense up; he rarely spoke about his private life, least of all with his colleagues. He certainly wasn't out at work, and didn't plan to be.

"I got into a fight with my roommate and he kicked me out," he muttered. "That's all, really."

"Shit. You've lived there for as long as I've known you. Did he get a girlfriend or something?" she asked.

"Something like that." Cameron shrugged.

"Do you need a place to stay?" she pressed.

"I'm spending a few nights in a hotel nearby so I can catch up on some sleep," he fibbed. "I just need a few good days of rest and I'll be fine again. I did the same when I was working in Newcastle to save travelling. You know how it is."

"Yeah, I know," she said, though she still looked worried. "If you need anything or want to talk, call me, ok?"

"Yeah, righto," Cameron muttered. "You had better go, it's 06:15 already."

"Alright hon, I'll leave you to it. See you in the morning."

Cameron watched her climb into her car and speed away, then stashed his suitcase in a safe spot. He pulled out his phone and sent Graham a quick message.

```
CAMERON: Just letting you know that
I'm moving in around a month. Don't
know when yet, but I'll keep you
updated.

GRAHAM: Damn, is everything ok? Where
are you moving to?

CAMERON: Yeah. Out West near Marsden
Park. Where are you working tonight?

GRAHAM: I'm on site in Parra until
20:00. So many hot birds here.
```

CAMERON: Don't let the staff catch you defiling their BBQ Chooks.

GRAHAM: lol smartarse

Graham was a short and skinny bloke, and as ugly as a hat full of arseholes. Somehow, he always seemed to be picking up women while working the supermarket floors. Graham was often asking Cameron if he'd picked anyone up, but his answer was always no. Cameron was there to work, not to get his dick wet, and given his circumstances, the thought of being with someone made him feel sick. He was better off alone.

* * *

Cameron knew that his streak of nil incidents wouldn't last for long. He was no stranger to dealing with whatever shit came up; he had been a security guard since he was nineteen, and had already faced it all. He had been spat on, punched, threatened with a knife, and stalked. He came across as a badass, and could be intimidating when need be. He wasn't fat, but he was solid, and knew how to handle himself.

The back dock only had a single light on since the tradies had knocked off. Cameron kept himself awake by pacing the length of the truck bays, and eyeing off the backpacker inn. A few people had come and gone, and every now and then he could hear laughter, but the building was mostly quiet.

Around 23:00, Cameron looked up in time to see movement in the garden. The mysterious figure had returned, and sat in the exact same spot as last time. *What on earth are they doing over there?* Cameron wondered.

It was only 01:30 when he heard a group of rowdy people walking along the road from the direction of the station. Cameron yawned and stretched, and turned his attention towards the voices.

There were six of them in the group, obviously drunk, walking on the other side of the road and raising a racket. One of them threw a glass bottle on the ground, and they all laughed when they heard the resulting smash. Cameron stood in the shadows with his hand on his phone, watching their every move. They seemed content in whatever they were doing, and for a moment he thought they would continue on their way.

One of the guys stopped and backed up a step, and said something to the person in the garden. Cameron couldn't quite hear what they said, but their body language showed aggression. The loner stood up and held out their hands.

"I don't want trouble guys." The voice belonged to a young man. He sidestepped the group and tried to walk off in the direction they had come.

"Don't walk away from me, prick!" one of the drunks yelled, grabbing his arm.

"I said I don't want trouble. Please, just leave me alone."

The drunk's fist shot out and punched the loner in the face, knocking him to the ground.

"Hey — back off!" Cameron yelled in his most threatening voice. He started to move towards the group of drunks, puffing out his chest and arms.

"Oh fuck, it's a seccy!" one of them yelled. "Run!"

The group scrambled and ran towards 7–11. Cameron glowered after them, making sure they were gone. A soft groan drew his attention, and he looked down to see the loner sitting up, holding his hand to his head.

"You ok, mate?" Cameron asked.

"Yeah," he mumbled.

Cameron put out his hand, and pulled him to his feet. "Thanks."

The man looked like he was early twenties; he had

dark hair tucked away under a beanie, and a short patchy beard. He was a little shorter than Cameron, and was dressed in a grey hoodie and torn jeans. His big brown eyes were the kind that mirrored the person's soul; their feelings, their mood. These eyes carried a deep sadness that resonated with Cameron's own pain, and for a moment he was mesmerised.

"Um. Can I go now?" Mr Loner asked, breaking Cameron's reverie.

"What? Oh. Yeah," Cameron mumbled and let go of his hand. "You probably should go and get checked out by a doctor. You know, concussion."

"No thanks. Thanks, anyway."

Before Cameron could say anything else, the young man turned and hurried away into the night.

* * *

By the time Sarah arrived to relieve him, Cameron was dead on his feet. He gave her a quick rundown of the night's events, and hurried to get his case.

"Is your hotel far from here?" she asked.

"It's only about a block away," he fibbed. "I can't wait to have a decent sleep for once."

"You definitely need it," she said. "Sweet dreams."

Cameron nodded and turned to cross the street. The tradies were already starting to turn up for another day of hard work. Cameron ducked down the side street next to the hostel, and slipped into the back entrance. He didn't want Sarah to know that he was staying there; his problems were his and his alone.

He opened the door, and the smell of freshly buttered toast wafted under his nose, making his mouth water. People were already up and moving about, getting ready for their day; footsteps from the floor above creaked and groaned, and the sounds of doors slamming echoed through the building.

The walls of the hallway were an off-pink colour, which clashed horribly with the brown and yellow carpet. Cameron followed the hall and turned to his left, and saw the reception desk opposite the staircase. He pulled his wallet from his pocket and stood waiting. Finally, an older lady bustled up to the desk.

"Morning," she said cheerfully. "What can I do for ya?"

"Hi, I'm Cameron," he said politely. "I was supposed to check in last night, but I was running late. The guy I spoke to on the phone said I could come in early this morning."

"No worries, darl, Yousef left me a note to expect you. I'm Maria by the way."

She pulled out a sheet of paper and pointed to a place for him to sign, then fetched a key from a cabinet.

"What's the maximum stay here?" Cameron asked.

"Two weeks usually," she replied. "Do you think you'll need longer?"

"Maybe," Cameron replied. "My apartment is being renovated, and I'm not sure how long it will take."

"If bookings are slow, I don't mind extending a stay," she said. "So long as you are courteous to other guests and don't cause trouble. It will be noisy here, but you should at least be comfortable during your stay."

"I'm usually so exhausted from work that I can sleep through an earthquake." Cameron shrugged. "So long as I can shower and wash my uniform, I'm happy."

"Here is a flyer on unofficial backpacker etiquette. A lot of our guests travel the world staying in places like this, and they have developed their own rules for sharing rooms with strangers. It's quite fascinating, actually. Anyway, come along and I'll show you your dorm."

Cameron followed her up the stairs, earning plenty of strange looks from some of the boarders thanks to his uniform. The floorboards creaked loudly under their feet as they walked.

"Here you are. Just swipe the card to unlock it, like so." She swiped the card and opened the door.

The room had two bunk beds on each wall, pushed end-to-end with four large lockers in between each set of bunks. One person was still asleep, and another guy was standing in his jocks staring at his phone. Cameron quickly looked away.

"Your bed is the bottom bunk over there next to the window. Linen is there, you can put your sheets and pillowcase on yourself. If you need another pillow or blanket, come and see me at reception."

"Ok."

"This locker is yours. The key is with your swipe card. Toilets and showers are down the hall, the kitchen and laundry are downstairs. Make sure you clean up after yourself. I think that's everything."

"Thanks heaps," Cameron said.

"You're welcome, darls. See you around."

Cameron hoisted his case onto his bed and unzipped it wearily. *I guess this is my home for the next few weeks. I may as well unpack and make myself comfortable. At least I get to sleep in a real bed for once,* he thought.

It didn't take long to unpack his stuff into the locker. He slipped the empty case under the bed, and looked around the room. The guy in the jocks had managed to put on some pants, and sat on one of the lower bunks staring at his phone still. The other guy had sat up and was rubbing his eyes. Cameron picked out a pair of shorts and an old tee to wear to bed, and turned his back to change. *Fuck modesty,* he thought. If he were in his own room, he would be sleeping naked.

Once he'd made his bed and plugged his phone in to charge, he finally crawled in under the blanket and pulled it over his head. The bed was surprisingly comfy. Cameron yawned; the image of the man he'd helped flashed before his eyes, and he soon drifted into a deep sleep.

Cameron woke with a start to the sound of his alarm tone blaring. For a second, he wondered where the hell he was. He reached out and turned off the alarm, and looked around. The dorm was empty except for him.

It was 16:00; eight hours of deep sleep was a rarity indeed. Cameron yawned and pulled himself out of bed, and peeked out of the window. To his surprise, he was directly opposite the hospital's loading dock; he could see Sarah talking to a group of tradies.

It was raining heavily outside, and Cameron sighed. It was going to be a long, wet, night.

Cameron didn't see the mysterious loner that night; he stood huddled in the dock, trying to stay warm. He was lucky that he had his thick waterproof work jacket, but his pants were thin black slacks, and they didn't warm much. Around 21:30, a car pulled into the dock, and with a sigh, Cameron dashed into the rain to investigate.

To his surprise, Graham climbed out of the car, brandishing a large umbrella with the company logo. For such a short guy, he looked ridiculous.

"How's it going, mate?" Graham asked, stretching the brolly higher so Cameron could duck underneath.

"It's going," Cameron grated. "Did you just get off?"

"Yeah, been over at Campsie," Graham yawned. "Barry needs me back in the office tonight, we have some bullshit audit coming up."

"Better hope the auditors don't uncover half of the dodgy shit you fuckers pull," Cameron said. "I don't think they'd like it if they knew we guards go a month or two without a day off."

"It's not me, mate, it's fucking Barry. He's got everyone wound up so tight, but won't hire more decent guards."

"Yeah, I know. He's lucky he has you, Sarah, and me to hold the place afloat."

"Yeah, mate. Anyways, how are you off for logbooks and report pads?" Graham asked.

"I could do with a new pocket log. This one is almost full." Cameron pulled a small dog-eared logbook from his pocket and flicked through to the incident from the night before. He had dubbed the mystery man as Mr Loner.

"I'll get you some from the car."

Graham opened the back door and rummaged around for a moment.

"Do you have more of those brollies?" Cameron asked.

"Yeah, we have two or three back in the office. You want one?"

Cameron plucked the umbrella from Graham's hand.

"I just got one, thanks." He managed a smirk.

"Fucking arsehole," Graham sighed. "Oh, you've been paid, I did the banking today."

"In that case, can you mind the fort for ten mins?" Cameron asked.

"Fine."

Cameron walked down to the 7–11 and bought two large coffees, and two pies. He bought a few more things while he was there, then hurried back to Graham.

"Shit, you bought out the whole store," he said, eyeing the bag of items.

"It's not like I get time out during the day to do this shit," Cameron said.

He handed Graham a coffee and looked around; no one was out in the rain, even the rough sleepers had moved on to find shelter. Still no Mr Loner.

"Right, I need to get moving," Graham said. "I'll probably crash at the office tonight, so if you need anything, yell."

"No worries." Cameron held up the brolly and walked him back to the car.

"Cya mate, thanks for the coffee."

Graham pulled the door shut, and Cameron dashed back undercover as he drove away. Sure, Graham was a pain in the arse, but he was a good bloke. Barry, the big boss, was the one who was responsible for all the shift changes and drama within the company.

Cameron leaned back against the wall of the dock and tucked into his pies. Oh, what he would do for a decent meal for once.

3

By Friday afternoon, Cameron was getting used to living in the shared accommodation. He had to admit to himself that staying opposite the site had been a good call. Despite being woken by someone vacuuming on Thursday, he was sleeping better, and had a few extra hours up his sleeve each day to manage his life. The other good thing was that the showers and laundry room were usually empty when he needed them after waking up.

Cameron made his way to the station to catch a train to Ashfield; he had worked in the supermarket there a few times, and knew that there was a barber in the centre. It was still raining, albeit lightly. He had ditched his uniform for his grey hoodie and his only pair of jeans. It felt strange dressing so casually after weeks of being in his slacks, business shirt, and heavy woollen jumper.

As he waited for his train, he looked across at the other platforms, watching the people staring at their phones like zombies. His eyes scanned the crowd, taking in every detail; years of being in security had him always on the lookout for theft and dodgy behaviours, a skill he couldn't switch off.

With a start, his eyes landed on someone familiar; dark grey beanie and hoodie, short dark beard. Mr Loner looked up just as Cameron's train pulled in at the platform, blocking him from view. By the time Cameron climbed to the top level and looked over, he was gone.

Who is he? Cameron wondered. *Who sits in a garden at night for hours like that?*

He sat pondering about the man, his curiosity distracting him from his own misery for a while. He found himself wanting to know the young man's story, to know what had caused the pain in those big brown eyes…

Cameron received a pleasant surprise when he checked his bank balance at the ATM; he had earnt a little over $1200 that last week. He calculated that he'd worked seventy hours in seven days; his next pay would hopefully be more, seeing as he would have worked eighty-four hours. After paying his bills, though, the balance was still depressing. *At least I have enough left for food, coffee, and a few luxuries,* he thought.

He treated himself to a haircut and Pad Thai, and sat savouring his first decent meal in almost two weeks. He thought back over his week; everything felt so surreal. It had only been a few days since he'd moved out, but it felt like it had been so much longer. Sure, the pain was still there, but he had it bottled up so tightly that it wasn't in the front of his mind at every waking minute. He was sure that if he pretended it wasn't there, it would go away on its own in time.

* * *

Much to his disappointment, Sarah wasn't at the site that night. He was greeted instead by Kulwinder, one of the guards that was always staring at his phone and letting people get away with shit. Cameron had seen him let a loaded trolley of groceries walk out of a supermarket under his nose once. Luckily, Cameron had been early for his shift, and was able to apprehend the thief.

"Hello," Kulwinder said happily.

"Hi, mate," Cameron shook his hand. "Anything to report?"

"Nothing today," he replied.

"Nothing ever happens through the day, anyway," Cameron said. "You may as well go."

"Thankyou, thankyou." Kulwinder made the namaste gesture, and smiled again. "See you."

Cameron bowed his head respectfully and watched him walk towards the station. Good or shit guard, Cameron was always polite and respected their customs. He was used to working with Indians, Pakistanis, and people from the Middle East; Sydney was a multicultural place, after all.

Cameron knew better than to hope for a quiet night on a Friday. He could hear the backpackers across the road laughing and yelling and carrying on in the dorms, despite the no alcohol rule. He wasn't too worried though, they would be settled down and hung over by the time he got to bed.

There was a lot more foot traffic to and from the station, but once midnight rolled around, the streets became quiet except for the hostel. Cameron took to his usual pacing to pass the time. *I should get a FitBit and see how many steps I do in a shift*, he thought. *I'd probably wear it out as fast as my shoes.*

Around 02:30, Cameron called the hospital security guys to cover him, and dashed inside for a quick loo break. Just as he resumed his pacing, his phone started blaring in his pocket, scaring the shit out of him. He pulled it out and froze; he was pretty sure he could feel the blood draining from his face.

Incoming video call — Paul.

Cameron stared at his screen and let it ring out. The familiar pains in his stomach returned as a wave of anxiety washed over him. Just as he was about to slide it back into his pocket, another call came through. Cameron frowned, and with shaking fingers, he accepted the call.

Paul's face appeared on his screen; it looked as though he was at a nightclub.

"What the fuck do you want?" Cameron hissed.

"It's nice to hear from you too." Paul pouted his lips. He was as pissed as a newt.

"I don't want to hear from you, ever," Cameron snapped. "Do us both a favour and lose my number, ok?"

"Don't be like that Cammy," Paul laughed.

Cameron cringed; he hated that nickname.

"Seriously, why are you calling me this late? It's almost 03:00."

"Can't you use AM and PM like normal people?" Paul asked. "Anyways, believe it or not, I miss you. I didn't think you would leave so soon."

"Let me guess, your new root has figured you out already and moved on?"

"No need to be snarky." Paul's face hardened. "Don't forget, I took you in and gave you a place to stay for all those years. We used to be in love."

Cameron felt his anger bubble to the surface; once upon a time, he would have buckled under Paul's guilt trips, but not this time.

"Get your fucking hand off it, Paul," he said angrily. "You have done nothing but fuck up my life since that first day I moved in."

"I was going to ask if you wanted to come back, but I don't think I will now."

"You fucking arsehole!" Cameron yelled, losing it. "You kicked me out, remember? Thanks to you, I'm homeless. Thanks to you, I'm $50k in debt. What gives you the idea that I would even want to come back? No, I have already sunk to rock bottom, I'm not giving you any more satisfaction."

"This was all your fault in the first place," Paul snarled. "You're just as pathetic as ever. I don't know why I even bothered to call."

"No, you're the pathetic one! You're a fucking narcissist, and you're not going to get any more pleasure from my pain!"

Cameron ended the call and threw his phone as hard as he could into the darkness.

He buried his face in his hands; he was shaking uncontrollably and felt as though his legs were going to collapse under him. An unpleasant taste rose in his throat; he staggered across to the side garden and threw up in the bushes as his anxiety took over.

You fucking idiot. Why did you have to answer his call? You've just given him more ammunition to treat you like dirt, he berated himself, as he brought up more of his stomach.

Cameron staggered back to the dock and cleaned himself up in the small sink up on the landing; he washed out his mouth and had a quick drink. It tasted like bile. *Fucking gross. How could I have been so stupid? What a waste of Pad Thai.*

He made his way over to Sarah's bench, and sat with his face buried in his hands. The image of Paul filled his thoughts, sneering as he always did when Cameron stood up for himself. Without warning, his eyes filled with tears, and he broke down into a quivering mess.

He didn't know how long he sat there in the shadows, crying his heart out. A cloud of darkness enveloped him, as though a part of him had died and would never feel happiness again. He was a failure, Paul was right. *I should just give up on life. I have nothing left to live for.*

The sound of footsteps behind him would usually have him spinning around, but in that moment, he wished it were someone with malicious intent. Cameron continued to sob into his hands, unable to stop.

A hand came out of nowhere and patted him on the shoulder, almost hesitantly. Cameron didn't move, he couldn't. Someone sat next to him and rested their hand firmly on his shoulder.

"Your ex is a real jerk," a young man's voice said quietly. "He really did a number on you."

Cameron managed a nod.

"So that's why a security guard, who spends most of his life at work, is living out of a backpacker's hostel instead of renting somewhere. How did you get into so much debt?"

Whoever it was had clearly been listening to his phone call. Cameron said nothing, and worked on getting his sobs under control.

"It's a long story," he managed.

"I have all night, and so do you. Spill."

Cameron crossed his arms on top of his legs, and stared down at his feet. Had he not felt so vulnerable, he would have told the man to piss off, yet for some reason the words tumbled from his mouth. The man's hand shifted from his shoulder to the middle of his back, which felt oddly comforting.

"Around three months ago, he borrowed my car without asking. He got into an accident and totalled mine and another car. A BMW."

"No insurance?" the man asked.

"I had third party insurance, but it only covered me as the driver, no one else. The other guy didn't have insurance, he had literally just bought it. It was Paul's fault, so the entire bill got sent to me."

"He caused the accident though, so why didn't he pay for it?"

"Because legally, it's my car, my responsibility who drives it, therefore my expense."

Cameron could feel himself trembling as the horrible

memories resurfaced.

"You should have gone fully comprehensive like I told you! You are so irresponsible; this is your fault and you need to deal with the consequences! I'm not paying one cent."

"Man, what a jerk. What did you ever see in him?"

"Dad died when I was twelve. Mum took her own life when I was sixteen. She couldn't cope without Dad anymore. I always blamed myself." Cameron shuddered. "Rather than go into foster care, Paul and his family took me in — we were childhood sweethearts I guess — and when we finished school, we moved into a place together. I have no one else."

"Damn, sorry to hear. That's harsh. How long do you plan to stay at the hostel?"

"It's only temporary." Cameron shrugged. "I have it booked for two weeks. I might have a place to rent in around a month, but until then, I'm homeless."

"Well there you go, that's something to look forward to and feel better about." The man elbowed him gently. "You know, I've come to realise something."

"What's that?" Cameron asked after a pause.

"Rock bottom is different for everyone. It could be a breakup for one person, a massive gambling debt, drugs, or living in the streets for another. No matter what it is, though, everyone's rock bottom is just as valid as the next. The only way to survive is to fight for the life you want. If you don't fight, you lose hope, and without hope, you have nothing to fight for."

Cameron sat mulling over the words. The man was right; he had something to hope for. He had to keep fighting.

The stranger stood and held something under Cameron's nose. It was his phone, undamaged except for a smear of grass and dirt across the screen. He took it slowly and looked up at the man.

"You!"

Mr Loner was looking down at him with a gentle smile that spread up his cheeks and into his eyes. Before Cameron could get over his astonishment and speak, Mr Loner had turned and walked away.

4

Cameron spent the rest of his weekend mulling over Mr Loner's words. He replayed the scenario over and over in his mind, all the while watching the shadows and hoping he would show again. He had beaten himself up for failing to at least get the guy's name.

On Monday morning, he was pleased to see Sarah back at work.

"Welcome back." He managed a slight curl of his lip. "How did you manage to get time off?"

"Time off, my arse. I had to guard a faulty generator while it received emergency repairs." She snorted. "You're looking a little better."

"I told you I needed sleep." Cameron shrugged.

"Have I missed anything exciting?"

"Nothing really," he said. "I was talking to one of the hospital guards last night, he thinks the job is going to go a little longer. Something about delays or some shit."

"I don't mind this site to be honest," she said. "I've had worse, put it that way."

"I hear ya." Cameron yawned. "I guess I'll see you tonight."

*

Monday night was much like any other night for Cameron, although it was much colder and windy. By midnight, his fingers felt as though they were frozen. He hadn't slept as well that day; he had been woken twice from a deep sleep, and was feeling tired. He pulled out his phone and messaged the hospital's security phone.

```
CAMERON: Hi guys. Would you mind
relieving me for 10?


SM HOSP SEC: Yeah mate, Bruce is
coming.
```

As soon as Bruce arrived to relieve him, Cameron dashed to the loo for a quick piss, then made his way back to the dock. Bruce stood out in the truck bay puffing on a cigarette, and scrolling through his social media. As Cameron walked down the ramp, the hairs on the back of his head prickled, as though he were being watched. He glanced around at the shadows almost by instinct. A familiar lone figure sat in the garden across the road, watching him.

"I'm just ducking down to 7–Eleven. Want anything?" Cameron asked, still eyeing Mr Loner.

"Nah mate, she'll be right."

Cameron turned and walked down the road. Only one rough sleeper was in the carpark that night, huddled in his blanket. His heart gave a slight lurch; the poor man's eyes looked vacant in the dim light. He knew from his training to never approach someone, unless they indicated they wanted to be approached. He stepped into the 7–11, and bought two large coffees, and two pies.

Mr Loner was still in the garden when he made it back to the loading dock.

"You thirsty or something?" Bruce asked, nodding at the two drinks.

"You could say that," Cameron replied. "I don't have a cosy office out here like you guys."

"Fair call," Bruce grinned. "Let us know if you need another break."

Cameron watched as Bruce disappeared back into the hospital, then turned to face the garden. He held up the coffees and beckoned, then walked purposefully over to Sarah's bench and sat down. He knew Mr Loner was watching him, and hoped that he would come over and say hi.

After an agonising minute, Mr Loner stood up and looked around, then shuffled across the street. Cameron wasn't the shy type, but seeing the familiar stranger walk towards him suddenly made him a little nervous.

Mr Loner sat down wordlessly on the seat, shivering. As Cameron handed him a coffee, their fingers brushed, sending a light jolt through his arm. They sat in silence, warming their frozen hands on their hot drinks.

"Do you have a name?" Cameron asked after a while.

"Everyone has a name," he said.

They sat in silence again, sipping at their coffees.

"Dalcian," he said finally.

"I'm Cameron."

"Ex still being a jerk?" he asked.

"I blocked his number." Cameron shrugged. "He can be a jerk on his own time."

"There ya go."

"What's your story?" Cameron asked.

Dalcian shook his head.

"There's not much to tell, really," he said. "Sleep by day, survive by night. Gotta keep fighting, right?"

"Right. How long have you been living like this?"

"Since I was sixteen, so three years." He shrugged. "Similar story to yours I guess."

"Did you lose your parents too?" Cameron asked.

"No. I ran away," Dalcian replied with a shudder.

"Why?"

His eyes seemed to zone out for a second, his thoughts far away. For a moment he looked haunted, as though he were terrified. Dalcian blinked and shook his head.

"I was sick of being his punching bag," he said quietly. "I don't talk about it."

"Sorry."

Cameron leaned back and stretched out his legs.

"Hungry?" he asked, offering him one of the pies.

Dalcian hesitated for a moment, then accepted the bag.

They sat in silence again as they ate their pies. Cameron brushed the crumbs off his uniform and took another mouthful of coffee.

"How does one so young survive on the streets?" he asked finally.

"There's a lot of support out there for those who genuinely want the help," Dalcian replied. "There's a café I go to that lets me work for a meal and a shower. The owner is really nice, she gives me some extra shifts for cash when she can."

"That's good of her," Cameron said.

"Yeah. Sleeping is tricky, as you can't defend yourself while you're out of it. The trick is to sleep during the day in a park, and stay awake at night when the predators are lurking. I have a spot that's well hidden and relatively safe. It's hard to find a place to hang out at during the night, though. Most places are guarded, and we're made to move on."

"If I hadn't been able to afford the hostel, I would have been out there too," Cameron said. "I honestly don't think I could survive it like you."

"The secret is to never trust anyone. It's better to be alone than to make friends. Those people are desperate for a meal or shelter, and will quickly turn on you to get what they want."

"I bet you get lonely."

"Yeah. I talk to some of the people at the café, but once our shift is over, we go our separate ways."

"I guess it's the same with my work. I talk to people every day, sometimes we have a laugh or whatever. At the end of the day, though, they're not my friends."

"I know what you're saying," Dalcian nodded.

Cameron stared into the darkness. He felt a warmth grow inside him at the thought that someone understood.

"Thanks for the other night, by the way. Those guys would have killed me." Dalcian shot him a smile.

"Why did they have a go at you?" Cameron asked.

"Who knows?"

"Well, thank you for the other, other night too."

They sat in silence again, each lost in their own thoughts.

"How much longer will you be working here?" Dalcian asked after a while.

"Another week and a half maybe," Cameron replied. "After that, I could be sent anywhere."

"How long have you been doing security?" he asked, looking closer at Cameron's uniform.

"Since I was nineteen," Cameron replied. "As soon as I finished school, I needed to work. The industry always needs guards."

"So what, ten years?"

"Geez, thanks," Cameron sighed. "Almost nine. I'm twenty-eight in a few weeks."

"Have you ever been injured at work?"

The rest of the night flew, as Cameron told him stories of his years in security. Dalcian sat listening to his every word, his eyes widening when Cameron described some of the fights he had gotten into or broken up.

"You're crazy," he said after a while. "I don't think I could do what you do."

"It's not for everyone," Cameron agreed.

"Crazy, but brave."

A smile crept into Dalcian's face. He unzipped his hoodie, then reached in and pulled out a small sketchbook. He flicked through some pages, then held it out. A comic scene depicted the incident from the other night, including a 'Whack!' where Dalcian's character had been punched. Cameron's character was portrayed like a superhero, though slightly more generous in the muscle department.

"You drew this?" Cameron asked, eyeing his new friend.

"Yeah. They're not that great, but they keep me occupied I guess."

"Mate, these are awesome. You have so much talent."

"Really?" Dalcian didn't look so sure.

"I wouldn't say so if I didn't mean it." Cameron stifled a yawn and looked at his phone. "Bloody hell, it's 04:45 already."

"04:45? Is that army time?" Dalcian asked.

"Yeah. It's used widely in security too."

"I never understood it," Dalcian admitted.

"It's easy. To convert the time between noon and midnight, you add 12. So 1 p.m. is 13:00, 5 p.m. is 17:00. To convert it back, just remove 12. That's how I learnt it, anyway."

"Oh, I see. The night sure went quickly," Dalcian said. "I need to get going."

"My offsider will be here in under an hour," Cameron nodded.

Dalcian shoved his sketchbook back into his hoodie and zipped it up to his neck.

"Thanks for the coffee and pie." He smiled, almost shyly.

Cameron felt his own face break into a smile; the first smile he'd had in three months. It felt strange on his face, almost foreign.

"I'll be here tomorrow night if you want to join me," he said hopefully.

"I'll keep that in mind. Who knows where the night will take me?" Dalcian leant over and kissed Cameron lightly on the cheek, and stood up. "You look cute when you smile. G'night."

The smile didn't leave him for the rest of the morning. When Sarah arrived at 05:45, she caught sight of his face, and looked him up and down suspiciously.

"What happened?" she demanded.

"What? Nothing," Cameron replied, trying to look normal.

"You look as though you got a blowjob in the bushes," she smirked.

"C'mon, you know me better than that," he groaned. "I was chatting to some dude and we had a good laugh, that's all," he fibbed.

"Whatever. See you tonight, mate."

"Cya."

Cameron was still smiling when he climbed into bed. His cheek still felt warm where Dalcian had kissed him, and he lay there for a while with his hand resting on the spot, picturing his smile, his eyes…

The warmth spread from his cheek down to between his legs, and his dormant unloved dick twitched to life. Cameron's eyes shot open; he hadn't even thought about touching it, nor had it moved, for months, and now it was coming to life with a vengeance.

With a yawn, he rolled over onto his side and willed himself to sleep. He wasn't ready for *that* yet.

* * *

Cameron's sleep was interrupted by the obnoxious sound of his phone ringing. He rolled over with a groan and fumbled to answer it.

"What?" he murmured.

"Sorry to wake you, mate. Can you talk?" Graham asked.

"Mhmm." Cameron rolled onto his back and managed to open his eyes.

"You're moving over towards Marsden Park, yeah?" he asked.

"Mhmm."

"One of our sites over that way needs a guard to cover a shift this arvo. Marsden Park Council, 13:45 til 22:00. We've got no one else who's inducted on that site." He paused for a moment. "The only way we can get around it is by throwing someone a training shift, and do the induction that way."

"You want me to go and get inducted at a site, for one shift?" Cameron yawned. "Can't you just send a ring-in?"

"We've just put in a tender for a contract while they undergo a major upgrade. If they secure the funding, that is. Early planning stuff. If you do this now, I can send you there if and when the job starts. It'll be twelve-hour night shifts."

"When does it start?"

"Around October, expected until March."

"What time is it now?" Cameron groaned.

"11:30. It should give you time to get there by 13:45." Graham had an edge in his voice, which Cameron knew meant there was more.

"And?" he grumbled.

"You'll need to get back to Stanmore by midnight. I have a ring-in covering you, but he's useless."

"For fuck's sake! I need to go now then, or I won't make it."

"Thanks mate, I owe you one."

"Whatever." Cameron hung up the call and groaned. "Fuck!"

He looked up the public transport planner, and groaned again. The only way he was going to get there on time was if he caught a cab or Uber once he reached Western Sydney. He quickly dressed and wiped down his shoes, and made sure he looked respectable. He was glad he'd at least ironed his shirt the previous day. He paired it with his woollen vest; council and office sites were usually uncomfortably overheated.

Cameron checked that he had everything he needed, and headed out the door. He had just enough time to buy a jumbo coffee from the station before his train came, then sat staring into space out the window. His phone dinged in his pocket, interrupting his music and making him jump.

```
SARAH: Did I just see you walking
towards the station?

CAMERON: Yeah. Fucking arseholes are
sending me to Marsden Park for an 8
hour, then back to Stanmore to finish
off the second half of my regular
shift.

SARAH: That's shit, hon. Did you get
much sleep before he called?

CAMERON: 5 hours. I've had less.

SARAH: Yeah. I'll see you tomorrow,
then.
```

5

The Marsden Park Council was a large imposing building that had been built around nine years ago. One of Cameron's first security shifts had been in one of the department stores in the nearby Westfield, and he remembered that the library had only just opened when he was there. The Westfield was only two years older, and the area had grown considerably since he'd been there last.

Cameron arrived at the council building with just five minutes to spare. He hurried inside, and almost bumped into the security supervisor.

"Ah, Cameron Greenwood?" he asked, putting out his hand.

Cameron shook it firmly and nodded.

"Frank. Let's go and get you signed in, and we'll get started. Have you done access control before?"

"Many times," Cameron nodded.

He followed Frank past a meeting room with a glass wall; a bunch of people were sitting around a table, and a taller well-dressed man with glasses was giving a presentation. Cameron shrugged and hurried to keep up with Frank as he strode towards the security office.

"You'll be two-up with me this afternoon. Usually, you and your offsider take in turns to patrol the library and council ends, and cross over in the middle like a figure of eight," Frank explained. "It's all the basic shit; make sure no one is sneaking into staff only areas, ensure teens aren't bonking in the fire escapes, that sort of thing."

Cameron nodded and stifled a yawn. It wasn't his first rodeo; he knew what he was doing. *Just get the fuck on with it,* he thought.

The only thing that got him through the shift was the thought of seeing Dalcian that night. He felt drawn to the young man; despite living on the streets, he still had an innocence about him. Cameron had never spoken so openly to someone before, and it had felt good to do so. Dalcian hadn't made fun of him for his mini breakdown the other night either, whereas Paul would have yelled at him to shut the fuck up.

Thankfully, after each patrol and door check, Cameron was offered coffee and biscuits. Once the council and library closed at six, their patrols shifted to perimeter checks. They let the people from the meeting out at 19:00, then spent the rest of the shift talking shit and drinking more coffee.

The library was stifling hot as he predicted, and he was soon sweating in uncomfortable places. *Hurry up 22:00, I just want to get the fuck out of here.*

* * *

Cameron struggled to stay awake on his train back to Stanmore. The carriage was overheated, which made him drowsier, but at least he could sit down. He slipped on his headphones and cranked up some music to help keep him awake. Despite his age, he loved older music, especially Roy Orbison; it was his go-to whenever he needed a cheer up.

He realised with a start that it was Tuesday; he had

been staying in the hostel for a week already. One week of being free from Paul's torment. He was far from over the hurt and pain, but he had to admit that he had been coping a little better lately.

He shifted his bag from his lap to the floor and grimaced; eight hours of walking around the council and library building had made him sweat between the legs, and he was sporting painful chafing on his inner thighs. He longed for a warm shower and to stretch out in bed.

By the time he got to Strathfield to change trains, Cameron also realised that he hadn't eaten all day, except for the few biccies he'd nibbled on in the security office. His belly rumbled rudely, reminding him of his poor eating habits. Had it not been for all the walking he did, he figured he'd be as fat as a walrus from all the pies and takeaway food that he lived off. Even when things had been ok with Paul, he rarely had the time to eat at home.

Cameron headed down the ramp to the concourse and ducked through the barriers, then made his way to a late-night pizza place that he'd been to many times. Wherever he worked, he knew where to get the best food at any hour.

The pizza place was open, and was empty except for the person behind the counter he didn't recognise. There were some ready-made slices of pizza on display, and he eyed them for a moment, pondering his choices.

"Mama Mia, Cameron my darling!" a woman's voice called out.

Cameron looked up in time to be swept into a big hug by Sofia, the owner's wife.

"Hello Sofia, long time no see," Cameron said, accepting her kiss on his cheek.

"I haven't seen you for long time, darling. How have you been?" she gushed.

"Overworked as usual," he replied. "Boss is still sending me here, there, and everywhere."

"Are you working here?" she asked, pointing her thumb towards the small shopping mall by the station.

"Nah, I'm at Stanmore for a bit. Just waiting for my train."

"How long do you have?" she asked.

Cameron checked the time on his phone.

"Twenty-six minutes," he replied.

"You've lost weight," she tutted. "You're not looking after yourself. I'll get Massimo to make you a fresh pizza."

"You don't have to—" Cameron started.

"MASS!" Sofia started yelling orders in Italian, and her husband scurried from the back to get working. He caught Cameron's eye, and his face lit up with a big smile.

"We no see you for long time," he called. "How you been?"

Cameron stood chatting to Massimo and Sofia. A year or so ago, he had walked in at precisely the right time, when someone was getting ready to assault Mass. Cameron had managed to diffuse the situation, and ever since, Mass and Sofia had adored him.

It wasn't long until the pizza was ready. Cameron took a bottle of Fanta from the fridge and pulled out his wallet.

"Don't take so long to come and see us next time, darling," Sofia said as she swiped Cameron's card. "Now get a move on, don't miss your train."

* * *

Mr Singh was sitting on the dock, talking to someone on his phone when Cameron arrived. He held up his hand to indicate not to rush the call, and sat his pizza and bottle of Fanta on top of a milk crate. He dashed to the loo; he had drunk too much coffee, yet at the same time, not nearly enough.

Mr Singh had finished his call by the time Cameron rejoined him on the dock. Mr Singh was not the man's real name, but had insisted on people within the company calling him that, as his real name was hard to pronounce. He was a nice enough guy, but he was another one of those guards that paid more attention to their phone than what was going on around him.

"Hi, mate," Cameron said, offering his hand.

"Hello, Cameron," Mr Singh said, shaking it firmly. "How have you been?"

"Good, mate. Anything happen?"

"Nothing to report," Mr Singh replied.

"Heading home or to another shift?" Cameron asked.

"Home for a bit. My next shift is at six in the morning."

"Alright then, Mr Singh, I'll see you around."

"See you."

There was no sign of Dalcian lurking in the shadows. Cameron couldn't help feeling disappointed. *Maybe he saw Mr Singh and thought I'm not working tonight,* he thought. He sat down on the bench with a sigh; he was too sore to patrol tonight. He sat the pizza next to him on the seat and took a slice. Massimo had made his favourite: supreme with extra pineapple, no anchovies or olives. *The anti-pineapple-on-pizza people would really hate me for this,* he thought.

Cameron sat staring across the dock, singing the words of *California Blue* in his head and chewing his pizza slowly. The lyrics of that song spoke deeply to him, as though it had been written just for him.

A soft step to his left made his head whip around and his body tense. Dalcian stood eyeing him with a smile, and he sat down softly on the other side of the pizza.

"You're jumpy tonight," he noted.

"In this job, I have to be," Cameron said. "There are a lot of people who would love to stick a knife in my back."

"I hear ya. I thought you'd stood me up."

"My boss dicked me around." He gestured to the pizza. "Help yourself."

Dalcian took a slice and sat picking off the chunks of pineapple; Cameron wordlessly took them and added them to his own slice.

"I took a paid shift at the café today," Dalcian said. "My boss reckons I should do a barista course."

"Is that something you want to do?" Cameron asked.

"Not really. But it means more paid shifts and I'll be more employable. I don't have a photo ID yet, which makes everything so much harder."

"Damn, just about everything is impossible without ID," Cameron mused. "Could you maybe reach out to your family for your birth certificate or something?"

"Out of the question." Dalcian frowned and shook his head. "I'm a missing person for a reason. He'll kill me if he ever finds me, and I'm not exaggerating."

"Oh. I'm sorry." Cameron paused for a moment. A part of him wanted to know the full story, to find out who *he* was, but he knew he had to respect Dalcian's boundaries. He changed the subject. "If you could choose any job or career in the world, what would you do?"

"I'd draw and publish comics," Dalcian said wistfully. "I'd love to move to the country someday, and focus on my drawing. What about you? What are your dreams?"

"I never really thought about it," Cameron admitted. "A job with regular hours in one location would be nice."

"Surely you have some wild dream, though?" Dalcian pressed.

"All I want right now is to be debt free, in my own home, and happy."

Cameron opened the bottle of Fanta and offered it to Dalcian; he took a deep swig and burped.

"Ok then, what makes you happy?" Dalcian asked, handing the bottle back.

"Let's see. Music." Cameron took a swig of Fanta and let out a burp of his own. "Pineapple on pizza. Sleep. Guys who aren't jerks."

"Am I a jerk?"

"I've known you for what, five minutes? So far I haven't noticed the jerk-gene in you."

"Well that's comforting." Dalcian smiled. "For what it's worth, I don't think you're a jerk."

Cameron's bladder decided to announce that once again, it was full. He groaned inwardly at the thought of having to summon the hospital security guys.

"I'll be back in a sec," he said.

Cameron ducked into a dark corner and relieved himself. It wasn't the first time, nor would it be the last. Just about every security site had a dark corner that was used as a urinal. He shook himself dry and tucked it away with a satisfied sigh.

"I hope the cameras didn't catch that," Dalcian smirked when Cameron returned from washing his hands.

"There's no cameras there, or here." Cameron pointed. "They capture pretty much everything in the lit-up area and the entrances."

"So…there's no way you can get in trouble for talking to me?"

"Fuck 'em," Cameron said. "So long as I'm doing my job, I'm fine."

"What if I did this?"

Cameron turned to look at him questioningly, and was met with a light kiss on his lips. Cameron's stomach fluttered, and he felt his cheeks flush. He was glad they were in the darkness so Dalcian couldn't see the other reaction he had on his body.

"Um…"

"Sorry, I shouldn't have done that," Dalcian apologised quickly. He stuffed his hands in his pockets and looked at his feet as though he were embarrassed.

"I-it's ok, I don't mind." Cameron's heart was pounding in his chest. He suddenly craved Dalcian's lips on his, to be kissed as though he mattered.

"I've never kissed anyone before," Dalcian admitted. "Properly, I mean."

"There's nothing wrong with that," Cameron said. He so wanted a proper kiss…

"You said music makes you happy," Dalcian said, changing the subject abruptly. "Tell me what music you like."

The rest of the night was spent talking about music and bands, songs and styles. Cameron's craving didn't go away, but he was a gentleman. He wasn't sure if Dalcian was being cheeky or impulsive. Deep down, Cameron was scared of being hurt again. *I don't want to do anything to scare him away or risk our friendship. He'll have to make the first move if there is to be a first move.*

Cameron was glad he had someone to talk to; the bond they shared from being homeless and alone had brought them closer together. When Dalcian was around, he felt happy, no longer alone.

05:00 came around way too quickly.

"I need to get going," Dalcian said, almost reluctantly. "Do you think you'll be working here tomorrow?"

"I hope so," Cameron said. "I don't suppose you have a phone?"

Dalcian shook his head.

"If I did, it would just get stolen. It's safer to not have things of value."

"Understandable. I guess I'll see you around, then."

Dalcian leaned over hesitantly, and kissed Cameron on his lips, ever so softly.

"Night, Cameron," he whispered.

"Night, night."

6

Cameron's elation that lingered after his night with Dalcian quickly waned and turned to worry. The next few nights, Dalcian didn't show. Cameron's anxiety skyrocketed, and found himself worrying that something bad had happened to him. He missed their long talks; everything seemed so much easier to deal with when Dalcian was around.

By Friday night, the weather turned sour; it was icy cold and bucketing down. Cameron stood huddled in the dock, breathing on his hands, and trying to stay warm. It was almost time to break out the winter woollies for night shifts.

The thought of Dalcian out there in the cold, all alone, made him worry even more. He had no idea where the boy went during his days and nights, nor where he worked. The thought of not seeing him again stirred an uneasy feeling deep inside him that he didn't like one bit. Dalcian had pulled Cameron away from the very brink of self-destruction, and probably didn't even realise it.

He's my guiding light, Cameron thought. *I probably wouldn't have made it this last week without him.*

*

Around 02:00, Cameron's phone dinged, alerting him to a message. He looked to see a photo of a pretty lady sent by Graham.

GRAHAM: I found someone to keep me warm tonight.

CAMERON: Fuck you. I'm out here in the freezing rain while you're getting nothing but your dick wet.

GRAHAM: Mate, I told you, you need to relax and find some fun.

CAMERON: One of these days you're going to get some weird STD and your dick will fall off.

GRAHAM: Ha. Well, don't call me. This one's wild, I'll be busy with her all night.

Cameron snorted and pocketed his phone. There was no one in the street; even the hostel was dark and quiet. *What's going on? There is no such thing as a quiet Friday night.* He scanned all the shadows for the millionth time, then settled back and stared miserably into the rain.

A muffled shout roused Cameron from his boredom, and he straightened himself up, straining to hear over the sound of the pouring rain. He unfurled his umbrella and stepped into the downpour to investigate.

Another shout floated to him from the direction of the station, followed by a pained cry. Cameron hurried towards the sounds, and spotted a man leering over someone on the ground.

"Hey! Step away!" Cameron bellowed in his most authoritative voice.

The man turned towards him.

"Stay out of this, seccy, it doesn't involve you!"

Cameron pulled out his phone to call the hospital guards for backup, but the man started towards him.

"Don't even think about calling the cops!"

Cameron quickly jammed his phone back in his pocket and held up his spare hand.

"I'm not calling anyone. You're on private property, you need to leave now." He took a step forward, hoping the man would get scared and run. Instead, he turned his full attention on Cameron and pulled out a knife.

"Come on, mate. Why don't you just turn around and leave? It's too wet and cold for this."

"Fuck you, pig dog. You need to learn to mind your own business!" he shouted.

Cameron groaned inwardly and tensed; the man wasn't going to back down. Up close, he looked like a junkie. Cameron tossed the umbrella aside, knowing all too well it would be useless as a weapon, and stood ready to defend himself.

The junkie lunged forward with the knife. Cameron caught his arm, and tried to twist his wrist to disarm him. His hands were too wet to get a decent grip, though, and slipped uselessly around the wrist. The junkie clung onto his blade; Cameron felt it pierce his shoulder, and managed to follow around with an elbow in the junkie's face.

The man let go of the knife, and shoved Cameron before he could regain his balance. Cameron slipped and fell roughly onto the ground, vaguely registering the knife skidding across the sodden concrete. The junkie took a step back, shaking his head; he looked at Cameron as though he were going to try again, but instead he turned and bolted.

Cameron was breathing heavy and shaking as the

adrenaline from the fight coursed through him. He could feel his heart pounding in his chest, and could hear the blood pumping in his head. He staggered to his feet and turned his attention to the person on the ground.

As he drew closer, his heart leapt into his throat. Dalcian was sitting on the ground with his knees to his chest, his hands covering his ears and rocking back and forth. Cameron knelt down and put his hand on his shoulder. Dalcian cowered and held up his hands to protect his head.

"Don't hurt me!" he whimpered.

"I'm not going to hurt you. It's me, Cameron."

Dalcian was distraught; his eyes were streaked with tears and looking far away, as though he were reliving some sort of nightmare. Cameron tore off his heavy jacket and draped it around Dalcian's shoulders, and pulled him into a tight hug.

"It's ok, you're safe," he said softly.

The rain was still bucketing down, and it didn't take long for Cameron to be soaked through to his skin. Dalcian finally took a shuddering breath.

"Cameron?" he whispered.

"I'm here. It's ok. We need to get out of this rain, though. Can you get up?"

"D-Don't know."

Cameron dragged himself up, and helped Dalcian to his feet. He was shaky on his legs; Cameron slipped his arm around his waist to help steady him. He paused to pick up the brolly, then helped him back to the dock.

He lowered Dalcian onto a milk crate and plonked down next to him.

"Are you hurt?" Cameron asked.

"Don't think so."

"Sit tight. I have to ring this in. You're safe now, ok?"

Dalcian's eyes widened, and he pointed at Cameron's shoulder. Cameron followed his gaze, and saw that his shirt was soaked in blood.

"Ah fuck. Wait here, it's ok."

Dalcian nodded, though he still looked scared. He was shivering from the cold, and pulled the jacket tighter around him. Cameron pulled a large wad of paper towel from the dispenser and held it to his wound, then called triple zero. Once he'd requested police, and called the incident in with control, he sent a quick text to the hospital security team.

He sat back down next to Dalcian to make one final call. His hands trembled slightly as he dialled Graham's number.

"This better be important." Graham sounded pissed when he answered.

"Would I be calling otherwise?" Cameron shot back.

"What's happened?"

Cameron gave him the rundown, and Graham's tone quickly changed.

"Shit mate, you alright?" he asked.

"I've been better," Cameron replied. "Control ordered me off the site to seek medical attention and have dispatched the on-call car."

"Fuck. Sit tight, they usually don't take long to get there," Graham said.

The sound of a siren caught Cameron's heightened hearing, and he could see the blue and red flashes of lights.

"The cops are here, gotta go," Cameron said as the car pulled into the truck bay.

"Righto. Call me tomorrow and let me know how you go. You'll have to have tomorrow night off too."

"Yep. I'll be in touch. Bye."

As he hung up the call, Bruce rushed out to the dock followed by a paramedic.

"You alright, mate?" he demanded.

"I'll be fine," Cameron said.

The paramedic gave him a 'what would you know?'

look, and cut off the sleeve of Cameron's work shirt. He busied himself with cleaning and dressing the wound, and asking a hundred and one questions.

"I've stopped the bleeding and cleaned it up, but you're going to need stitches," he said. "Rather than sit in A&E for hours, go home and get yourself dried off and get some sleep. Go to your GP first thing in the morning to get it stitched, ok?"

"Alright," Cameron nodded.

"It needs to be stitched within ten hours, so don't leave it until tomorrow night. It's going to be painful once the adrenaline wears off, so you might want to have some Panadol handy. I'll just check the other chap while I'm here."

Dalcian looked at Cameron, his fear showing in his eyes. He had a few stray tears running down his cheeks.

"It'll be ok," Cameron whispered.

"What about the cops? They're going to want my details." Dalcian was still shivering; Cameron wanted so much to put his arm around him to comfort him, but until the incident had been handled, he was still on the clock.

"You can tell them who you are. You're over eighteen, so they won't tell your family or anyone that you've been located. You're safe."

"Not from *him*. If they ask, my name is Thomas."

"Alright," Cameron relented. "I need to go and talk to the police. I'll be just over there."

Cameron left Dalcian with the paramedic and approached the officers and Bruce.

"I'll go with Bruce and review the footage. You can stay here and get their statements," the senior constable was saying.

"No worries. Oh hi, Cam."

Cameron recognised the constable, and shook his hand.

"Hi, mate. How you been?"

"Same old," Constable Washburn sighed. "You'd think the rain would wash the dregs away, but it only seems to bring them out more."

"Shit floats downstream," Cameron pointed out.

"True." The constable laughed, then turned serious. "Righty-o. So what happened here?"

Cameron recounted the incident, giving as much detail as he could.

"You said he dropped the weapon. Where is it now?" Constable Washburn asked.

"It's still over there." Cameron pointed.

"Who's the kid?" the constable asked.

"I only know him as Thomas," Cameron replied. "He comes over for a chat every now and then. He's a good lad."

"I've seen him around. I'm pretty sure he's homeless. Do you know where he's staying?"

"Yeah. He's been staying at the hostel over there, I think," Cameron fibbed.

"Thanks, mate. I'll go and get his statement."

The paramedic, satisfied that Dalcian was not experiencing shock or concussion, nodded to Cameron and Washburn and headed back inside. Cameron hovered as close as he could to Dalcian while the constable questioned him.

As his body began to cool down from the excitement, the freezing cold air started biting at Cameron's skin, causing his wound to start aching. He rummaged around in his bag and found some Panadol, as Bruce returned to the dock brandishing two hot cups of tea with the senior in tow. He handed one each to Cameron and Dalcian, then turned his attention back to the senior.

"Are you ok?" Cameron whispered, sitting back down on the milk crate so that their knees touched.

Dalcian shook his head.

"Can I stay with you tonight?"

"I'm staying in an eight-person dorm on a single bunk," Cameron pointed out.

"Please? I don't want to be alone."

Cameron saw the silent pleading in his eyes, and nodded. He didn't want to be alone either, and he certainly didn't want Dalcian to have to fend for himself in the streets. A small car branded in the security company's logo pulled up next to the police car; a guard climbed out and hurried into the dock.

"I'll just finish up with these guys and we can go," Cameron whispered.

Constable Washburn had collected and bagged the knife, and was wrapping up with Bruce. Cameron shook their hands and thanked them, and quickly conducted handover with the replacement guard.

"Right. I'll help our friend here back over the road, then I'll be off," Cameron said.

"Let us know if you need anything," Bruce said, shaking his hand.

"Thanks, mate."

Cameron fetched his backpack and brolly, then helped Dalcian to stand. He was a still a little unsteady on his feet, so Cameron slipped his arm around his waist for extra support, and held the brolly over them both.

"This is all my fault. I'm so sorry," Dalcian said once they were out of earshot.

"Why is it your fault?" Cameron asked.

"Apparently, I looked at him wrong," he replied. "He chased me from the station, and I slipped. I'm lucky you were working tonight and not one of the other guys."

Cameron's blood ran cold at the thought of that.

Once they were inside and sure that no one was at the reception desk, Cameron snuck Dalcian up the stairs and across to his dorm. As they tiptoed inside, seven loud snores greeted them. Cameron fished a spare towel and shirt from his locker, and handed them to Dalcian. He turned his back respectfully and peeled off his sodden uniform, drying himself off as he went. The frigid air of the dorm stung at his already cold skin. He slipped on his shorts and turned back to Dalcian; he was bent over and drying his long hair.

Cameron reached over and pulled back the blanket. Dalcian crawled in and shuffled over as far as he could, and lay facing the wall, shivering uncontrollably. Cameron climbed in after him and lay on his right side; he pulled the blanket up to their necks and willed himself not to touch so much as one hair on Dalcian's body.

A throbbing sensation between his legs made him groan inwardly. *Now is not the time to be thinking with your dick, for fuck's sake,* he berated himself. He wanted to roll over, but his left shoulder was too painful. He managed to cross his arms awkwardly in front of his chest, but he doubted he would be able to sleep.

He knew not how long he lay there in the darkness, listening to the others snoring and the rain belting down outside. He was still hyper-alert after the incident. He could hear Dalcian's breathing; he was still shivering. Cameron wanted to reach over and warm him up, but the poor man had been through so much that night already. He yawned and tried to get comfortable.

"Cameron?" Dalcian whispered softly.

"Yeah?"

"I'm so cold."

Dalcian rolled over so that they were facing each other in the darkness. Cameron's breath caught in his throat as Dalcian reached out and tugged at his arms. He slowly unfolded himself, and Dalcian pressed himself against Cameron's body. Cameron wrapped him in his arms and held him protectively. Despite his cold skin, it felt good to cuddle and feel close to someone again. After the night they had, Cameron felt comforted too.

It was only after Dalcian eventually stopped shivering, that Cameron realised that he was naked. He concentrated hard to force his body to behave itself; just when he thought he'd mastered it, Dalcian reached out and brushed his fingers lightly against Cameron's cheek. A light shiver travelled down his spine and made him tingle.

Dalcian tilted his head and found Cameron's lips in the darkness. Cameron's heart started beating wildly as Dalcian kissed him ever-so-softly. He hovered for a moment, then kissed him again, this time with his lips slightly parted and with more intent. Cameron's insides squirmed; it had been so long since he had been kissed, so long since he had tasted another man. He tilted his head, and as Dalcian found him a third time, Cameron kissed him back, teasing his lips open with his tongue.

It took Dalcian a moment to get the hang of kissing with tongues, but once he figured it out, Cameron was in heaven. He tasted like mint toothpaste, and he could smell a hint of Lynx body scrub, as though he had showered not too long ago. He became lost in Dalcian's spell, the magic of his gentle touch. Cameron ran his hands across his back, enchanted by the feel of their bodies touching. It felt as though Dalcian was melting into his arms, as if he, too, were entranced by the magic forming between them.

Cameron had only kissed two other guys, and neither of them compared to the kiss he shared with Dalcian. His first kiss with a boy was when he was ten during a game of truth or dare, and had made him realise he liked boys. Paul was the only other person he had kissed, and that only happened when Paul wanted to fuck. Despite being a badass, Cameron was soft at heart, and craved cuddles and tenderness.

Dalcian pulled his lips away and rested his head on Cameron's shoulder. He ran his fingers through Cameron's chest hair and stifled a yawn.

"You're a hero," he whispered. "No one has ever helped me before."

"I'm no hero," Cameron whispered back. "I'm just a decent human being, that's all."

"You're *my* hero," Dalcian breathed. "You're the only person I can trust. Thank you."

Cameron leant down and kissed his forehead, and yawned. Dalcian soon drifted off to sleep in his arms, and Cameron wasn't far behind him.

7

Cameron woke to the sound of the vacuum cleaner roaring obnoxiously around the room. He could hear people talking and laughing, and doors slamming on the upper floor. The sun was shining through the gap between the window and the blind; Cameron grimaced and pulled the blanket up over their heads.

Dalcian was still wrapped in his arms, sleeping soundly. He looked at peace, as though he had no care in the world. Cameron instinctively reached out and brushed a stray lock of hair from his eyes, revelling in his beauty. He thought about their kisses the night before, and the memory filled him with something that he couldn't identify; he longed to kiss him again, to never let him go from his arms.

The more time he spent with Dalcian, the less he thought about Paul and his past. His relationship had been over for months, if not years, and the pain of their final breakup was finally fading. The freedom Cameron had felt after leaving intensified, filling his gut with a sense of happiness that felt strange, yet welcome.

The vacuum came closer and was almost unbearable. Dalcian squirmed and opened his eyes; he looked confused for a moment, then smiled sleepily and looked up at

Cameron. Cameron held his finger to his lips, and could feel himself smiling back.

"I was having the best sleep," Dalcian whispered with a yawn. "You make a good pillow."

"You kept me warm," Cameron agreed. "How are you feeling?"

"Tired. But better."

"Wanna hang out today?" Cameron asked.

"I'd like that." Dalcian smiled.

After what seemed like an eternity, the vacuum cleaner was shut off and wheeled from the room. Cameron cautiously peeked out from under the blanket; there were only two other guys left in the room. One was lying on his back on a top bunk staring at his phone, and the other was tying his shoes.

"I need to piss," Cameron whispered.

"Me too."

"We could both do with a shower too. Wait here a sec and I'll get you something to wear."

No one batted an eye when Cameron left the dorm with his extra guest. It was only 08:30, but Cameron felt surprisingly awake. Once they'd relieved themselves, he dashed downstairs and put their wet clothes in the wash, then showed Dalcian to the showers. There were three cubicles, and only one was unoccupied.

"You can go first if you like," Cameron offered.

"Or…we could go in together?" Dalcian asked a little nervously.

"Ok." Cameron wasn't sure if he was nervous about asking, or if he was scared to be alone. Either way, he didn't mind sharing.

Inside the cubicle was a built-in bench seat and a shelf. Cameron sat his toilet bag on the shelf and hung up their towels on the hooks behind the door.

Dalcian sat on the bench and took off the baggy shirt Cameron had lent him. His skin was pale and tight across his ribs, accented by a soft layer of dark patchy hair sprouting on his chest. He could have looked like a gorilla and Cameron still would have thought that he was beautiful.

Cameron tore his eyes away and stripped off, all too aware that every inch of his body was being scrutinised. He reached into the shower and turned on the water, being careful not to wet the dressings on his shoulder. He held his hand under the stream until it was the right temperature.

When he turned back, Dalcian was naked and standing awkwardly, looking shy. Cameron took his hand and guided him into the shower, resisting the urge to check out his lower regions.

"How's your shoulder?" Dalcian asked.

"Sore," Cameron admitted. "I'll live, though."

"You're so strong and brave. My hero," Dalcian sighed. "I was so scared. I'm not nearly as manly as you."

"Being manly doesn't involve getting into fights with people. You're manly in other ways. Don't put yourself down."

"Do you ever get scared?"

"Of course I do." He didn't want to admit that there was a moment last night when he'd been absolutely terrified.

Cameron tried to reach behind to wash himself, but the pain from his shoulder made him flinch.

"Bloody hell," he grumbled.

"Do you need help?" Dalcian asked.

"Yeah. If you don't mind."

Dalcian took the soap, and Cameron turned around. He leant his forehead on the tiles and closed his eyes, enjoying the feel of the soap gliding across his skin. His whole body ached from his fall, but the hot water felt soothing. As Dalcian reached his butt, he paused as though unsure of himself, then almost timidly ran the soap between his cheeks.

Cameron felt his body reacting to Dalcian's touch, but he knew his attraction was so much more than lust. Dalcian was young and innocent, and Cameron didn't want to do anything to break the trust that had formed between them.

Once Dalcian had finished, he rinsed the soap off Cameron's back and legs, then stood back. Cameron turned around and watched as Dalcian washed himself. His eyes dropped lower, and he stood staring at Dalcian's body. He had a nice circumcised dick, thicker and longer than Paul's. Dalcian looked up and blushed when he caught Cameron staring. He handed over the soap and turned around.

Cameron ran the soap slowly over his back and shoulders, and paused. His breath caught in his throat as he noticed a number of scars etched into Dalcian's back, consistent with a belt or something long and slender. A horrible feeling rose in his stomach; he ran his fingers along the scars, as Dalcian's words echoed in his head: *"I was sick of being his punching bag."*

He knelt down and washed the rest of his back, though he couldn't stop staring at the scars. *What kind of a sick fuck abuses a child?* Cameron thought darkly. *No wonder the poor boy ran away so young.* He stood up and sat the soap in the holder.

"There you go," he said gently.

Dalcian turned around slowly; his eyes once again had that far-away haunted look, a lone tear creeping down his cheek. Cameron brushed it away gently and pulled him into his arms. No words were needed as they stood there in the shower, sharing a moment of silent understanding.

The sound of voices entering the bathroom interrupted the tender moment. Cameron sighed and reluctantly let him go.

"We'd better get moving," he said. "Come on."

*

Once they returned to the dorm, Cameron dressed in his jeans, an old shirt, and his hoodie, then deposited Dalcian on his bed. He was wearing Cameron's tee and shorts that were way too big for his slender frame.

"I'm just going downstairs to put your clothes in the dryer," he said.

"Ok," Dalcian replied. He looked as though he didn't fancy being left alone.

"Here's my phone. There's YouTube and a few games on there that should keep you from being bored," Cameron offered.

"Thanks," Dalcian replied.

Cameron threw Dalcian's clothes plus his own wet jocks and socks into a dryer, and added two dry towels as well. It was a trick he'd learnt that greatly reduced the time needed to dry a small load. He set the timer for forty minutes, then checked his uniform. His jumper and jacket both had holes from the knife and were stained with his blood. He bundled them up in a garbage bag with his destroyed shirt, and tied the top firmly. He would have to return them to Graham and have them replaced.

Dalcian was lying stretched out on the bed, staring at Cameron's phone when he returned to the dorm. He shimmied over to make room, and Cameron lay down next to him. Dalcian squirmed and rested his head on Cameron's shoulder, and held up the phone.

"I found some videos with tips on drawing," he said. "So cool."

"I admire anyone who can draw," Cameron said. "I don't have a creative bone in my body."

"You're the only person I've ever showed my work to," Dalcian admitted. "Did you really like it?"

"Of course," Cameron said. "I'd love to see more of it. If you want to show me, that is."

"My sketchbook is in my locker at work," Dalcian

said. "I'm glad I didn't bring it last night or it would have been ruined."

Cameron ran his fingers through Dalcian's hair absentmindedly, enjoying their close contact and feeling content. For once, he didn't feel alone in the world.

"Have you ever watched *Yogi Bear?*" Dalcian asked once his video had finished.

"Oh, he's smarter than the average bear," Cameron quoted with a grin. "Why's that?"

"I used to sneak out to the TV and watch Saturday morning cartoons when I was little. I liked Yogi because he was always trying to escape from the park, and stealing picnic baskets. It's what got me started on drawing."

Dalcian searched through YouTube and found a playlist; it wasn't long until they were both laughing at the antics of Yogi and Boo-Boo.

"It's so silly," Dalcian snorted. "You're so Yogi, we just need to get you a hat."

"I'm not that hairy, am I?" Cameron laughed. "I like to think I'm smarter than Yogi, but ok. I guess that makes you Boo-Boo."

It felt good to laugh again, and Dalcian seemed much more relaxed. Before he knew it, it was time to check on the washing. The dorm had emptied, and he hadn't even noticed.

"I'll go and check the washing. Be right back," Cameron said.

The washing was dry enough thanks to Cameron's towel hack. Dalcian stripped off and pulled on his warm clothes, no longer shy with his nakedness. Cameron went to pass Dalcian his light grey shirt, and realised it had a patch of blood on it.

"Oh no, I ruined your shirt," he said, feeling bad. "I'm so sorry."

"It's ok," Dalcian shrugged. "It's not like you didn't save my life again."

"Do you have any other clothes?" Cameron asked.

"I have pants and a shirt in my locker at the café. They're my uniform, though."

Cameron made sure he had his wallet, phone, and hostel key, then stood up.

"We'll do some shopping after we go to the doctor," he said. He put on a mock Yogi voice; "Let's go Boo-Boo, we have things to do!"

It was still chilly outside, despite the bright blue sky. As they disembarked the train, Cameron spotted a familiar security guard on the platform. He grinned when George smiled and waved.

"Habib! I haven't seen you for long time," he said, shaking Cameron's hand fondly. He reached out and shook Dalcian's hand too. "Hello, young man."

"Hi," Dalcian replied.

"How have you been, George?" Cameron asked.

"Same old," he replied. "We had an incident last night. Some junkies were fighting on the platform and one fell on the tracks. It delayed the network for around an hour."

"Shit," Cameron replied. "It must have been a night for it."

He told George about his incident the night before.

"Wollah! You need to be careful!" George said. "Are you still living around here?"

"Nah. I'll be moving out near Marsden Park soon," Cameron replied.

"Hopefully I'll see you around," George said. He shook their hands again.

"You will. Bye, George."

Cameron's regular medical centre was a short walk from the station. The place was quiet for a Saturday. He held the door for Dalcian, and made his way to the reception desk.

"Can I help you?" The lady smiled.

"Hi." Cameron handed over his Medicare card. "Can I see Dr Solomon, please?"

"Sure. There's only one person in front of you. Let's see…Paul or Cameron?"

Cameron flinched at the mention of Paul's name. He had forgotten that they were both on the same card, and made a mental note to get him removed.

"Cameron," he said quickly.

"Has your address changed since your last visit?" she asked.

"Oh, yeah. I'll be moving in a few weeks. Hang on."

He opened Kristy's email on his phone and handed it over so the receptionist could copy it.

"Done. Take a seat and the doctor will be with you shortly," she said.

Cameron sat with Dalcian outside Dr Solomon's room and waited patiently. His shoulder was aching, and he was craving a coffee. Dalcian was fidgeting as though he was nervous; Cameron patted him on his thigh to reassure him.

Finally the door opened, and Dr Solomon poked his head out.

"Cameron Greenwood," he called.

Cameron stood up and took a step, then turned to Dalcian.

"Coming?" he asked.

Dalcian nodded and followed him into the office.

"How are you, Cameron?" Dr Solomon asked, shaking his hand warmly.

"I've been better," he replied.

"Still doing security?"

"Unfortunately," Cameron said.

"Ah. Let me guess. Another work incident?"

"Yeah. Got stabbed," Cameron said casually. "How's your sewing skills?"

"Bloody hell, Cameron," the doctor sighed. "Trust you

to come in here on a Saturday needing stitches and blood work. Lie down on the bed, I'll be back in a moment. Did you think to fast before coming in?"

Cameron nodded. He had been visiting Dr Solomon since he started doing security, and they had built up a friendly banter over the years. Cameron stood up and took off his hoodie and shirt as Dr Solomon slipped out of the room. He looked at Dalcian and winked, then climbed onto the bed and lay down.

Dr Solomon returned to the room pushing a small stainless-steel trolley loaded with supplies.

"When did it happen?" he asked, removing the dressings carefully.

"Around 03:30 – 04:00 this morning," Cameron replied.

"At least you didn't leave it too late to come in," Dr Solomon sighed.

Cameron looked at the roof and gritted his teeth as the doctor injected him with a local anaesthetic and a tetanus shot. For a badass, he hated needles.

"How's Paul?" Dr Solomon asked as he worked.

"Oh, we're done," Cameron replied.

"I'm sorry to hear that," he said.

"Don't be. You know he was an arsehole," Cameron said. "I just wish I woke up sooner before he messed up my life so much."

"What did he do this time?"

Cameron told him about the car accident and subsequent events. Dr Solomon shook his head.

"I told you last time, it's mental abuse," he said. "You should lawyer up and take him for half of everything. I can write a letter to confirm your depression and anxiety to support your case."

"I just want to get on with my life," Cameron said. "I don't think I could handle going through all of that. Besides, I can't afford to take a lot of time off from work."

"It's your choice. But think about it, you're in a lot of debt because of him, and it's not even your fault. I know a good lawyer who could help you. I'll give you his number before you go."

"Yeah, whatever," Cameron said.

"Speaking of depression. Have you been taking your tablets?"

"I ran out a few weeks ago and didn't have time to come in," Cameron confessed. "I've been much better, though."

"You should know better than to go off them without coming to see me," Dr Solomon scolded him. "If you want to go back on them, I'll write you some repeats. Remember to start with 50mg the first week, then increase to 100mg the week after. And don't stop them cold turkey."

"I think I'll be ok for a while," Cameron said. "I promise I'll come in if I need to."

"If you need another script, call me. I can fax one to your nearest chemist."

"Thanks, Doc."

"There we go, all done. No fighting or anything rough. I'm putting you on light duties for a week. Come back in two weeks to get the stitches out."

Dr Solomon sat at his computer and tapped away at his keyboard. Cameron hopped off the bed and replaced his shirt. He caught Dalcian's eye, and shot him a grin. Dalcian looked relieved that Cameron was ok, and smiled back.

"Here you go. A letter for your boss, that covers you from last night until Monday. A script for antibiotics, your usual antidepressant should you need it, and request for full blood test. If there is anything nasty, I'll call you, otherwise you can get your results when you come in to get your stitches out. Anything else?"

"That should do me for today. Thanks, Doc."

"Oh, here's the lawyer's number. See you!"

* * *

By the time Cameron had finished his blood test, he was tired, hungry and craving caffeine. Dalcian looked just as tired, if not more. Cameron dropped his script into the chemist, and they had thirty minutes to kill before it was ready. He checked his phone and realised it was already lunchtime.

"What would you like for lunch?" he asked.

"Whatever," Dalcian shrugged.

"You can choose. It can be anything you like."

"Anything?"

Cameron nodded, and Dalcian looked thoughtful for a moment.

"Asian pork dumplings," he said finally. "I've always wanted to try them. That's if there's a noodle shop around here though, I don't want to be a hassle."

"You're not a hassle," Cameron said. "I know just the place."

He led Dalcian to the lifts and took him to the level four dining precinct. He had done a lot of work in the centre, and of course he knew where the best food was. They passed a number of different restaurants and stopped at Happy Noodle Dumpling King.

"Here we are," he announced.

The shop was open-faced with tables out the front. Cameron led Dalcian inside to a snug corner that was somewhat private. The table had booth-like seats; Cameron slid in next to Dalcian. One of the waitresses approached with a menu, and smiled when she recognised Cameron.

"Hello! I haven't seen you for a long time," she said. "Are you working here today?"

"It's been a while," Cameron agreed. "Day off today."

"How lovely."

She placed some forks and spoons in a decorative bucket on the table, and disappeared.

"You know everyone," Dalcian noted.

"I get around a lot," Cameron said. "I used to come here sometimes for lunch. Their Pad Thai is amazing."

"I've never had that," Dalcian mused, looking at the menu. "There's too much to choose from. Surprise me."

"Ok." Cameron grinned. He took the menus and placed their order, then hurried back to the table.

"I can't remember the last day I had off to just hang out with someone," Cameron smiled.

"I hope I'm not too boring."

"Not at all. I enjoy having you around," Cameron said truthfully. "Thanks for coming to the doctor with me."

The waitress placed two hot steaming trays in front of them and hurried off again.

"What are those?" Dalcian asked, pointing at one of the trays.

"Long Bao. They're a dumpling thing with soup inside."

Dalcian blew on one for a moment, and put it in his mouth. Cameron watched with a grin as he bit into it, and his eyes widened as his mouth was filled with soup.

"Wow! How do they make them?"

"I have no idea," Cameron replied. "They're so good, though. Wait until you try the dumplings."

Cameron had ordered way too much food, but he didn't care. He ordered combination Pad Thai, teriyaki chicken, and Mongolian lamb, just so that Dalcian could try a diverse range of foods. The look of delight on his face as he tried the different flavours made Cameron feel warm and fuzzy inside.

"I'm so full," Dalcian gasped. "I don't think I've ever eaten so much before."

"Me too," Cameron groaned, rubbing his belly. "At least we have plenty left over for dinner."

"Urgh, I don't want to even think about eating for a while."

"We could always go downstairs and walk it off,"

Cameron suggested.

"I don't think I can move," Dalcian sighed.

"How about you wait here while I go and pick up the stuff from the chemist?"

Dalcian looked around as though unsure.

"Ok," he agreed reluctantly.

Cameron handed him his phone and kissed him on the forehead.

"Won't be long."

* * *

As a rule, Cameron hated shopping centres. His years in security had gifted him with an eye for theft and negative body language, and he couldn't switch it off and relax, especially in a shopping centre where he had worked so much. Everywhere he looked, he recognised people he'd apprehended before. Judging by the nasty looks he got from some, they recognised him too.

Dalcian walked close to Cameron's side, their hands brushing every now and then. His eyes were sweeping around as though trying to take in everything all at once. Cameron pointed out the stores he had worked in, and quietly told him some of the stories that he'd experienced. They made their way down to level two, and Cameron steered him towards one of the large department stores.

The door greeter saw him, and started waving excitedly. Cameron grinned and walked towards her.

"Oh my god, hi Cam!" she said, pulling him into a hug. "Are you working here again?"

"No, day off," he replied. "How are you?"

"Same shit, different day," she smirked. "Who's your friend?"

"This is Dalcian," he replied. "Meet Annie."

"Hello," Dalcian said politely.

Annie stepped away for a second to check someone's

bags.

"Since when do you get a day off?" she asked when she returned.

"We had an incident last night," Cameron said quietly. "Stabbed. Twelve stitches. Just been to the doctor, I'll be fine."

"Shit, no way! Come and work here instead," she said. "We're so sick of the shit guards we get."

Cameron laughed. If he had a dollar for every time someone asked him that…

"As I always say, you'll have to ask the boss." He leant forward and lowered his voice. "The guy and girl just there in the confectionary aisle. Three boxes of Favourites under the pram."

"Oh for fuck's sake," she sighed. "I'm on it, thanks. Take care, guys."

8

Dalcian was quiet on the train ride back to Stanmore. Cameron slipped his arm around his shoulders and squeezed him gently.

"Are you ok?" he asked. "You're quieter than usual."

"Yeah." He sat there in silence for a moment, then sighed. "Just a little overwhelmed, I guess."

"What about?" Cameron asked.

"I'm not used to people caring about me," he said. "I've been alone for so long, fighting to survive. Anything I've ever needed, I've worked hard for. Not once have I ever begged or asked for anything. And then you come along and spoil me."

"I wouldn't say I spoilt you. I got you a few things you needed, and bought you lunch," Cameron said. "I did it because I care."

"I know. I'm just not used to that. You saved my butt twice in two weeks."

"You saved mine too," Cameron confessed. "I probably wouldn't be here today had I not met you when I did."

"How do you mean?"

Cameron thought back to the night Paul had called, and how close he had been to doing something stupid. Dr Solomon was right to scold him for going off his medication.

"I've had bad depression for a couple of years now," Cameron admitted. "I was close to doing something irreversible that night Paul called."

"I had no idea," he said. "I mean, I heard your doctor talking about it, but back then I didn't know."

"I'm not ashamed to admit that my mental health isn't great," Cameron said. "There's so much stigma surrounding it. But since I've met you, I've been feeling so much better."

Dalcian kissed him lightly on the cheek, then blushed when a guy a few seats down sneered at him. Cameron glared at him, and the guy quickly got up and changed seats.

"Would you like to stay with me again tonight?" Cameron asked.

"Yeah, but only if you want me to," Dalcian said.

"Please? I don't want to be alone tonight either. And besides, you keep me warm."

"Ok. Let's be alone, together."

Cameron leant down and kissed him on the forehead, then stood up as the train started slowing to a halt. He helped Dalcian to his feet, and gathered up their bags of shopping.

As they stepped onto the platform, an icy gust of wind greeted them. Dalcian paused and zipped up the warm jacket that Cameron bought him, then walked alongside him, looking happier.

"Coffee?" Cameron asked once they'd passed through the station barriers.

"Yes, please." Dalcian smiled.

"I'd like to drop in and see Sarah, if you don't mind," Cameron said. "She'll be wanting to hear about last night."

"Ok."

Cameron pulled out his phone and sent Sarah a message.

CAMERON: Coffee?

SARAH: Have I ever said no? Tall soy latte, 2 sugars.

Cameron ordered the drinks from the station café. Before he could object, Dalcian took the cardboard tray and carried it with a smirk.

Sarah was sitting on her seat with her legs stretched out in front of her, hands behind her head. Cameron shook his head, and she held out her hands as though to say 'what?!'

"It's about time you came to see me," she said as they approached. "I've been waiting to hear from you all day."

"Been busy," Cameron said. "Be thankful that I brought you a coffee."

He sat the bags of shopping down and took the tray of drinks.

"This is Dalcian. Sarah," he said, handing Sarah her latte.

"Hi, hon," she greeted, smiling.

"Hello." Dalcian sat on the opposite end of the seat, and Cameron handed him his coffee.

"So, what happened last night?" she asked. "Graham didn't tell me much."

Cameron recounted the story, and finished up with a gory description of his stitches.

"Bloody hell, Cam," she sighed. "Did Graham give you time off?"

"Yeah, I messaged him earlier," Cameron replied. "I've gotta call him tomorrow, he's on a covert ops today. I have a feeling he's going to pull me from this site and put me somewhere easy."

"Oh yeah, we're here til Thursday," she added. "Graham told me that you're moving. Any news on when?"

"Not yet," he replied. "I'll call the real estate on

Monday and see how it's coming along."

"What's the holdup, anyway?" she asked.

"Landlord wanted to fix a few things first." He shrugged.

"Do you need any furniture?"

"Um…like what?"

"I have a few things I've been looking to clear out of the garage," Sarah replied. "If you want them, they're yours. I'll send you some pics when I get home."

"Alright. Thanks," Cameron said.

"Hubby has a ute, so we can deliver to you," she added. "Just let me know when, ok?"

* * *

When they returned to the hostel, Cameron made his way to the reception desk while Dalcian snuck upstairs. Maria smiled when she saw him.

"How are ya, darl?" She beamed.

"Not bad, thanks," Cameron replied. "Am I able to extend my stay? The apartment is taking a little longer than I'd like."

"Let's see." She tapped on her keyboard for a moment and frowned. "The longest I can extend for is nine days, which will be the morning of Friday the 31st checkout. After that, the place is booked out."

"Yes, please," Cameron said quickly.

"No worries, darl. Did you want to pay now?" she asked.

Cameron nodded and handed over his bank card.

"All done." She smiled. "Cya round."

"Thanks heaps." Cameron turned and hurried up the stairs.

One of the backpackers was leaving the dorm as Cameron reached the top step, and stood holding the door open.

"Thanks, mate," Cameron said.

"No worries." The guy nodded and headed towards the bathroom.

Dalcian was lying on the bed with his shoes off and staring at Cameron's phone again. Cameron kicked off his shoes, and paused to hang a towel from the top bunk.

"What's that for?" Dalcian asked.

"Privacy. I read it somewhere." Cameron crawled onto the bed and lay on his back.

"It's a good idea," Dalcian said. He handed back Cameron's phone and yawned. "It feels a bit like a blanket fort."

"It does a bit," Cameron agreed.

Dalcian propped himself up on his elbow and ran his fingers along Cameron's cheek.

"Thanks for everything today," he said.

Cameron's heart started beating a little quicker at his touch. Before he knew it, Dalcian was leaning down and kissing him. Cameron wrapped his arms around him, and pulled him on top of his body. They spent the rest of the afternoon wrapped in each other's arms, making out as though nothing else mattered in life.

It wasn't until around 20:00 that they surfaced, and realised they were hungry. They made their way down to the kitchen, and ate the leftover noodles for dinner. A few other boarders were sitting at the tables, chatting and laughing with each other as though they'd been friends forever. He had noticed that the people who stayed in the hostel seemed to be outgoing and inclusive, and were always greeting strangers as though they knew each other. Staying in the hostel had definitely opened Cameron's eyes, and his opinion of such places had changed drastically since living there.

There was something else on Cameron's mind as they ate, and he wasn't sure how to approach it. He had a new craving, one which involved exploring more of Dalcian's body. Judging by the boners they'd both been grinding against all afternoon, he was pretty sure that Dalcian was keen too. Cameron couldn't remember the last time he'd had a sexual release, but it was a long time, and he was definitely ready for that next step.

By the time they headed back upstairs, Cameron was starting to feel drowsy. He could see that Dalcian was sleepy too. They changed out of their clothes and into their new boxers, and climbed into bed. As much as Cameron needed sexy time, he didn't want to do it in a room with seven strangers. Dalcian deserved better than that.

Cameron pulled him into his arms and kissed him one final time.

"G'night, Yogi," Dalcian whispered.

"Night, Boo-Boo."

* * *

Cameron couldn't remember the last time he'd had a Sunday off work, let alone two days off in a row. Knowing that he had another full day and night together with Dalcian filled him with excitement he hadn't felt for a long time.

"What do you feel like for breakfast?" Cameron asked once they were dressed.

"We could go to the café where I work," Dalcian suggested. "I get staff discount if I order from the menu. Besides, I should probably check my roster."

"Where exactly do you work?" Cameron asked.

"Dirty Bean Café in Burwood," he said. "It's right next to the station."

"I think I got coffee from there once when I was working down the road," Cameron mused.

The weather had at least improved; the sun shone warmly with an occasional cool breeze. Cameron and Dalcian had ditched their jackets and shoved them in

Dalcian's new backpack just in case the weather turned cold.

The café was bustling with activity when they arrived. The atmosphere was buzzing with an air of Sunday morning catch-ups with friends. Cameron wasn't expecting such a modern layout; apart from one table in the corner where a group of shaggy people sat together sipping coffee, he would never have known that the café was friendly to homeless people.

"Have a seat, I'll be right back," Dalcian said, pointing to the only spare table.

Cameron sat down and watched as an Indigenous fellow greeted him with a big smile and handshake. Dalcian chatted to him for a moment then disappeared into the kitchen. Cameron turned his attention to the menu, and flicked his way through the pages. He sure hoped the food tasted as good as it smelt. He looked up just in time to see Dalcian and an older woman walking towards him.

"Cameron, this is Jill, my boss," he said with a smile.

"Nice to meet you," Cameron stood and put out his hand, but she swept him into a hug and kissed him on the cheek.

"Likewise," she said warmly. "Dalcian's told me all about you."

Cameron saw a slight blush creep into Dalcian's cheeks.

"All good, I hope," Cameron said.

"Of course! Thanks for looking out for him. Most people don't blink an eye when something happens to homeless folk."

"I'm not most people." Cameron shrugged.

"Well, thanks again." She smiled. "You both get staff discount off the menu. I need to get back to work, lots to do."

"Thank you."

Cameron sank back into his chair as Dalcian sat across

the table from him.

"She seems nice," Cameron said.

"She is. I got my roster, she needs me for lunch shifts all week. Paid shifts."

"That's good!" Cameron smiled.

"Yeah. I might not get to see you as much, though."

"It'll be ok. I'll give you my number so you can call if you need me."

Dalcian unzipped his backpack and pulled out his sketchbook. He opened it to the last page and slid it across the table. Cameron took a pen from his bag, and wrote in his full name, mobile number, and future address.

"There you go," Cameron said. "Now, what do you recommend for breakfast?"

* * *

Cameron emerged from the café holding his belly and groaning.

"I ate too much," he announced.

"Me too," Dalcian said. "What are we going to do now?"

"I guess I should call Graham," Cameron sighed. He pulled out his phone and dialled.

"How are ya, mate?" Graham answered.

"Yeah, not bad. Twelve stitches," Cameron replied. "Doctor doesn't want me to work until tomorrow. Light duties for a week."

"Shit, mate. Are you free to drop into the office sometime today?"

"Righto." Cameron looked at Dalcian as he nodded. "I'll come straight over. Cya then."

"K, mate."

Cameron hung up the phone and sighed again.

"I have to go into the office and see Graham," he said. "Wanna come? It's over in Leichardt."

"Sure," Dalcian said.

It took them just under an hour to get to the office in Leichhardt. From the outside, the building looked just like every other office building in the area. There were no logos or listing to indicate so much as the name of the company, let alone the nature. On the intercom panel, the company name had been deliberately left blank.

Cameron pressed the intercom button and waited.

"Yeah?" the scratchy voice sounded like Graham.

"It's me," Cameron said.

The lobby door clicked open, and Cameron led the way inside and down a hallway to a plain door. It was already ajar when they got there. Cameron went straight in and closed the door behind them. Barry and Graham were hunched over Graham's computer at the far end of the room.

"Phaw, nice tits," Barry was saying. "How do you manage to score all the hot birds?"

"Nice to see you two are working hard as always," Cameron said.

Barry jumped, then stepped forward to shake his hand.

"How are ya, mate?" he asked.

"Oh, great," Cameron said sarcastically.

"Don't be like that," he said.

"This is my mate, Dalcian. I'm staying at his until I can move into the new place."

Graham shook his hand firmly.

"I'll leave you to it," Barry nodded and walked over to his side of the office.

Graham stood up and cleared off two chairs that were covered in files. His large desk was a mess and disorganised as always.

"Sorry, mate. We've been doing a guard audit. You've got your RSA, don't you?"

"Of course," Cameron replied. He sat down and

pulled the bag of destroyed uniforms from his backpack.

"We've had a few guards kicked off sites for not having theirs at all. Fucking idiots know they can't work in alcohol stores without it." Graham looked stressed as usual.

"Not our friend Mr Singh again?" Cameron asked.

"Nah. Kulwinder and Manpreet so far," he sighed. "What's this?"

"I need more uniforms." Cameron undid the bag and fished out his destroyed shirt. Even though the shirt was dark grey, Cameron's blood had soaked into the shoulder fabric that hadn't been cut away by the paramedic.

"Bloody hell. Good thing I have some on hand. Are you able to return to work tomorrow?"

"Yeah. The doc said it has to be easy work, nothing that can put me in the line of another attack."

"Shit. You've had two incidents at Stanmore now, haven't you?"

"Yep," Cameron replied.

"The site wraps up on Thursday. It's hardly worth sending you back," Graham said thoughtfully. "Are you ok to do covert?"

"Regular or ops?" Cameron asked.

"Ops. Just follow and call the cops to handle the apprehensions."

"Yeah, piss easy," Cameron nodded.

"Gimme a sec, I'll see who I can shift around and where to send you."

Cameron sat looking around the office while Graham rummaged through a stack of paperwork. The couch where Cameron had slept was covered in Graham's clothes; he had obviously stayed there the last few nights. Dalcian was sitting quietly, taking in the office with interest.

"When are you moving?" Graham asked.

"Still no word," Cameron sighed. "I'll call the real estate tomorrow. Oh, while I think of it, I have to go back to the doc in two weeks."

"Where are you staying at the moment?"

"Stanmore."

"Righto. I'll send you to Parra tomorrow, 08:00 til 20:00. The cops are after a specific syndicate who are targeting health and beauty."

"Let me guess, sensitive toothpaste and electric toothbrushes?" Cameron asked.

"Yeah."

"I busted them over at Castle Hill nine months ago." Cameron frowned. "I guess they're still supplying the junkies for their sore teeth."

"More than likely. I'll text you the roster this arvo when I get it all sorted. Now, what uniform do you need?"

Cameron stood up and helped himself to the piles of shirts on the uniform shelf. He picked out three shirts in his size, a new jumper, and a new jacket.

"Bloody hell, leave some for the rest of us," Graham grumbled.

"I'll have a beanie and cap too," Cameron grinned, pointing to a stash hidden on top of a filing cabinet. "Thanks. Always a pleasure doing business with you."

"Fucking smartarse."

Cameron stuffed his new uniform into his backpack, and pulled it onto his back. He winced as the strap brushed against his stitches.

"Right. We're off," he announced. "Talk to you tomorrow."

9

Once they were outside and away from the office, Cameron stopped and looked at Dalcian.

"What would you like to do now?" he asked.

"We're not far from Balmain, are we?" Dalcian asked.

"Not really. If I remember right, there's a bus we can catch from Allen Street," Cameron replied. "Is that where you want to go?"

"If that's ok with you," Dalcian nodded. "I'd like to show you something."

"Alrighty."

Cameron led the way towards the bus stop.

"What's covert ops?" Dalcian asked as they walked.

"Covert means undercover, plain-clothed work," Cameron explained. "Ops means that I'll be working with the police to catch someone in particular. I pretty much just witness the person conceal something and discretely follow them until they leave without paying. The police then swoop in and make the arrest."

"That sounds dangerous," Dalcian said.

"It can be. I'll be ok, though."

Much to their luck, the 445 bus arrived soon after they reached the stop. Dalcian slid into the front seat, and sat watching for their stop. Cameron sat behind the driver, pondering the week ahead of him. Luckily, he was going back to day shift and wouldn't have to stay up all night to readjust back to nights. He pulled out his phone to message Sarah.

```
CAMERON: I've been taken off the
hospital site. Covert ops starting at
Parra tomorrow.

SARAH: Energy drinks again?

CAMERON: Nah, toothpaste and electric
toothbrushes. I think they're the
ones I apprehended in Castle Hill.

SARAH: Good luck. Let me know how you
go. Oh yeah, I'll send you those pics
of the furniture tonight. Don't let
me forget.
```

The sound of the buzzer drew his attention back to the present, and he looked to see that Dalcian was getting ready to stand up.

"This is us," he said.

Cameron followed him off the bus, then stood looking around and gathering his bearings. The buildings in the street looked old, and some were run down. It felt like a rough area. Dalcian hesitated for a moment, then shyly took Cameron's hand. Cameron squeezed it gently and walked alongside him. His hand was warm and sweaty, but Cameron sure didn't mind.

Dalcian led the way along the road a bit, then turned down a narrow side street lined with parked cars. To their right, a large abandoned building loomed over them. Every window in the upper level had been broken, and most reachable surfaces were covered in lewd graffiti. The perimeter had been boarded up, as though it had been marked for demolition. Dalcian stopped by a low brick wall, and sat down without a word. He tugged Cameron's hand to sit next to him, then let go and glanced around.

The houses that lined the other side of the street looked older, but neat and tidy. Cameron watched as a car pulled away from the curb and drove away in a hurry. He heard a rustle behind him, and turned to see Dalcian crawling into the bushes and disappearing from sight.

"Don't let anyone see you!" he whispered from the darkness.

Cameron glanced around, then quickly followed him into the bushes. Dalcian was crawling through a large hole in the wall. Cameron's heart started beating a little faster; he was all too aware of the laws on trespassing, and risked losing his security license if he were caught. He shrugged off his bag and squeezed through the hole.

Once they were inside, Dalcian helped him to his feet. They were in the carpark of the abandoned building; just about every surface was covered in more graffiti. A small amount of light filtered through from the upper levels, allowing them to see.

"This way," Dalcian whispered, taking his hand again.

The sounds of the traffic on the main road echoed around the concrete walls; somewhere, water was dripping in tune with a chorus of frogs and crickets. The place was creepy and smelt terrible. Cameron shivered uneasily.

Dalcian led the way down to the next level of the carpark, then stopped as though getting his bearings. He frowned, then kept going towards the darkness of the underground section. Cameron pulled out his phone and turned on the light.

"Over there!" Dalcian pointed.

Cameron followed his finger with his light. A lone blue armchair lay on its side in a corner; the legs had been broken off, and the cushion was missing. Someone had even tagged the chair with white spray paint. Dalcian hurried towards it, and dropped to his knees. He pushed the chair over, and started poking around for something. Finally, he held up a small box.

"Got it," he whispered. "I can't believe it's still here."

"What is it?" Cameron asked.

"I'll show you when we're outside." He shoved the box inside his hoodie, then fished his jacket out of his bag and slipped it on. "Can I borrow your phone?"

Cameron wordlessly handed it to him, and Dalcian aimed it around the carpark.

"When I ran away from home, this is where I stayed for a while. This small area was mine. There used to be a few others living here too, but there are too many vandals and explorers that break in and attract the police." He swept the light across to another corner. "I knew it was time to move on when I saw Old Blue overdose just over there. He was such a nice guy, just down on his luck. He was addicted to heroin, and that was the end of him. From that day I swore I'd never touch the stuff."

"Bloody hell," Cameron sighed. "No one should have to live like this."

"I know. It was scary, but nowhere near as bad as home. Most of the other people here were quite welcoming and took care of me."

"What happened to…his body?"

"We all said our good-byes to him. When it got dark, some of the elders carried him outside and left him somewhere for the police to find. Sadly, no one mourns when a homeless person passes away. We don't get a funeral, and very few will remember us."

"That's so sad," Cameron breathed.

"Yeah. Most of these people just have mental health issues, but they're too scared to ask for help. So long as they have a warm safe place to sleep, they're happy."

"Wouldn't it have been warmer to have stayed inside

the actual building?" Cameron asked.

"No. The place is totally trashed, and there's mould in there. Even homeless people know the risk of breathing that in."

The sound of laughter carried eerily down the ramp, and Cameron felt the hairs rise on the back of his neck.

"We should go," he whispered.

"Yeah."

Dalcian's eyes were miles away as they sat on the bus headed towards the city. He sat clutching the bulge in his hoodie protectively, as though he were guarding it with his life. Cameron sat with his hand on Dalcian's leg, watching where they were going. Once he saw Darling Harbour from the window, he hit the buzzer and waited for the bus to stop.

They hopped off not far from Sydney Town Hall, and Cameron steered him towards Darling Harbour. They walked slowly along the dock, each trapped in their own quiet thoughts. Cameron had many questions he wanted to ask, but once again he respected Dalcian too much to start prying. *I wonder what's in the box? Why is it so important? Oh, settle down Cameron, you'll find out soon enough.*

Together they rode the escalators up to Pyrmont Bridge, and found a seat overlooking the water. They sat in silence, their bodies touching, watching the boats and ferries below. After a while, Dalcian pulled out the box and sat staring at it.

It was a rusty old biscuit tin, with nothing but a shadow of an Arnott's logo on the lid. With shaking fingers, Dalcian pried it open.

A folded piece of paper sat on top. He carefully removed and unfolded it; it was an A3 sized poster of a superhero, with large muscles and a well-endowed crotch area. It was a little water damaged, but Dalcian seemed satisfied. He refolded it and handed it to Cameron to hold.

The next item he removed was an A5 visual arts diary that looked undamaged. He didn't open it, but sat it on his lap. Underneath the book were a $5 and $10 note and two plastic cards. He handed the cards and money to Cameron, and carefully replaced the book and poster before slipping it into his backpack. He then took the cards back and sat staring at them. Cameron reached over and unzipped Dalcian's pocket, and slipped the money safely inside.

"This was me in year ten. I ran away on the last day of school."

He handed Cameron his school library card. He looked much younger without the beard, and his hair was much shorter. He looked sad, and Cameron could just make out a hint of a bruise on his neck. *Dalcian Lang. DOB: 19 December, 1999. Warwick Farm High School.*

"We lived at 9 Mannix Street, Warwick Farm. The day I ran away, I caught the train into the city, and a bus out to Balmain. At the time, I had no idea where to go or what to do," he said quietly. "I was scared."

"Why did you go there of all places?" Cameron asked.

"I had heard a group of guys in my class bragging about tagging the place. I knew that if I stayed down in the Liverpool area, *he'd* find me. The farther I go from that place, the safer I'll be."

"I'm guessing you have a good reason for not going to the police?"

Dalcian nodded, but said nothing.

Cameron handed back the card, and Dalcian handed him a bank card with the same name. The expiry date was February 2020.

"Do you think these will help me get ID?" he asked.

"It should be enough to get you a KeyPass ID," Cameron said thoughtfully. "They work the same way as a license would. Then you can use it to get your name on a lease or utility bill, register to vote, get a Medicare card, and so on. It's the first step."

"Ok. I'll do that."

Dalcian didn't seem ready to talk about the rest of his treasures. He put the cards in a separate pocket and made sure they were safe. Cameron looked at the time on his phone; it was almost 14:30.

"Are you hungry?" he asked.

"I'm still full from breakfast," Dalcian replied. "Getting thirsty, though."

"Let's go and get something to drink, and catch the ferry around to Circular Quay," he said.

"Ok. I've never been on any of the ferries," Dalcian mused. "I always stayed away from tourist and crowded areas."

"We've got time to kill. Let's go and be tourists."

The afternoon felt surreal for Cameron. They walked hand-in-hand along the Sydney Harbour Bridge in contented silence, licking at their ice creams and watching the world pass by around them. Dalcian stopped once they reached the middle, and stood gazing out across the iconic Opera House. Cameron looked across at the Navy base, admiring the large warships.

His thoughts turned to Dalcian, and he attempted to define the relationship that seemed to be forming between them. He wasn't sure exactly what they were to each other; were they friends who kissed and held hands, or were they already more than that? *How do you define two lost souls who are completely alone in the world except for each other?* he pondered. *I don't think this is love. Not just yet, anyway. But I do adore him, and he clearly adores me too. He needs someone to care for him, to show him how life should be. He's even more lost than I am...*

"Your ice cream is about to drip," Dalcian said, interrupting his silent contemplation.

Cameron quickly licked the melted parts and got it back under control.

"Oops," he said sheepishly.

Dalcian reached up with his napkin and wiped the corner of Cameron's mouth.

"Wanna go somewhere we can be alone together?" Dalcian asked.

"Do you know of such a place in Sydney?"

"I've lived on the streets for three years," Dalcian reminded him. "I know a nice place that isn't far from here."

"Alrighty." Cameron found Dalcian's hand and walked along beside him.

The thought of being somewhere alone, just the two of them, made Cameron's heart beat a little faster. *If only I had that bloody apartment already, we would definitely be alone there. Should I ask him to move in with me? God, I've only just met him.* He nodded to a security guard as they walked past, then stood aside as a cyclist came speeding towards them. *There's too many people in Sydney.*

Cameron finished his ice cream by the time they reached the bridge stairs. He looked at Dalcian; the young man looked as though he were deep in thought too. *Whatever he has in mind, am I even ready for this? Oh fuck it, I was over Paul and his shit years ago. Dalcian is nothing like that arsehole. He's a sweetheart. Yeah, I'm ready for this.*

* * *

The sun was just starting to slip towards the horizon by the time they reached a quiet, empty garden. Construction fencing had been set up around the block, closing it off from the surrounding streets. Dalcian eyed the fence for a moment, then pushed on one of the sections to create an opening. Before Cameron could argue, Dalcian had already slipped inside. With a sigh, Cameron quickly followed him and closed the fence.

Dalcian led him along a winding brick path, until they found a cosy nook overlooking Lavender Bay. They could see the Harbour Bridge across the water, and the twinkling lights of the city as they started flickering to life.

"I found this place by accident," Dalcian said. "I was being chased by some guys from the North Sydney station one night. I hid in here, and they eventually gave up looking for me."

"Are you ever *not* being picked on by someone?" Cameron asked. He took off his bag and sat down at a wooden picnic table with one leg on each side of the seat. He patted the seat between his legs, inviting Dalcian to join him.

"The streets are dangerous." Dalcian shrugged. "It's hunt or be hunted. I try and stay out of trouble, but it's not always easy."

Dalcian took off his backpack and sat between Cameron's legs; Cameron pulled him back against his chest, and Dalcian put his feet up on the seat. Cameron buried his face in his hair; his familiar scent was mingled with the slightest hint of sweat, just enough to drive Cameron wild. The closeness of their bodies soon made Cameron's come to life.

"I don't like it when you're out there all alone," Cameron said softly.

"I do what I have to, to survive." Dalcian shrugged. "I can't say it's not my choice or my fault, because I totally made the decision to leave when I did. I don't regret that decision either. Anything is better than where I came from."

"You could stay with me." Cameron kissed his neck, and felt a shiver pass through Dalcian's body.

"I don't know." Dalcian tilted his head to the side, and Cameron kissed him again, a little farther up and a little more suggestively.

"Just think. You can come home each day to a roof over your head." Cameron could feel Dalcian melting into him. "Have a hot shower, sleep in a nice comfy bed."

"Do I sleep with you, or do I get my own room?" Dalcian breathed.

"It's your choice." Cameron found his ear and nibbled it gently. "You could stay with me. Or you could stay in your room and come over for sleepovers."

Dalcian groaned softly as Cameron ran his tongue around his earlobe.

"I'll have to think about it." He turned his face to look at Cameron, and was instead met with his lips. Cameron ran his fingers along Dalcian's jaw and kissed him deeply. The faintest hint of rum 'n' raisin ice cream lingered on his tongue. Cameron closed his eyes; he could feel himself growing hard, as had become the norm for his body whenever Dalcian kissed him.

Cameron slowly ran his hand down Dalcian's body and rubbed the bulge between his legs. A shudder passed through his body, and he groaned against Cameron's lips.

"Tell me if you want me to stop," Cameron whispered.

"Don't stop!" he gasped.

Cameron undid the button and fly of Dalcian's jeans, and traced the length of his cock with his finger. Dalcian was already hard, fighting against the constraints of his underwear. Cameron massaged him through the fabric, making him even harder.

Dalcian tore his lips away and set himself free, then pulled Cameron's face back to his and kissed him hungrily. Cameron reached down and took his cock in his hand, earning a soft moan and shiver. He stroked it gently, delighting in the reactions his touch had on Dalcian's body.

Cameron let go of his cock and pulled his lips away. For a moment Dalcian looked confused; Cameron gently guided him upright, then clambered off the seat and sank to his knees between Dalcian's legs. Cameron ran his tongue around the tip of his cock, teasing him with what was to come.

Once Dalcian realised what was happening, he leant back against the table and closed his eyes. Cameron took him into his mouth, and started sucking him hard. At first, he was a little self-conscious, and Paul's words came floating back into his head: *"You're really not good at this, are you?"* A quick glance up at Dalcian reassured him that he was doing just fine, though, and he pushed the thoughts from his mind. Dalcian was softly moaning as though he was in heaven, and the look of pleasure on his face gave Cameron all the confidence he needed.

Dalcian reached down and locked his fingers with Cameron's spare hand.

"I'm going to cum!" he gasped.

Cameron squeezed his hand and kept going; he wanted to taste him in his mouth, to swallow every drop he was gifted.

Dalcian tensed, and with a loud groan, he blew his hot load into Cameron's mouth. He tasted a little bitter, but not unpleasant.

"Oh my god!" Dalcian panted.

Cameron licked Dalcian's cock clean, then pushed himself up from the ground and kissed him roughly. He could feel Dalcian's tongue tasting himself.

"Was that ok?" Cameron whispered.

"Amazing," Dalcian replied. "Your turn."

Cameron undid his jeans and sat on the end of the picnic table, and leaned back on his hands. Dalcian helped himself to Cameron's aching cock, and was soon exploring every inch with his tongue and mouth. Cameron wasn't used to being on the receiving end, let alone by someone who eagerly wanted to please him. For his first time ever sucking cock, he was much better than Paul had ever been. Cameron felt a wave of euphoria course through him, and a soft moan escaped from his lips. He thought about Dalcian bending his legs back and burying his dick in his arse; the idea of bottoming and being pounded hard excited him…

"Oh fuck! I'm—" Cameron gasped as he shot with little warning into Dalcian's mouth. He felt as though he were going to explode as an intense orgasm rocked through him.

Dalcian choked on the unexpected load, but quickly regrouped in time for the next. As soon as he swallowed, Cameron filled him with more and more. He couldn't remember ever shooting so much cum before, nor such an intense release.

He managed to pull up his jeans, and settled back on the table, breathing heavily and looking at the sky. It was streaked with bright orange patterns as the sun continued dipping down towards the horizon. Dalcian climbed up next to him and snuggled into his arms. Cameron held him tightly as they floated back down to earth.

"Was *that* ok?" Dalcian asked after a while.

"Can I be honest?"

"It was bad," Dalcian sighed.

"No. It was amazing," Cameron replied.

"You're just saying that," Dalcian said.

"I won't ever lie to you," Cameron stated firmly. "You already know that my ex was a jerk. He was selfish in bed too."

Dalcian was quiet for a moment.

"What's sex like?" he asked finally. "I mean. Wouldn't it be…messy?"

"If it's done properly it can be incredible." Cameron shrugged. "As for mess… The bottom should prepare first. A quick douche and shower before sexy time ensures that everything is nice and clean. No one wants something embarrassing to happen during a moment of intimacy."

"Does it hurt?" Dalcian asked.

"It can at first. The trick is to go nice and slow, use lots of lube, and work up to it with fingers or toys. Don't believe what you see in porn."

"I only ever watched porn once," Dalcian said. "Only the straight porn sites were blocked on the school computers. I snuck on there one day after school when I was supposed to be studying."

"You rebel," Cameron chuckled.

Once again, Cameron was struck by his innocence. He knew that the boy had clearly lacked a proper father-like figure in his life. The thought of growing up all alone with no support made him feel sad. He pulled Dalcian closer and ran the back of his hand down his cheek.

"Are you a top or bottom?" Dalcian asked, interrupting his thoughts.

"I've always topped," Cameron replied. "I never bottomed for Paul. I never felt that he deserved to be somewhere so intimate within my body. That spot is reserved for someone special. In saying that, I used to have some toys for alone-time."

"He really is a jerk."

Cameron nodded his head in agreement.

"I lost my drive while I was on the tablets," he admitted. "Antidepressants can do that. I haven't had sex for well over a year, maybe two."

"Do you think we could…you know?" Dalcian asked shyly. "I mean. I always pictured myself as being a top, but I could try and bottom, I guess."

Cameron felt the euphoria stir in his belly again; he certainly wanted to.

"Are you ready for that?" Cameron asked. "I don't want you to feel pressured or anything. I was pressured into my first time, and it sucked."

"I'm almost twenty years old. I'm more than ready," Dalcian declared.

"Alrighty. We just need to go shopping and get a few

things first." Cameron slapped at his cheek and felt the body of a mosquito crumple under his palm. The sun had finally disappeared, and it had grown dark. "Bloody mozzies are out already."

Dalcian sat up and stretched.

"It's getting cold. Let's get out of here."

10

Monday came around all too quickly. The euphoria that Cameron had felt the night before hadn't left him, and he knew he was walking with an extra pep in his step. He walked slowly up and down the aisles of the supermarket, pretending to do his shopping, while keeping his eyes open for the telltale signs of theft. By 16:00, he had already apprehended someone trying to steal baby formula, and another person trying to sneak out with a pack of steak hidden up their jumper.

As he made his way into the health aisle, he noticed someone loading up their trolley with suspicious quantities of vitamins and other items. Cameron paused and pretended to choose a razor as he discreetly watched his suspect. The sound of his phone ringing made him jump. He threw the razor into his basket and quickly answered the call.

"Hello?"

"Hi, Cameron. It's Kristy from the real estate. How are you?"

"Good thanks, you?"

"I'm well. I have some happy news for you."

"Oh?" Cameron felt a hint of excitement stir inside him.

"The landlord said that you can move in on Saturday 1st June," she said.

"Excellent!" Cameron breathed.

"Are you free next Monday to come and inspect the apartment?"

"Um." He watched as the dude with the trolley turned and hurried towards the back of the store and turn to the left. "Can I call you back? I need to check with my boss."

"Sure, no problem," she replied.

"I'll call you back shortly. Bye."

Cameron hung up and hurried to catch up with his suspect. He was hovering in the fruit and veg section, eyeing the front entrance. Cameron took cover at the end of the next aisle and waved over the duty manager. His previous good mood had been replaced by his serious work-mode.

"What's up?" Clarissa asked.

"I've got one. I need you to call Tony away from the entrance."

Clarissa nodded and reached for the microphone.

"Tony to the service desk. You have a call on line 6." Clarissa's announcement blared across the speakers.

Cameron quickly called the detective in charge of the operation as Tony hurried towards the service desk.

"Yea?" Senior Constable Saunders answered.

"I need you guys. We're about to have a trolley walk," Cameron told him.

"Shit mate, we're not in place right now."

"You better get your arses here, then," Cameron barked. "He's walking now. Hurry up!"

Cameron's suspect was making a beeline for the entrance. Cameron dumped his basket next to a drink fridge and pushed his way through one of the checkouts. He walked purposely towards the trolley and cut him off.

"Excuse me, mate." Cameron flashed his security license from his pocket. "Can I see your receipt for these goods?"

"How about you go fuck yourself?" the man hissed. "I threw it in the bin back there."

"Well actually, I saw you load the trolley and walk out the entrance without paying, and we have the CCTV footage to prove it," Cameron said. "I need you to come back inside and have a chat."

The guy looked pissed, as though he were going to put up a fight. Cameron glared at him and nodded towards the entrance; the guy took a few steps back as though he were going to comply, but instead, he charged at Cameron with the trolley.

Cameron was ready, and easily stopped the trolley with his body. The guy threw his hands up in anger.

"What the fuck is your problem?" he demanded. "Get the fuck out of my way!"

"Not gonna happen, mate," Cameron said. He was vaguely aware that a number of staff and customers stood watching him. He looked over the man's shoulder and could see a number of plain-clothed officers running towards him.

He stood his ground and braced himself. The man stepped forward and shoved him, but Cameron swept his hands aside. Just as the man went to take a swing, Senior Constable Saunders grabbed his arms and wrestled him to the floor.

"Where the fuck were you?" Cameron demanded.

"We were on our break," one of the other officers said sheepishly.

Cameron shook his head and snatched the trolley. He had worked with Saunders many times, and they had built up a working banter. He pushed the trolley over to the service desk and started unloading the contents onto the counter. Clarissa's eyes widened as she scanned up the items.

"$972.37," she said, handing him a printout. "Good

work, Cam."

"Thanks. It would have helped if Detective Dickhead over there wasn't off having a coffee break," he grumbled.

He helped himself to the large report books on the counter and followed the cops and thief inside to write his report.

By the time the police left, Cameron was hungry and craving a decent coffee. He headed back to the front of the store and motioned to Clarissa that he would be back in fifteen.

As he walked through the entrance, he pulled out his phone and called Graham.

"Yeah, mate?"

"You know those guys the cops wanted to get?" Cameron asked.

"Yeah?"

"I just got one of them." Cameron grinned. "Almost a grand out the door."

"Bloody hell, well done!" Graham said.

"I doubt they'll hit again this week. The guy was pretty pissed, he was getting ready to go at me."

"Saunders will call me later and let me know the plan," Graham said. "The op ends tomorrow, but I might keep you at Parra til the end of the week."

"While I think of it, I need a favour," Cameron said quickly. "Next Monday I have a house inspection that I can't get out of. Any way you can swing me night shift that week?"

"You're pushing it," Graham sighed. "I'll see what I can do."

"You owe me, remember?"

"Righto. I'll call you when I figure out Monday."

Cameron hung up, then stopped as he noticed a familiar face smiling at him from the customer seats opposite the supermarket. Dalcian was sitting cross-legged with his sketchbook and pencil in hand. Cameron felt his face break into a smile and hurried over to him.

"Hello, you." He grinned. "Just in time for a quick break."

Dalcian unfolded himself and leapt to his feet. Cameron took his hand and led him down the escalators towards the café below. "How long have you been here?"

"I had just sat down when I saw you chasing that guy," Dalcian replied. "You're such a badass."

"I'm just glad the cops got there when they did," Cameron admitted. "That guy was going to try and fight me."

"Are you ok? I was worried about your shoulder."

"I'm fine," Cameron assured him.

The café was quiet and getting ready to close for the day. Cameron ordered a coffee and pie each, then stood to the side.

"How was your day?" he asked.

"We were busy, but I have some exciting news," Dalcian replied. "Jill wants to hire another barista. She said that if I do the course, she'll put me on the books and I'll get paid properly. I told her I'll do it."

"That's great news," Cameron gushed. "I can't wait to perve on you in your sexy barista uniform."

Dalcian chuckled.

"I just need to apply for a tax file number, and book in for the course. It only goes for five hours which is good, and I have enough money saved for it."

"I'm so excited for you, Boo-Boo." Cameron pulled him into a tight hug. "Do you need a hand with anything?"

"Not really. I just need to use a computer to fill in the applications." He shrugged. "I could go to the library for that."

"Order ready for Cameron," the server called.

"Thanks," Cameron said.

He led Dalcian back to the seats out the front of the

supermarket and sat down with him.

"I'll go for a walk and do all of that while I wait for you," Dalcian smiled.

Cameron quickly scoffed his pie and brushed the crumbs off his jeans.

"I better get back to work," he sighed. He leant over and kissed Dalcian on the lips. "See you soon."

The rest of the week turned into a routine that Cameron had never experienced before. Each morning, he and Dalcian showered together and took care of each other's morning wood, then parted ways at the station. Once Dalcian finished work, he would meet Cameron and wait for his shift to finish.

Cameron felt as though his future was looking brighter each day, and for once he felt happy and positive. Although Dalcian hadn't mentioned about moving in with him, Cameron held onto hope that he would. He knew he was falling for the young man, and was sure he wouldn't get hurt again.

By Saturday afternoon, though, Cameron started to worry. There was no sign of Dalcian anywhere. He scoured the food court and downstairs café during his break, but he was nowhere to be found.

Once he knocked off, Cameron walked around the centre and checked the lower food court, but Dalcian was not there. The familiar knot of anxiety in his gut started churning uneasily, making him feel nauseous. Cameron forced himself to remain calm. *Maybe he's working late. Or he's back at the hostel,* he thought.

Cameron made his way back to Stanmore, feeling worried and confused. He replayed the morning over and over in his head; they had showered together as usual, and Cameron had gotten ready for work. Dalcian didn't have to leave until later, and had offered to stay back and do their washing. Cameron had kissed him goodbye and looked forward to seeing him later.

Cameron couldn't think of anything that could have upset him, though deep in the back of his mind, he was pretty sure it was his fault.

There was no sign of Dalcian at the hostel. Their clothes had been dumped on the bed in a pile, though some of Dalcian's were missing. Cameron went back downstairs and sat in the garden where he'd first seen him and waited. The hospital dock was locked up and shrouded in darkness now that the work had finished; working there felt like a lifetime ago. He waited and waited, but Dalcian didn't show.

Where are you? Cameron wondered. He sat biting his nails until he had none left. Just after 22:00, the first few drops of rain started to fall. With a heavy sigh, Cameron went back inside and climbed into bed. *Please, please be ok.*

* * *

Cameron barely slept that night, and when he finally did get to sleep, his dreams were plagued by nightmares. The sound of his alarm blaring was almost a blessing for making the dreams stop. He stumbled into the shower and tried to wake up; the thought of Dalcian being hurt and alone somewhere made him feel like throwing up.

Cameron's phone rang, making him jump. He turned off the water and snatched it from the bench next to his toilet bag. His heart fell when he saw that it was Graham.

"Yeah," Cameron mumbled.

"Hi, mate. Did you still need Monday night shift?" Graham asked.

"Yeah," Cameron said again.

"Good. I'm putting you at Granville for a while. One of the guards has fucked off to India to visit family, so we'll need the site covered."

"Alright," Cameron nodded.

"It's an empty site, but the company is concerned about vandalism. You'll be in a heated gatehouse and only need to patrol once an hour." Graham said.

"What facilities are there?" Cameron asked. He had learnt to ask the important questions.

"Coffee, fridge, microwave, TV, couch. You'll have to take any food you need, as there are no places to buy from in the area."

"Couch?" Cameron asked.

"Yeah. Someone dumped it across the road. Ibrahim and I dragged it inside last time I dropped by for an inspection."

"Fuckers probably sleep on it instead of working," Cameron sniggered.

"Better bloody not be, or I'll burn it. You'll also have the support of the roving on-call guy if anyone does break in. Standard drill."

"Too easy," Cameron replied. "What time?"

"19:45 for handover. 20:00 til 08:00."

"Alright. Thanks, mate."

The morning dragged on, and by 11:30 Cameron couldn't take it any longer. He whipped out his phone and Googled the Dirty Bean's number, and called.

"Dirty Bean Café, Jill speaking."

"Hi Jill, it's Cameron. Dalcian's — um — friend."

"Oh hi, Cameron. What can I do for you?" she asked.

"Um. I'm a bit worried about him. He didn't show last night, and I haven't heard from him. Is he working today?"

"He's fine. He's here right now and is working, but he's flat out at the moment," she replied.

"Oh ok. Would you mind giving him a message for me?" Cameron asked.

"Sure."

"Tomorrow night I'll be going back to night shift. 8pm til 8am, in Granville." He quickly told her the address.

"No worries, I'll pass it on as soon as he's free."

"Thanks, Jill. Bye."

Cameron hung up feeling relieved, but still confused. *Is he upset at me for something?* he wondered. *He has my number. Why hasn't he called me? What's going on?*

Dalcian didn't show Sunday night, either. Cameron kept himself awake for most of the night, overthinking anything and everything. The bed felt empty and cold without him, and Cameron felt his loneliness come flooding back.

He was woken at 11:00 by his alarm blaring on his phone, and rolled over groggily to turn it off. The last time he'd looked at the time was 06:51. He sighed and dragged himself out of bed. He felt shit, and the thought of facing night shift without a decent sleep made him feel stressed before his day had even started.

After his shower, Cameron sorted through his dirty pile of clothes, and finished folding the clean pile he had dumped into his case under the bed. He separated his and Dalcian's clothes into two neat piles, and as he pulled his hoodie out, something solid fell out with a *thunk*. He reached down and picked up Dalcian's sketchbook.

That's strange. He guards this with his life, it's not like him to forget it. He opened it to the back page where he had written his number, and saw that Dalcian had sketched Yogi and Boo-Boo holding hands underneath. *So that's why he hasn't called me. I wonder what's made him leave and not take this with him? I'm such an idiot, I should have given Jill my number. Fuck! If I call again, though, she'll probably get shitty at me for being a pain. Urgh.*

He slipped the book into his backpack and carried his washing downstairs. Once he'd set up the machine, he made his way to reception.

"Morning, darl," Maria greeted him cheerfully.

"Morning," Cameron replied. "I finally got the date for my apartment. I can go in on the 1st of June. Is there any chance I can extend my stay for one more night?"

"Let me see." She looked at her screen for a moment. "Still all booked out. There have been no cancellations. Vivid Sydney started on the 24th, so the chances of finding a place will be pretty slim."

"Damn." Cameron's heart fell.

"If anyone cancels, I'll let you know." She smiled.

"Thanks," Cameron nodded.

It was hardly worth booking a room somewhere for a day. The idea of crashing on the couch at the office didn't appeal to him either; the phones were constantly ringing, and guards were always coming in and out for uniform or disciplinary meetings. Cameron pushed the thoughts from his mind and busied himself getting ready for the inspection.

* * *

The apartment was only a ten-minute walk from the Marsden Park light rail station. The neighbouring suburb was a well-known low socio-economic area; Cameron felt uneasy walking past the commission houses, knowing all too well that he had apprehended many people from the area. He had his hoodie on over his uniform and had the hood pulled up so that no one would recognise him.

He found his way to the apartment building; it was one of many on the block, and looked as though they were built fifty years ago. An abandoned shopping trolley lay on its side next to a pile of broken household goods adjacent to the letterboxes. Cameron screwed up his nose and walked along the rows of car spaces until he found number 23. He stood with his hands in his pockets, waiting.

A white car that looked way too expensive for the area turned into the driveway and pulled up next to him. A pretty lady in a business skirt and blouse climbed out of the car, and fished out a clipboard.

"Hi, I'm Kristy," she said, and held out her hand.

"Cameron." He shook her hand politely and pulled down his hood.

"Are you ok?" She frowned.

"What? Oh, just tired," he said quickly. "I'm back and forth between days and nightshift."

"Damn, I bet that's hard," she said as she led him over to the apartment. "Well, that's your parking space back there. The area is a bit rough, but if you leave them alone, they'll leave you alone."

"I've apprehended half of this suburb," Cameron murmured as they climbed two flights of stairs. "I'm not even exaggerating."

"Jesus," she said.

Kristy led him down the second storey corridor to number 23 at the far end.

"The door has already been replaced. It had a fist-sized peep hole in it," she said as she jiggled the key in the lock. "It's a corner unit, so you get two views instead of one."

They stepped into a decent sized living area that encompassed the kitchen, dining, and lounge areas. The walls were painted a pale yellow colour, which clashed horribly with the brown linoleum. The softest hint of stale piss hung in the air.

"Don't worry about the smell," she said quickly. "The lino is being replaced with carpet tomorrow."

Cameron walked into each of the bedrooms in turn; the piss smell was stronger in the smaller room. A section of the wall had been replaced with unpainted gyprock sheets. He squeezed his nose and quickly retreated.

"Were they using that room as a urinal or something?" Cameron asked.

"God only knows," she sighed. "There were fist holes in the bedroom walls, and rubbish all over the floors. It was disgusting. But don't worry, once the floor is pulled up, they're going to paint the place and have it all nice for you. I've told them that you're a responsible renter, not like their usual tenants."

"Thanks," Cameron said. He drifted into the bathroom and was pleased to see a bath as well as a shower.

As he backtracked, his eyes fell on the large windows next to the kitchen bench. The curtain rod had half fallen off the rail, and was hiding a large crack in the sliding door. A lone magpie was sitting on the balcony, and fluttered away as Cameron approached.

"At least I have a nice balcony," he said with a hint of sarcasm. His view was taken up by other apartment buildings.

"You've got a brand new kitchen," she pointed out. "New stove and benches. The drawers and cupboards were rotting away."

"It looks good," Cameron nodded.

He poked his head into the laundry and was glad that there was room for a dryer as well as a machine, and a large sink for soaking his shirts.

"So, are you still interested?" she asked as he joined her in the kitchen.

"Of course," he said quickly. "It's actually not that bad. Anything is better than being homeless."

"Great! I have the application form here for you." She handed him the clipboard and he started filling it out. "I've already pre-approved you, but we just need this for our records."

"I have a letter from my boss with my employment details instead of pay slips. Is that ok?" he asked.

"Oh yeah, that'll be fine," she said. "Just email me a copy of your bank statements and a photo of your ID. It'll make the lease signing quicker."

"Ok."

He reached the field that asked for other occupants, and hesitated.

"Need some help?" Kristy asked.

"Um. My…*friend*…is thinking about moving in with me, but he hasn't made up his mind yet. Do I need to list him now or can I wait until I sign the lease?"

"It's best to list him now and be upfront with the landlord," she said. "You can always supply his references, statements, and pay slips before the signing."

"Er…he doesn't have any of those," Cameron said. "He is technically homeless. He volunteers in a café in exchange for basic essentials."

"Oh." Kristy paused as though pondering options. "He's not an addict, is he?"

"What? No!" Cameron said defensively. "He's the sweetest guy I've ever met, and he wouldn't do anything to cause damage or harm to another's property. He's only on the streets because he was abused as a child, and ran away to protect his own life."

Kristy looked horrified as she held her hand to her mouth.

"I'm sorry, I didn't mean to sound insensitive. Given the fortune the landlord has spent to fix this place up, he's asked me to ensure that he gets responsible tenants this time. If you vouch for him, I'm happy to take your word for it."

"I deal with fuckwits every day. There is no way I would invite one to come and live with me," Cameron said. "If you need references, I'll happily swear my life on his good nature. I'm sure his boss would be able to write a letter too. He's just been offered a full-time job which he's accepted. He has worked bloody hard to get where he is, despite almost being beaten to death. He has the scars to prove it."

Cameron felt a tear spring to his eye, and quickly reached for his phone to hide it as he blinked it away. *Where are you, Boo-Boo?*

Kristy put her hand on his arm.

"I'm so sorry. He's more than a friend, isn't he?"

Cameron nodded.

"I haven't heard from him for two days," he admitted. "I'm just really worried about him, that's all."

"Fill in what details you can, and we'll list him as your spouse. I'll let the landlord know that you're supporting him financially while he's getting on his feet, and I'll back you both."

Cameron filled in Dalcian's details and handed back the pen.

"Thank you," he said.

"Are you sure you're ok?" Kristy asked. "You look terrible."

"I'll be fine," he said. "I haven't slept much in the last two days, and I have a twelve hour shift ahead of me tonight."

"Where are you working?" she asked as she gathered all of her paperwork together.

"Granville," Cameron said.

"I'm heading over to Parramatta next. Would you like a lift to the station?"

"Are you sure?" Cameron asked.

"Of course. Come on."

11

Cameron arrived at the work site almost five hours early. Kristy ended up driving him all the way to work; she had been so engrossed in his stabbing story that she just kept driving. Cameron waved as she drove off, and turned as Ibrahim hurried out of the gatehouse to greet him, with confusion written over his face.

"Hello, Cameron," he said, shaking his hand. "Has there been a shift change? I wasn't expecting you until 19:45."

"Hi, Ib. No change, I'm just early," Cameron replied. "My day got messed around a bit, and it wasn't worth going home."

"All good. Come, I show you around."

Cameron followed him into the gatehouse, and his eyes immediately fell on a couch that was pushed up against the far wall. A monitor showing the security camera streams sat on the desk next to a small TV, and there was a bench with the most important feature: the jug, coffee, and sugar.

Once Ibrahim showed him the patrol route and filled him in on the workings of the site, Cameron settled down on the couch with his feet up. It really was comfy; he closed his eyes to rest them for just a second, and before he knew it, Ibrahim was shaking his shoulder.

"What?" Cameron grumbled.

"Sorry to disturb you. It's almost eight, I need to sign out and head off."

"Shit, already?" Cameron's eyes flew open, and he sat up quickly.

"Yes. You must have been tired, you were snoring."

"Sorry, mate," Cameron yawned.

"All good. I did a patrol ten minutes ago, so you're all set for the next hour."

"No worries. Catch you later."

Cameron grabbed a torch from the bench and followed Ibrahim to the gate. He heard a soft crunch in the garden next to the gatehouse, and felt the familiar sensation that he was being watched. Cameron felt his heart start beating faster, and he leaned casually against a post, pretending that he hadn't heard it. He watched Ibrahim get into his car, and soon his tail lights were disappearing down the road.

"Am I going to have to arrest you for trespassing?" Cameron called. He spun around and shone the torch into the garden, lighting up his stalker mid-step. Had he not been so emotional, he would have laughed at the look of surprise on Dalcian's face at being caught. He turned off the torch and rushed over to him.

"I was going to try and sneak up on you," Dalcian confessed.

Cameron dropped the torch and picked him up easily off the ground; Dalcian wrapped his arms and legs around him, and buried his face in Cameron's neck.

"Where have you been?" Cameron demanded. "I've been worried sick about you."

He could feel tears in his eyes, and fought to keep them under control.

"I'm so sorry," Dalcian said. "I feel so bad. I wanted to call, but I didn't have your number on me."

"What happened, Boo-Boo?" Cameron turned his head and kissed him softly.

"After you left on Saturday, I got caught at the hostel by the grumpy guy who works there," he said. "He yelled at me and demanded that I leave immediately, or he'll call the police. I left before there was any trouble."

Cameron carried him into the gatehouse and sat him down on the couch. Dalcian wriggled out of his backpack, and as soon as Cameron sat down next to him, Dalcian threw himself into his arms.

"I missed you," he sniffed. "I would have come to see you, but I was working. I had to get to my park before the gates were locked for the night."

Cameron held him tightly. He could feel himself shaking from his own heightened emotions.

"I only have three more sleeps at the hostel," he said finally. "I check out Thursday night when I leave for work. Moving day is Saturday."

Dalcian pushed himself up and studied Cameron's face. His eyes were rimmed with red, and he looked as though he hadn't been sleeping much either.

"What about Friday? Do you have a place to stay?" he asked.

Cameron shook his head.

"I'll take you to where I sleep," Dalcian said.

"Is it…safe?" Cameron asked hesitantly.

"Yes. I'm the only one who knows about it."

"Alright," Cameron agreed. He ran his thumb along Dalcian's beard. "You've had a trim," he noted.

"Yeah. Once a month a barber comes around and gives everyone a free haircut." Dalcian pulled off his beanie; his hair was much shorter than usual and well groomed.

"You're so gorgeous," Cameron sighed.

Dalcian leant forward, and Cameron met him with a kiss.

"I almost forgot!" Dalcian tore his lips away and sat

up straight. He snatched his bag off the floor, rummaged around inside it for a moment, and extracted an envelope.

Cameron opened it and pulled out a plastic card.

"You got your KeyPass!" Cameron gasped. "Oh my god!"

"I have my tax file number too." He grinned. "They needed a fixed address, so I got them sent to the café. Jill didn't mind."

"I'm so proud of you, boo," Cameron gushed.

"My course is on Friday the 7th of June," Dalcian added. "If all goes well, I start officially on Monday the 10th as a barista. It feels like everything is happening all at once. It's a little overwhelming."

"I know," Cameron agreed. "What days are you working this week?"

"I have Friday and the weekend off," he replied.

"Perfect. You can sleep here on the couch while I'm working."

"Are you sure?" Dalcian asked.

"I insist. I don't want you out there all alone anymore." Cameron looked at the clock that hung above the camera monitor and sighed. "I'm going to go and do my patrol. I'll be back in fifteen."

"Ok."

Cameron kissed him on the forehead, then headed outside to fetch the torch he'd dropped. The night was humid with the threat of rain. He walked around the site and checked that everything was locked and that no one was hanging around, then hurried back to the gatehouse.

Dalcian was already asleep when Cameron returned. He looked so peaceful and innocent. Cameron draped his thick jacket over him, and turned the main lights off. The outside lights illuminated inside enough that Cameron could make coffee and stay awake. He set up his phone to quietly play some music; with a yawn, he wheeled the office chair next to the couch, and sat watching over

Dalcian as he slept.

Thank God he's ok, Cameron thought as he ran his fingers through Dalcian's hair. *I don't think I could have handled losing him. Those two days alone were horrible. He clearly means so much more to me than I realised. Maybe it is love?*

* * *

The weather turned sour around 06:00. Cameron made it back from his patrol just as the sky opened up with a heavy downpour. He leant the gatehouse's brolly against the wall and took off his jumper just as a loud clap of thunder shook the building and echoed around the complex.

Dalcian yelped and bolted upright, his eyes darting around the room.

"It's ok, it's just a storm." Cameron sat next to him on the couch and motioned for him to lie back down. Dalcian rested his head in Cameron's lap and yawned.

"I don't like storms," he whispered.

"I'm here. You're safe," Cameron said.

"I know. Bad memories, that's all."

"Oh, Boo-Boo." Cameron sat rubbing his shoulder gently, watching the lightning flicker outside, "Here comes another one."

Dalcian covered his ears and flinched as another rumble shook the gatehouse.

"Tell me a story," he said.

"What kind of story?" Cameron asked.

"Something about your life that you haven't told me yet."

"There's not much you don't already know," Cameron said. "Let's see. I used to go to the gym a lot, up until I started working so many hours. I was strong, healthy, and happy. Lived in a nice house, had a nice car. In the early days, things were actually good."

"What was your house like?" Dalcian asked.

"It was single storey and nice. Had a decent backyard and a pool. I wanted to get a dog, but Paul wouldn't let me."

"Sounds expensive," Dalcian mused.

"It cost us around $800,000 at the time. It would probably be worth around $1.2 mil now," Cameron replied.

"How were you able to afford that straight out of school?" Dalcian asked incredulously.

"When my parents passed, their money was put into a trust fund for when I turned eighteen. I put in most of the money for the house, and Paul's parents put in the rest. His family is loaded."

"So…you're paying off his debt, and he's living rent-free in a house that he didn't pay for," Dalcian summarised. "That doesn't sound fair. You need to fight back!"

Another rumble echoed through the sky, but it was farther away and Dalcian didn't flinch.

"Can I tell you a secret?" Cameron asked.

"Of course," Dalcian nodded.

"I'm scared of him," Cameron admitted. "Absolutely terrified. He is the master of mind fuckery. I'm scared that if I try and fight back, he'll just ruin my life even more. He's threatened me with physical violence, and a few times he indirectly crossed the line."

Dalcian squirmed onto his back and looked up at Cameron.

"What did he do to you?"

"That's the thing. Technically nothing. One time I had just mopped the floor in the kitchen. We got into an argument and he took a step towards me. I stepped back onto the tiles, slipped and hurt my wrist. Then he would twist it around in my head that I was clumsy and it was all my fault."

"He sounds like a psycho," Dalcian said fiercely. "You were way too good for him."

"Yeah, I guess."

"I still think you should fight back. You have worked so hard to get to where you are. Why should he have everything for nothing? You seem to have nice people around you to back you up. Plus me, so you won't be alone."

"I don't know," Cameron sighed. "I guess I need to think about it for a bit. I'm not quite ready to face him yet."

* * *

The last few sleeps at the hostel were much better knowing that Dalcian was safe. Cameron still missed snuggling with him, but at least he got some much-needed sleep.

He woke up an hour early on Thursday afternoon so that he could shower and shave, then took his time packing up his clothes. His wardrobe had increased during his stay at Stanmore, plus he still had some of Dalcian's clothes. He packed what he could into his suitcase, and the rest into a green reusable Woolies bag.

Cameron took one more glance around the room, then closed the door of the dorm one final time. *Time for a new chapter in my life,* he thought as he walked down the stairs. *One rough sleep tomorrow, then I'll finally be in my own home.*

Yousef was at the reception when Cameron handed back his swipe card and locker key. Dalcian was right; he was a grumpy prick. Cameron was tempted to say something nasty, but thought better of it. *I'm better than that. I'm out of here, there's no need to stoop to his level.* Instead, he forced the biggest smile he could muster, wished Yousef a fabulous day, and walked out with his head held high.

117

*

Cameron decided to make a pit stop at Strathfield, and wheeled his case to the pizza shop. Sofia rushed out from behind the counter when he walked inside and smothered his cheeks in kisses.

"Cameron, my darling! How are you?" She beamed.

"I'm good," he said. "I'm moving into an apartment out West on Saturday."

"Oh, how wonderful! You look much happier than last time," Sofia ducked back behind the counter. "What would you like, darling?"

"I'll get a chicken supreme, but large. And can you leave half with no pineapple?" Cameron replied.

"Half with no pineapple? Are you sharing with someone special?"

"Yes. I've met someone I can class as special." He smiled.

"Mama Mia! What is her name?" Sophia asked.

"Actually, he's a man. His name is Dalcian and you'll love him."

"Oh my darling, that's wonderful!" she gushed. "You had better bring him here to meet us."

"I will, I promise." Cameron grinned.

"MASS!"

A few groups of people walked into the shop, drawing Sophia's attention away. Cameron took a seat and checked his phone.

SARAH: We still all good for
Saturday?

CAMERON: Yup.

SARAH: I'll be free after 11. What
time do you want me to meet you?

```
CAMERON: I need to sign the lease
and get the keys, then go and get
my stitches out. How about 12:30 -
13:00ish?
```

```
SARAH: Perfect. See you then!
```

Cameron stared at his phone, feeling the excitement growing in his belly. He opened up the saved photos and scrolled through the furniture that Sarah was bringing. A queen size mattress, two bedside tables, a three-seater couch, a small TV unit, three bar stools, and a simple desk with the world map printed on it. There was also a fridge, washing machine, and clothes dryer. It wasn't much, but to Cameron, it was everything.

As he scrolled past the last image, he landed on a photo that he definitely hadn't taken. He felt his face break into a smile as he looked at the cheeky selfies that Dalcian had snapped and left for him to find. In the final photo, he was staring at the camera with a smouldering look, one which captured the raw emotion in his eyes. Cameron felt his insides squirm in a good way, and set it as his wallpaper just as his name was called.

He said his farewells to Mass and Sofia, and hurried to catch his train.

Thursday night seemed to fly. Although he was tired, Dalcian sat up with Cameron for most of the night and kept him company. Despite being at work, Cameron had fun, and was almost disappointed when it was time to sign out and hand over to Ibrahim.

"Ah, you have a visitor," Ibrahim said as he entered the gatehouse.

"Yeah, this is my mate Dalcian. He just finished work and dropped in," Cameron fibbed.

"Hello." Ibrahim shook Dalcian's hand.

"Alright, we're off. Catch you later." Cameron gathered his suitcase, and Dalcian beat him to the bag. "Oh, there's a slice of pizza left in the fridge of you want it. It's halal, there's no ham on it either."

"Thanks, Cam! See you tomorrow."

Cameron led Dalcian towards the station. As soon as they were out of sight from the gatehouse, Dalcian slipped his hand into Cameron's.

"I've never had someone stay over at 'my place' before." Dalcian grinned. "Just a word of warning, though, the couch in the gatehouse is much comfier."

"So long as you're with me, I'll be fine." Cameron smiled.

"Why didn't you leave your suitcase there for the day?" Dalcian asked.

"I don't trust anyone in security apart from Sarah. There are a lot of corrupt guards in the industry. Besides, I don't want to sleep in my uniform. Where are we heading?"

"Ashfield," Dalcian replied.

Cameron was about to speak, but was cut off by his phone ringing. He sighed and let go of Dalcian's hand to answer it.

"Hi, mate," Cameron said when he saw Graham's name on the screen.

"How's it going?" Graham asked.

"Same shit different day," Cameron replied. "Just finished my shift at Granville."

"You're moving Saturday, aren't you?" Graham asked.

"Yep," Cameron said. "I don't suppose you're calling to give me that night off?"

"What do you think this is, Christmas?"

"Feels like it for me." Cameron grinned.

"Well…I need you over at Parra on Sunday for uniform. They're still having trolleys walk." Graham sighed. "I can't put a shit guard there or we'll lose the contract."

"Good ol' Cameron to save the company's arse again," Cameron said sarcastically. "Where's Sarah next week?"

"I've got her on covert in supers," Graham replied.

"She's helping me move, so don't dick her around," Cameron said.

"You'll be right, mate. Shit, got one, gotta go." Graham hung up.

"Your boss?" Dalcian asked.

"Yeah," Cameron replied. "Guess what?"

"What?"

"I have Saturday night off as well." Cameron wanted to jump for joy. "Back to dayshift on Sunday."

"There you go."

Once Cameron pocketed his phone, Dalcian did not let go of his hand again, except for when they passed through the station barriers at Granville, and again at Ashfield. As they walked past the Ashfield shopping mall, Cameron could feel his stomach starting to knot again. *It'll be ok,* he told himself. *I'm sure it's just like camping.*

Dalcian turned and led him down a side street, lined with Victorian-style homes on their left. A large sporting ground lay nestled amongst the houses as though the suburb had sprouted and grown around it. As they got closer, Cameron could see an ornate grandstand looming over an oval.

"They play AFL football and cricket here," Dalcian said. "It's pointless to try and sleep here when they have games on over the weekends, but during the week it's quiet and safe."

"Where do you sleep on weekends, then?" Cameron asked.

"It all depends on the weather and time of year," he shrugged. "The Botanical Garden is nice on warm days. Sometimes an abandoned house or shed if it's raining. There are so many factors to consider too, such as territory and law enforcement."

Cameron said nothing as they crossed the road and walked through the gates of the park. Apart from a lone jogger running laps around the oval, no one else was around. Dalcian led him towards the rear of the grandstand, and stopped by a low, solid-looking wooden gate embedded in the brickwork. He fiddled with the latch, opened it, and ducked inside. Cameron had to squat low to fit under the ledge, but once he was inside, there was plenty of room to stand. Dalcian closed the gate behind them, and slid a piece of wood across to lock it.

It took a moment for Cameron's eyes to adjust to the darkness. A small vent on their right allowed a sliver of light inside; the walls were solid brick, and the floor was dirt. It smelt earthy, though Cameron was sure he caught a slight hint of mouse for good measure.

Against the left wall was a stack of dusty gymnastics mats that Dalcian had clearly used as a bed. An upturned milk crate with a small shelf on top held a collection of personal care items, including deodorant, mouthwash, and a comb. Dalcian flipped the top mat over and laid it on the ground, revealing a clean mat to sleep on. He sat the green bag on top of the mat on the ground, and Cameron wordlessly sat his suitcase next to it.

Seeing first-hand how Dalcian lived made Cameron appreciate everything he had ever had in life so much more. He slowly took off his uniform and got changed into track pants and his hoodie, as the reality of Dalcian's situation hit him. *How many people are out there, living like this? It's so unfair. No one deserves to not have a safe, clean place to live. Something better needs to be done.*

"Sorry it isn't much," Dalcian whispered, breaking Cameron's thoughts. "It's better than sleeping at Central Station or Martin Place, though."

Cameron turned towards him; Dalcian looked embarrassed and quickly glanced away.

"Do you know what it reminds me of?"

Dalcian shook his head.

"A bear cave. It's dark, warm, sheltered, and should hopefully keep humans away."

Dalcian climbed onto the pile of mats and lay facing the wall. Cameron set the alarm on his phone for 16:30, and lay next to him. He wanted to pull Dalcian into his arms, but he seemed lost in his own thoughts. Cameron reached down and grabbed his security jacket to use as a pillow, and rolled onto his left side. The wound in his shoulder no longer hurt to lay on it; he squirmed around until he got comfy, then stared into the darkness.

As tired as he was, Cameron couldn't fall asleep. He thought back over the last month, and the events leading up to Saturday. The thought of Paul sleeping in the house that Cameron had invested his parents' money on, while he was sleeping beneath a grandstand, made him feel a range of emotions. On one hand, he was angry and felt the injustice. On the other hand, though, he was proud of how far he had come since he had escaped Paul's grasp.

A soft yawn behind him brought Cameron back to the present.

"Boo-Boo?" Cameron whispered.

"Yeah?"

"Are you ok?"

"Yeah, I guess. I can't sleep," he sighed.

Cameron rolled back over and tentatively rested his hand on Dalcian's hip. Deep in the back of his mind, he half-expected an angry response for invading Dalcian's space when he obviously didn't want to be disturbed. But the man he was laying with was Dalcian, not Paul; instead, Dalcian sighed softly.

"Just thinking, that's all," he said. "I hope you don't think less of me now that you've seen how I've been living my life."

Cameron's heart lurched when he realised what Dalcian was saying.

"Come here. You're too far away," Cameron whispered.

Dalcian shuffled backwards, and Cameron pulled him gently against his body. His hair still had the gentle scent of the shampoo he'd used the night before.

"I could never think less of you," Cameron said softly. "More than anything, I admire you even more for being strong enough to make that decision to leave home in the first place, and follow through with it. To go from having everything to nothing, not even a place to stay, is bloody terrifying. Many would have given up, but you kept fighting to get somewhere. I would have been sleeping rough, too, had I not been lucky enough to have a job to pay for that hostel. And I was pretty close to giving up on everything before I met you. If anything, you're *my* hero."

"I never thought I'd be saying my good-byes to this place."

Dalcian's statement caught Cameron off-guard.

"So, you're coming with me?" he asked.

"If the offer is still there," Dalcian replied.

Cameron felt his over-stressed emotions bubble to the surface again. He tried to hold back the tears, but this time he couldn't. With a shuddering breath, they rolled down his cheeks and into Dalcian's hair. A soft sob echoed from Dalcian, and before he knew what was happening, Dalcian had rolled over in his arms, and they were holding each other tightly, sobbing together. Cameron could feel their bond strengthen a hundredfold; it was their final sleep while being homeless.

* * *

Neither of them spoke when the alarm jolted them awake. Cameron kissed Dalcian tenderly, then busied himself with getting ready for work. Dalcian gathered up his few belongings and packed them into his bag, then stood watching Cameron as he slipped on his clip-on tie and fixed his collar. Once he was ready, he zipped up his case and sat it by the door. One twelve hour shift to go, and they could finally get the keys for their new home.

Dalcian replaced the lone mat neatly onto the pile, and opened the gate cautiously. He took one final glance around the small room that was once his home, then scrambled through the door without looking back.

Part Two

June 1st, 2019

12

The real-estate was still closed when they arrived at 08:45 Saturday morning. Cameron leaned against the side of the building, sipping his coffee and tapping his fingers subconsciously on his leg. He felt anxious, and found himself imagining all sorts of scenarios that would prevent him from moving into the apartment. *What if they're closed today? What if the landlord rejected my application? What if someone better came along and demanded the apartment? What if…*

"Relax, Yogi," Dalcian said. "You're starting to make *me* nervous."

He reached out and took Cameron's hand.

"Sorry." Cameron tapped his thumb against his coffee instead.

After what felt like a lifetime, but was really only a few minutes, the lights inside flickered on, and the doors were swung open. Cameron downed the rest of his coffee in one large gulp, and tossed the empty container in the bin. He grabbed his suitcase with his spare hand and nudged Dalcian towards the door.

The receptionist was already on the phone when they walked inside. Cameron stood nervously by the desk, still holding Dalcian's hand.

"Hi, Cameron!"

He looked up to see Kristy poking her head out of one of the offices. She hurried out and shook his hand.

"Morning," he said. "This is Dalcian. Kristy."

"Hiya!" She smiled and shook his hand also. "Let's go and get this paperwork signed, and it's all yours."

The next half an hour was a blur as Cameron went through the paperwork and signed what felt like a hundred pages. He paid the bond money, and finally, she handed over two keys, and a folder containing their copy of the documents.

"All done." She smiled. "I bet you're excited."

"Honestly, I'm so tired that it hasn't hit me yet," Cameron admitted.

"Well, you'll be in your own bed in your own place tonight," she said. "Are you heading straight there?"

The thought of bed was certainly appealing; he hadn't slept too well beneath the grandstand, and of course he hadn't napped while working.

"Gotta get the stitches out and do some shopping first," Cameron replied. "I don't want to get there and realise we don't have any toilet paper."

Kristy laughed and walked them outside.

"My personal mobile number is written inside the folder. Call me if you need anything."

"Alrighty. Thanks so much for everything," Cameron said. "I really appreciate everything you've done to help me out."

To his surprise, she pulled him into a hug and kissed him lightly on the cheek, and hugged Dalcian too.

"It's my pleasure. Next time you're over this way, message me and we'll get coffee, ok?"

The next stop was Dr Solomon. Cameron was looking forward to getting the stitches out; they were itching him like crazy. As luck would have it, he was called in straight away.

"Hi, Cameron," Dr Solomon shook his hand.

"Hi, Doc," Cameron replied. He sat in the chair closest to the desk, and Dalcian sat next to him.

"We got your blood results back. All good there, no HIV or anything funky," he said.

"Well that's a relief," Cameron replied.

"Are you going on a holiday?" Dr Solomon asked when he noticed the suitcase and bags.

"We're moving into an apartment today," Cameron said. "We've just been to sign the lease."

"That's exciting." Dr Solomon smiled at Dalcian and back at Cameron. "Let's have a look at those stitches."

Cameron stripped off his jumper and shirt and lay down on the bed. It felt like months had passed since he had been there last, yet it had only been two weeks. Dr Solomon slipped on some gloves and armed himself with a sharp blade.

"How's your mental health been?" he asked as he removed the dressings and examined the wound.

"Fine," Cameron fibbed. He really didn't want to go back on tablets.

"Did you get around to calling that lawyer?"

"Not yet. I've had a lot on my mind over the last few weeks. I need to have a good think about it first," Cameron replied.

"Fair enough. Don't leave it until it's too late," he said.

Cameron turned his head and watched as the stitches were removed one by one. He yearned to be able to scratch it; the itchiness was even worse once they had been removed. Dr Solomon wiped something over the top that stung a little, but felt good at the same time.

"No scratching it," he said, as though reading Cameron's mind. He stuck an adhesive dressing over the top and pulled off his gloves. "All done."

Cameron re-dressed and yawned.

"Thanks, Doc," he said.

"No worries. Stay out of trouble for a while, and all the best with your new place."

The final thing on the list for the day was to go shopping. He had enough money left in his savings after paying the bond, plus some left over from his pay, to buy some much-needed essentials for the new place. He led Dalcian to a large department store, and made his way towards the trolley bay.

Dalcian let go of his hand and darted ahead, and pulled out a trolley from the bay. He smirked at Cameron and gripped it tighter.

"I'll push."

"Cheeky bugger." Cameron grinned. He paused and sat the green bag in the baby seat.

As they weaved through each of the departments, Cameron felt his nervousness turning into excitement as they picked out their tea towels, dinner set, bedding, and all the important things they needed. Cameron's eyes lingered on a shiny new coffee machine, but instead picked out a cheap jug. He was happy with instant coffee for the moment.

"Do you need anything from over there?" He pointed at the stationary aisle.

"I hadn't really thought about it," Dalcian replied.

"Go and have a look, I'll be back in a sec."

Cameron slipped back to the home area and picked up a desk lamp that he'd spotted. He hid it in the trolley without Dalcian seeing.

Dalcian picked out a few pencils and markers for his drawing, and they headed to the checkout. It was only 11:00; they still had plenty of time before Sarah was due.

Cameron was surprised that they hadn't spent nearly as much as he'd expected. As they walked outside, his thoughts turned to the adult shop in the shopping centre opposite the department store.

"I'll quickly duck over the road and get a few groceries to do us for a day or two. Are you ok to wait here with the trolley?" Cameron asked.

"Ok," Dalcian replied. "Hurry back."

* * *

Cameron's emotions were all over the place as they stood outside the apartment door with their piles of shopping. He pulled the keys from his pocket and handed one to Dalcian with shaking fingers.

"You can do the honours," he said.

"No. You should do it," Dalcian argued.

"Go on. Please?"

"Together," Dalcian said.

He slipped the key into the lock, and waited until Cameron's hand was on top of his. Together, they turned the key and unlocked the door to their apartment. The smell of fresh paint and carpet greeted them as the door swung open.

Dalcian took a step inside, his eyes wide in surprise.

"Wow," he breathed.

"Welcome home." Cameron picked him up and spun him around. "Our home!"

Dalcian wrapped his arms and legs around Cameron and helped himself to a kiss. Cameron could feel happy tears forming, but he blinked them away. Reluctantly, he returned Dalcian to his feet.

"You get to pick our bedroom," he said.

Cameron busied himself with bringing their shopping inside; he still couldn't believe that he was finally in the apartment. The fresh carpet felt soft under his feet, and the walls had been painted white, which made the place look so much more modern and less like a dump.

"This one," Dalcian called.

Cameron loaded his arms with their bedding and joined him in the master bedroom.

"I can't believe this is actually happening," Cameron blurted out. "I was so sure that something bad was going to happen and we'd be out there still."

"I know, hey," Dalcian replied.

Cameron took his hand and showed him the rest of the apartment.

"This is like a mansion compared to where I used to live," Dalcian said as he looked out from the balcony. "I can't believe we actually live here now."

Dalcian drifted back inside and stood staring into space as though he were overwhelmed. Cameron picked him up and sat him on the kitchen bench. Dalcian blinked, then grinned, and pulled Cameron closer so that he was standing between his legs. He was a little bit taller than Cameron while sitting on the bench; Cameron wrapped his arms around Dalcian's waist as their lips came together in a passionate kiss. Cameron could feel his legs turning to jelly as it finally hit him; he and Dalcian were together in their own home. The butterflies that had taken up residence inside him all took flight at once. If there was such a thing as a perfect kiss, Cameron was pretty sure that that kiss would be it. Dalcian's body melted into his…

"Jeez, get a room you two!"

Cameron jumped and spun around at the intrusion; he felt his face turn red when he saw Sarah smirking at him from just inside the door with her arms crossed.

"Don't you know how to knock?!" Cameron gasped.

"Don't know how to close and lock your door?" she countered with a laugh.

Cameron didn't know where to look; while he was more than comfortable with his sexuality, being sprung during an intimate moment by a work colleague left him feeling flustered and embarrassed. He heard Dalcian slip to the floor behind him, and silently cursed himself for forgetting to close the door in the first place.

Sarah crossed the floor and pulled him into a big rough hug.

"What are you all embarrassed for?" she asked.

"Graham. Barry…" Cameron murmured.

"Oh, fuck those two," she said, releasing him. "You do you. I already guessed that your roommate wasn't your roommate."

Cameron clammed up; he was surprised by her reaction, and for once he didn't know what to say. Dalcian materialised from behind him and shyly took his hand.

"There you are. Don't be shy, hon." She reached out and gently pinched him on the cheek. "Let's go and unpack the furniture."

Cameron stationed Dalcian inside as the door opener, and helped Sarah's husband Ron to carry everything upstairs. As they carried the final piece towards the door, Cameron paused and looked inside. Dalcian was in the bedroom; Cameron nodded to Ron and they snuck into the spare room with the desk.

"This'll do," Cameron said.

They pushed it under the window, and Cameron unboxed the lamp he'd bought. It had a pen cup built into the base which he thought was cool. He plugged it in and sat Dalcian's pencils and markers on top of the desk, and stood back to admire his work.

"Looks good, mate," Ron said.

Cameron closed the door to the spare room just as Dalcian joined them.

"Don't go in there yet," Cameron said.

"Oh, ok."

"I guess we'll be off, then," Ron said.

"We'll walk you down," Cameron nodded. "Let's go."

Cameron waved as Sarah and Ron drove off, then dragged his arse back upstairs. His body was sore from carting everything up two flights of steps, and he desperately wanted a long hot shower. He followed Dalcian back inside and stretched.

"What's in the spare room?" Dalcian asked curiously.

"A surprise," Cameron said. "Do you want to see it now?"

"Yeah."

Cameron covered his eyes with his hands and guided him into the room.

"Ok. Ready?"

Dalcian attempted to nod, and Cameron removed his hands.

"Ta daa!"

Dalcian stood staring at the desk for a moment, then drifted over and turned on the lamp.

"It's not much, but I thought you'd like your own space to hang out in, work on your drawing and stuff," Cameron said.

Without a word, Dalcian turned and threw himself into Cameron's arms.

"Thank you," he said. "It's awesome."

"I'm going to go and have a shower," Cameron said. "Wanna join me?"

"Of course," Dalcian replied.

Cameron slowly peeled Dalcian's shirt over his head, and teased him with a kiss on his nose. He was pleased to see that in the couple of weeks that he had been eating more regularly, Dalcian's body had filled out a little and was looking healthier. He ran his hands around Dalcian's back and waist; he was still tiny compared to Cameron's larger frame.

By the time they made it from the spare room to the bathroom, they were both naked, and a trail of clothes and shoes lay strewn across the floor. Cameron fumbled with the taps, his lips never parting from Dalcian's, and managed to get the temperature right.

Although he was dead tired, he could tell that Dalcian had more in mind than blowjobs; where they would usually wash each other and chat, this time they were silent and washed themselves as quickly as possible. When they weren't washing their bodies, Dalcian was all over him, his boner grinding against Cameron's as he nibbled and kissed Cameron's neck.

Cameron turned off the water and clambered out of the shower. He could feel himself shaking with anticipation; he didn't even bother to finish drying himself. As Dalcian bent over to dry his legs, Cameron dropped his towel and put his hands on Dalcian's waist, and pressed his dick against his arse to tease him. Dalcian stood up slowly, and Cameron ran his hands from his waist up to his chest. He kissed from Dalcian's shoulder up to his neck, earning a soft moan from his lips. Cameron steered him from the bathroom and into the bedroom.

Dalcian had already put the sheets on the mattress, though the doona cover lay in a heap on the floor. Cameron crawled onto the mattress and rolled onto his side as Dalcian joined him. He pulled him into his arms and kissed him passionately; all thoughts in his head were gone except for the desire he felt for the man in his arms.

Cameron ran his hands over every inch of Dalcian's body, as though touching him for the first time. The feeling of Dalcian's body against his, the taste of his lips, and his passionate kisses all made Cameron drift away into a sea of bliss. He could feel a deep emotion forming in his chest, much stronger than he had ever felt, and for a moment it consumed him. He gripped onto Dalcian and rolled onto his back, pulling him on top of his body.

Dalcian tore his lips away and straddled Cameron's body, then started licking and sucking on his nipples. Cameron felt a soft moan escape from his lips, and closed his eyes, permitting Dalcian to do whatever he pleased to his body. Dalcian was soon making out with Cameron's cock and slurping on his balls.

He pushed Cameron's legs back and immediately started exploring his hole with his tongue. It was something Cameron had never received before, but the sensation of Dalcian's warm damp tongue working its magic sure felt amazing.

There were many things Cameron wanted to do and explore with him, but being Dalcian's first time, Cameron wanted to make it memorable for him. As Dalcian came up for air, Cameron pulled him back up the mattress and switched positions. Dalcian was soon moaning softly as Cameron sucked his dick. As much as shower blowjobs were fun, being in the privacy of their own bed made everything feel so much better.

Cameron was so aroused, so turned on, that blowjobs just wouldn't do. He could see the hunger on Dalcian's face that echoed his own desires. He reached out for the bag of sexy stuff he'd bought, and fished out the lube and condoms. Cameron had bought a few toys, too, but they were for another day. He shimmied back up the bed and kissed Dalcian hungrily.

"Would you like to top?" Cameron whispered.

"Are you sure? I thought that was for someone special."

"You are so special to me." Cameron kissed him again to prove his point.

Dalcian scrambled to change positions again, and Cameron rolled on the condom for him with shaking fingers. He could feel his heart beating faster inside his chest at the thought of what he was about to do. Dalcian pushed him roughly back onto the mattress with a grin.

Cameron pulled his legs back again, and watched as Dalcian applied the lube — somewhat clumsily — then slowly pressed a lubey finger into Cameron's hole. He worked up to a second finger; Cameron was no stranger to having toys in his arse, but it had been a long time. He closed his eyes and bit his lower lip as Dalcian slowly pressed his cock against his hole, and slid inside. For a moment he felt a little pain, but that pain was soon replaced by pleasure, and the look of bliss on Dalcian's face said everything.

There was no way that Cameron could ever describe the feelings that washed through him. He wasn't used to being in control during sex, and felt somewhat vulnerable. Being able to trust someone so much, to share that control, was empowering and liberating. To share something so intimate with someone he cared deeply for made the moment even more special.

Cameron was vaguely aware of himself grunting and groaning as Dalcian slid in and out of his arse; none of the toys he'd used even came close to how amazing Dalcian's dick felt inside of him.

"I'm going to cum!" Dalcian gasped.

"Cum for me, babe."

Cameron started playing with himself as Dalcian closed his eyes and pushed himself in as deep as he could go; with a loud groan, he released and came.

"Oh my god!" he exclaimed.

Seconds after, Cameron came too, with Dalcian still deep inside him. He shot load after load onto his chest, until finally he was done.

"Wow," he breathed.

Dalcian pulled off the condom and passed Cameron the doona cover to wipe himself down with, then collapsed next to him, panting as though he'd just run a marathon. Cameron pulled him into a tight hug, and held him as they floated in their post-orgasmic euphoria.

Dalcian kissed Cameron's chest, then tilted his head back to peer into Cameron's eyes.

"Was that ok?" he asked.

"Better than ok," Cameron said smiling. "It was amazing."

"I dunno. I think I'll need more practice."

Cameron chuckled, and pulled him closer for a kiss.

"You're so amazing. I think I lo—" The obnoxious sound of Cameron's ringtone cut him off and made him jump. "Oh, for fuck's sake!"

"You better answer it, it could be important."

Cameron sighed and pushed himself up off the mattress. He followed the sound out to the living room, and fished his phone from the pocket of his discarded pants. It was Graham.

"Of all the times to call, you had to call now," Cameron hissed when he answered.

"What, did I catch you with your pants down?" Graham asked.

"You could say that."

Graham cracked up laughing.

"It's about time you got yourself some arse. She any good?"

"Fuck you." Cameron couldn't help but grin. He loved the banter they shared.

Dalcian floated from the bedroom and cuddled him from behind. Cameron put the call on loudspeaker and stared into space.

"So, the reason I'm calling. A big job has come up this Wednesday night. A new flagship store is opening in Barangaroo at midnight with a massive sale. They're anticipating crowds to rival the biggest Myer crowds."

"Shit. How many of us are going to be on site?" Cameron ran his spare hand over Dalcian's.

"Six of us. I'll be on the door. One will be patrolling the registers and checking bags. Two will be patrolling inside, and I have you and Sarah in the tech department. They're going to be selling some really cheap shit, so we could be seeing idiots fighting over TVs and phones. It's formal uniform too. Do you have one?"

"No."

"I'll drop one off to you tomorrow."

"What's my roster for the rest of the week?" Cameron asked.

"Tomorrow til Tuesday, uniform at Parra. 08:00 til 20:00. Wednesday, Parra, 08:00 til 16:00. Go home and get some rest, then Barangaroo midnight til 12:00. I know you will hate me for this, but I'll need you back at Parra til 18:00."

"Are you fucking kidding me?" Cameron demanded.

"It's bullshit I know. We are short on guards at the moment, and Barry won't hire any temps to fill the void."

"This company will be the death of me," Cameron grumbled.

"I know, mate."

"Tell Barry I'm having Saturday off, then," Cameron said.

"What's happening on Saturday?" Graham asked.

"I'm going to live my life, that's what. I gotta go, I'll see you tomorrow."

"Alright mate, catch ya later."

Cameron hung up and groaned.

"I'm so sick of this bullshit," he sighed.

"You're going to be so tired," Dalcian pointed out.

"Yeah. I'll be ok though, I'm used to it." He looked at his phone; it was already 16:00. He sighed and set his alarm with a yawn. "Speaking of tired, I'm dead on my feet."

After a quick wash and glass of water, Cameron finally climbed into bed, followed closely by Dalcian. He plugged in his phone and stretched out on his side of the mattress.

"This is so much better than the hostel," he said sleepily. "I'll see if I can get a second-hand bed from somewhere."

"This is just fine," Dalcian said, snuggling into his chest. "Night, Yogi."

"Night, Boo-Boo."

13

Cameron's Sunday flew. Morning shower sex, breakfast with Dalcian on their couch, and the anticipation of going *home* had Cameron bouncing off the walls. The few incidents that day had mostly been school kids trying to pinch snacks and drinks, and Cameron took the opportunity to put the fear of God into them. For most school kids, the threat of their parents finding out was usually enough to stop them from reoffending, and Cameron knew it was his opportunity to steer the kids away from a life of crime.

Being a uniform shift, Cameron had too much time to think. He couldn't remember ever being so happy in his life; sure, the early days of exploration with Paul were fun, and when they moved into their house, he had been excited. Even as a child, before his parents died, though, he couldn't remember ever being so happy.

As he walked through the supermarket on his hourly patrol, he realised with a start that everyone he had ever cared about were gone from his life. Dad, Mum, Paul, all gone. Cameron tried to push his anxiety aside and stop overthinking things, but deep down he was scared that something would come between him and Dalcian. He knew he had almost slipped out with the big L word in his post-orgasmic euphoria, and was still struggling to define their relationship.

What if Dalcian doesn't feel that way about me? What if he just sees me as a friend, and falls for someone else? Should I tell him how I feel? What if I upset him? Bloody hell Cameron, you always have to over-complicate things.

With a sigh, he pulled out his phone and scrolled through the pictures that Dalcian had taken. He was pretty sure he had nothing to worry about, but the horrible double-guessing of himself thanks to his anxiety still had him worried.

He was saved by the arrival of Graham, around twenty minutes before he was due to knock off.

"I was starting to think you'd been called to another job and weren't coming," Cameron smirked.

"Mate, don't get me started," Graham sighed. "How's the new place?"

"It's great," Cameron replied. "It would be nice to have some time off to actually enjoy it, but hey, at least I get to sleep there."

"I haven't been to my house for over a week," Graham said.

"Yeah, but you pick up a different sheila every night, you don't need a house."

"That's true," he laughed. "So I hear you're seeing someone now."

"Bloody hell, news travels fast." Cameron frowned. "Let me guess. Sarah?"

"Nah, Clarissa. She's gossip central."

Cameron groaned and slapped his forehead; he felt his face growing hot. Clarissa would have seen him and Dalcian together quite a few times, but he hadn't thought of her to be one to gossip.

"For fuck's sake!" he groaned.

"Mate, don't worry about it," Graham waved his hand. He looked tired and preoccupied. "Now, about

Wednesday. I've got your uniform in my car. Sarah said she can pick you up and bring you into the city, and drop you off at Parra the next day."

"That'll be handy," Cameron managed.

"You're going to love this. We're being issued with radios for comms."

"You're kidding me," Cameron scoffed. "Those were being phased out back when I first started."

"I know. Given the anticipated crowds, and the number of guards on site, it will be handy. It's a bit hard to call each other when we're six-up." Graham looked at his watch. "It's almost time for you to sign out. Want a lift home?"

The thought of getting home to Dalcian sooner was certainly appealing.

"Alright. Sounds good," Cameron nodded. "I'll just go and get my stuff. Back shortly."

* * *

The new department store was unlike anything Cameron had expected. Where he had envisaged a Myer-type setup, Global So was more like an oversized Kmart or Big W spread out over two levels. The lower floor was mostly clothing, tech and kitchenware, whereas upstairs held the Manchester and furniture section.

Cameron stood next to Graham and Sarah, listening to the store manager ramble on about her expectations and the policies they had to enforce. Ms Jones was an arrogant bitch, but Cameron wasn't bothered. Once the doors opened, he knew he wouldn't see her again unless the shit really hit the fan. Ms Jones handed them all a radio each, and briefed them on proper protocol.

Finally she was done, and hurried off to yell at her staff. Graham let out a deep breath followed by an eyeroll.

"Right. Keep the chatter to a minimum and remember

your callsigns. That idiot will be listening in, so I don't want to give her an excuse to make the night hell." Graham nodded as though giving a cue, and everyone switched on their radios and hooked their earpieces in. "Doors open in twenty minutes. You all know what to do, so go do it."

Cameron fist-bumped Graham, then turned and followed Sarah to their post. Frazzled staff were milling about all over the store, getting ready for the doors to open and the subsequent rush.

"These bloody suits," Sarah complained as they walked. "How are we supposed to tackle people when we're wrapped up like monkeys?"

"We're not supposed to tackle, remember?" Cameron snorted. "Observe and report. At least we'll look good, though."

"Says he who got stabbed," she laughed.

"Come to think of it, can you take a photo of me for Dalcian?" Cameron handed her his phone, and posed in front of a stack of TVs.

"Got it. Now turn around," she ordered.

"Why?"

"I'm sure he'll want to perve on your arse."

Cameron sighed and turned around, then slipped his phone back in his pocket.

"Mike One to Delta One — what's your status? Over." Ms Jones' voice came through the radio, making them both jump.

"Delta One in position and standing by. Over," Graham replied.

"Mike One to Roving One — what's your status? Over."

Cameron rolled his eyes as she cycled through to every guard on the frequency.

"A simple 'You all ready?' would suffice," Sarah smirked once they'd both called in.

"I wonder if Graham's tried to hit on her yet." Cameron grinned.

"Mike One. All teams stand by. Doors open in ten minutes. Over."

"I might have to buy one of these TVs if there are any left tomorrow," Cameron said, eyeing the $99 price tag. "Hopefully I can get Dalcian a cheap phone too."

"How're things going with your boyfriend?" Sarah asked.

"He's not really my boyfriend," Cameron blurted out. "I mean, I don't know what we are."

"You certainly looked the part when you were eating each other's faces off," she said.

"I'm actually really confused," Cameron admitted.

"What about?"

"All of this just…happened. It's like we're in a relationship, but nothing is official. I don't know if I should ask him out to formalise it, or just go with it."

"I don't think there is any doubt as to how you feel about each other," Sarah noted.

"I'm more worried that if I don't formalise it, someone might come along and sweep him off his feet," Cameron sighed. "I'm also worried that if I just come out and ask him what we are, he might get upset. I don't know. It sounds so silly."

"Why don't you just take him out to dinner and tell him how you feel?" she suggested. "You need to be honest with him. Stop overthinking it and just do it."

"You're right," Cameron sighed. "I—"

"Delta One to Mike One. The crowd is substantial and rowdy. Be prepared for a surge. Over."

"Mike One. Roger that Delta One. All teams stand by, doors opening in thirty seconds. Over."

"Here we go. Good luck," Sarah smirked.

Cameron could hear the crowd once the doors opened, and watched as a sea of heads flooded into the store. A large group of shoppers headed straight to the tech department, and made a beeline for the cheap TVs.

Most of the shoppers were well behaved. Cameron only had to argue with around ten people who wanted more than the one-per-family limit, and Sarah didn't have to tackle anyone. By 04:00, the crowds thinned, and the staff ran around frantically, restocking as much as they could before the next rush.

The next surge came around 06:00, and this time the crowd were more desperate for what bargains were left. It wasn't long until the stack of TVs dwindled down to just one, and before Cameron could flag down a staff member about it, two women were fighting over the final unit.

"I saw it first!" one of the women yelled, yanking on one end of the box. "Let go!"

"I picked it up first, it's mine!" the other woman, shorter with a blonde bobbed haircut yelled. "Where's the manager?!"

Cameron and Sarah rolled their eyes, and before they could intervene, the two women were fighting and pulling at each other's hair.

"Tech Two to Roving One and Two. Get your arses here quick," Cameron yelled into his mic, not giving two shits about protocol as he tried to pull back the blonde woman.

"Mike One to Tech Two. That was inappropriate! What's going on? Over."

"What's going on, Cam?" Graham demanded.

Cameron didn't get to reply; the woman's husband joined in and punched him in the jaw just as the two patrolling guards came running to help. Cameron let go of the woman, and managed to tackle the husband to the ground. One of the guards grabbed the woman, and the other guard helped Cameron to drag the husband to his feet.

"Tech Two to Mike One. Please call the police. We have just broken up a fight and will require assistance. Over," Cameron panted into his mic.

"Mike One to Tech Two. I'll be right there. Over."

Cameron's phone rang, and he quickly answered.

"Fuck the radios. What happened?" Graham asked.

"Two bitches fighting over a TV and the husband joined in," Cameron replied. "We're all fine."

"The idiot is on her way over, she just called the cops. Send Sanjeep or Arjun up here and I'll come down."

"Righto, mate. Here she comes." Cameron quickly hung up, and took a hold of the husband's arms.

"Go up front and cover Graham, mate," Cameron said to Arjun.

The guard nodded and hurried off towards the front, as Ms Jones materialised out of the clothing racks.

"What on earth is going on here?" she demanded.

Both of the women started shouting about how the TV was theirs and their treatment was unfair. Cameron hid his smirk as Ms Jones' face mirrored her panic. For a moment she froze as though she didn't know what to do.

"May I suggest we go out the back and out of sight from the rest of your customers?" Sarah said politely.

"I was about to say that," Ms Jones said quickly. "This way."

"May I also suggest you bring the TV and hold it off the floor?" Cameron added. "We don't want any more fights over it."

Ms Jones wordlessly picked up the TV and led them out the back to await the police.

Thankfully, the rest of the shift was a breeze. After the police left, Ms Jones was a lot nicer towards the security team, and even gave Cameron permission to purchase the last TV. He collected a few things they needed for home, then made his way to the registers to pay and sign off.

"Good job, everyone," Graham yawned once he'd briefed the two dayshift replacement guards. "I'll be back at the office having a nap. Catch you all later."

Cameron said his good-byes and followed Sarah to

her car.

"Let's stop in at Maccas and get coffee on the way. You owe me a drink," Sarah said.

"Actually, let's swing by Burwood. Dalcian's working today, and they do good coffee."

"Oh, he'll love that," she agreed. "Let's went."

The café was packed when Cameron and Sarah pushed their way inside. A group of homeless people sat at a table and eyed their uniforms suspiciously. Cameron nodded politely, and caught sight of Dalcian behind the counter, taking someone's order. He was dressed all in black, and had a tea towel hanging from his back pocket. He stuck his pencil behind his ear, and took the customer's payment.

Cameron stepped forward and stood patiently with a grin on his face; Dalcian handed the written order to the barista, then turned back to the register.

"Hi. What can I get you?" he asked, not looking up.

"You should know how I like my coffee by now." Cameron grinned. "You look sexy in your uniform."

Dalcian frowned and looked up; his face broke into a huge smile when he realised who it was.

"Yogi! Oh my god. Hi, Sarah."

"Hi, hon." She smiled.

"We're just on our way over to Parra," Cameron said. "Thought we'd drop in for coffee."

"Tall soy latte, yeah?" Dalcian asked Sarah.

"He's good." Sarah grinned. "You should keep him."

Dalcian blushed and handed the order to the barista. Cameron went to hand him his card, but Dalcian shook his head.

"My treat," he said.

Cameron sat a small gift box on the counter and pushed it across to him.

"I know you're busy, so we won't hold you up. Here's something to play with when you get off work tonight."

"Oh, ok. Thanks, Yogi."

Cameron winked and stood out of the way. He could see Jill through the rectangle window of the kitchen, and didn't want to get Dalcian in trouble. The barista had around six orders to make in front of theirs; Cameron could see why Jill wanted to hire another staff member.

"Here's your order," the barista smiled, handing over two large takeaway mugs.

With a start, Cameron realised that Dalcian had asked him to make their order first. Dalcian looked over and waved with a cute smile.

"See you tonight, boo," Cameron mouthed.

Cameron struggled through his shift in Parramatta. He was exhausted and sore, and couldn't wait to get home and crash. Around 16:00, his phone buzzed with a message from an unknown number. Cameron grinned; he already knew who it was.

```
UNKNOWN: Hi sexy.

CAMERON: Hello sexier. Surprise!

DALCIAN: You're too good to me. You
didn't have to do this.

CAMERON: I wanted to. Now I can send
you dick pics.

DALCIAN: lol

CAMERON: When do you finish work?

DALCIAN: Already finished.
```

CAMERON: Oh. Are you coming to see
me?

DALCIAN: No.

For a moment Cameron felt disappointed. He stared
at his phone for a second, contemplating a reply. He
started to type a message, but deleted it. Someone tapped
him on the shoulder, scaring the shit out of him. Cameron
jumped and spun around. Dalcian laughed, and Cameron
felt his face break into a smile. Dalcian handed him a
coffee; Cameron glanced around, then helped himself to
a quick kiss.

"You cheeky shit," Cameron said sheepishly. "You
totally got me."

"I know," Dalcian chortled. "You should have seen
your face!"

Cameron took a deep swig of his coffee. It was just the
right temperature.

"Speaking of your face. What's with the bruise?"
Dalcian asked.

"What bruise?"

He lightly traced his finger along Cameron's jaw and
cheek.

"Oh, *that*. We had a bit of an incident last night.
Nothing serious," Cameron said quickly. "I'll tell you
about it on the way home."

"Ok." Dalcian pulled his shiny new phone from his
pocket and looked at it. "I still can't believe you bought
me a phone."

"It's nothing fancy, but it was cheap and too good
to pass up on." Cameron shrugged. "It has a prepaid sim
card, and you'll be able to hijack the shopping centre or
library Wi-Fi."

"And send you dick pics," Dalcian smirked.

Cameron laughed.

"I need to do a patrol. Come for a walk."

He steered Dalcian inside the supermarket, and together they walked through the store as Cameron checked what needed checking.

"Are you working on Saturday?" he asked as they walked along the frozen section.

"No, I have the weekend off," Dalcian replied.

Cameron stopped by the frozen chips and turned to face him. There was only one customer in the aisle, and he was too busy reading the back of a frozen pack of peas to be paying them any attention.

"I have Saturday off," Cameron said. "Do you want to head over here and do something?"

"What do you mean?" Dalcian asked.

"Go shopping, watch a movie, hang out. We could go to the restaurant at the RSL club for dinner." Cameron hoped that Dalcian couldn't notice his nerves. *You idiot. This is nothing to be nervous about Cameron.*

"Ok, that sounds like fun. If I pass the course tomorrow, we can celebrate."

Cameron breathed a silent sigh of relief, and quickly scanned the aisle again. The pea man was now studying a pack of carrots. Cameron pulled Dalcian in closer for a quick lingering kiss, then swept him from the aisle.

"Where are you doing the course and what time does it start?" Cameron asked as they walked along the back of the store.

"It's here in Parramatta, a place along Church Street, and starts at 7:30 in the morning," Dalcian replied.

"Perfect. I'll get up early and see you off before work."

"I'd like that."

18:00 couldn't come quick enough. Had Cameron been required to work until 20:00, he doubted he would have been able to stay awake and finish the shift. He dozed off twice on the train ride home, but thankfully Dalcian nudged him awake and ensured he didn't miss their stop.

Finally, they arrived home just before 19:00. Cameron busied himself setting up the new TV so that Dalcian had something to do while he was home alone, then sank onto the couch, exhausted.

"Do you want something to eat?" Dalcian called from the kitchen.

"I'm too tired to eat, but I am hungry," Cameron sighed as he kicked off his shoes.

"I'll make you some two-minute noodles."

Cameron managed to drag his arse off the couch and strip off his uniform. He had a quick wash and slipped on his trackies and hoodie. The night was cold, and there was a chill in the air inside the apartment.

He slumped back to the couch, and Dalcian sat his noodles and a mug of tea on their make-shift coffee table.

"Thanks, Boo-Boo," Cameron yawned.

"Apartment, TV, phone. We're really moving up in the world," Dalcian marvelled.

"Totally. You know, it still hasn't sunk in that we're here. I keep thinking I'm going to wake up from a dream at any minute."

"It's all real, Yogi."

"Stanmore feels like a lifetime ago," Cameron mused. "Come to think of it, we've known each other for a month now."

"A month already? Are you sure?"

"The first time I met you was the 8th of May when that guy punched you. I know the date because I had to report the incident."

"It feels like so much longer. Maybe because I'd seen you around a lot before then," Dalcian admitted.

"Really?"

"Yeah. I saw you take down two big guys by yourself in Pitt Street one time. Another time you bumped into me at Strathfield station. I promise I wasn't stalking you or anything weird."

Cameron frowned and tried to remember that particular incident. Finally it dawned on him.

"Wow, I actually remember that. I was heading up to Gosford to do a twelve-hour shift. I only had three hours sleep, and was a total zombie. The idiots behind me almost pushed me over trying to get to their train, and I almost knocked you over. I tried to turn back and apologise, but you were already gone with the crowd. I never got to see your face."

"Well, you get to see my face every day now." Dalcian grinned. "You'll get sick of it soon."

"I could never get sick of your pretty face. Or you."

Cameron forced himself to eat his noodles, and almost choked when *The Big Bang Theory* started up on TV.

"Oh my god, I love this show!" Cameron said. "I haven't seen it for so long."

"I've never seen it," Dalcian said.

"You'll love it. I used to have the entire set on DVD."

Cameron finished his noodles and sat sipping his tea, with Dalcian lying with his head in his lap. He must have dozed off; Cameron vaguely remembered being shaken awake and being dragged to the bedroom. As soon as his head hit the pillow, he fell into a deep sleep.

14

Cameron woke up shivering and cold. He reached out and checked the time on his phone; it was only 02:15. With a sigh, he rolled over and put out his arm to pull Dalcian closer. The bed was cold and empty. With a start, Cameron vaulted upright and scanned the room. Once his eyes adjusted, he could make out a faint light spilling into the room. He dragged himself off the mattress, and went to investigate.

The light was coming from the spare room. Cameron squinted as his eyes adjusted to the brightness, then looked to see Dalcian hunched over his desk, wrapped in one of the throw blankets they had picked out together. On the wall next to the window, Dalcian had blue-tacked the poster of the mysterious superhero that was in the metal box.

"Are you ok, Boo-Boo?" Cameron asked from the doorway.

Dalcian jumped and furtively covered something on the desk.

"You scared me," he said, turning around.

"Sorry."

With a yawn, Dalcian turned off the desk lamp and shrugged the blanket off his shoulders. He wrapped his arms around Cameron's neck and buried his face into his shoulder.

"I can't sleep," he sighed.

"Oh, boo. Come back to bed where it's warm."

Dalcian tightened his grip and raised one leg. It took Cameron a second to catch on; with a sleepy smile, he lifted Dalcian effortlessly off the ground and carried him to the bedroom. Once they were beside the mattress, Cameron lowered him to the floor, and Dalcian reluctantly let go and crawled into bed.

"What's troubling you?" Cameron asked once he'd pulled him into his arms protectively.

"I haven't been in a classroom for years. What if I fail the course tomorrow?" he blurted out.

"You won't fail. You're good at your job and you're smart. What makes you think you won't pass?"

"I'm scared I'll forget everything they teach us, and not have a clue what to do on Monday. I don't want to let everyone down."

"Listen to me." Cameron ran his fingers down Dalcian's cheek to draw his full attention. "You're not going to fail. You will go in there with pen and paper, take notes and write everything down. If you get stuck, ask the teacher for help. I know you can do this."

"I already did the online part of it on the computer at work," Dalcian said. "I passed but Jill had to help me."

Dalcian stuck his cold feet on Cameron's, and wriggled closer. He was shivering; Cameron yanked the doona up to their necks and squeezed him gently.

"I guess I'm just nervous," he sighed after a while. "I struggled a bit at school. I always scraped through with a pass, but I think the teachers felt sorry for me or something."

"Did they know about your home life?" Cameron asked gently.

"I think they suspected it, but I lied about the bruises."

Dalcian yawned and seemed to relax a little. "Tell me a story. What was school like for you?"

"Gee, that feels like such a long time ago," Cameron said. "Dad died when I was in year six. I missed a lot of school that year because Mum kept me home. The school wanted me to repeat year six, but I begged Mum not to keep me back, and she managed to convince them to let me go on to high school.

"It was hard. Mum worked hard to put meals on the table and to pay for books and uniform. Most of the family money was tied up in assets, so we only had her income. I never went without, though. We both missed Dad. I got to see the school counsellor when everything got to me, which helped.

"Anyway. I wasn't popular, I was one of the weirdos. We all hung out at the back of the oval and had a good time. While the popular kids were fighting over who slept with whom at parties, we were jamming to Metallica and talking shit. Some of them smoked, so we would all stand in a circle and block them from view from the teachers."

"Did you smoke?" Dalcian asked.

"When Paul came along in year nine, he convinced me to try it. I'd have an occasional drag just to shut him up, but it wasn't until Mum died that I started smoking for a while. It helped to calm me down, and Paul's parents didn't care. They bought us what we wanted."

"I didn't figure you as a bad boy," Dalcian said sleepily. "Badass, yes. Smoking is gross."

"I wasn't a bad boy, I just let myself get peer pressured. I quit cold turkey when I finished school, and started going to the gym to get fit and healthy. I actually had a decent body back then, and looked pretty good."

"I think you have the sexiest body right now," Dalcian murmured. "Did you pass your classes?"

"I was a nerd. I got good grades, and was top of the class in English and science. Had things been different,

I would have gone to university and probably studied forensics—" Cameron broke off as a soft snore floated from Dalcian's lips. "G'nite, Boo-Boo. Sweet dreams."

* * *

Dalcian looked tired and nervous as they stood outside the training centre. They had awoken to an icy frost, and as they waited their breath steamed in the air. Dalcian patted his pocket for the hundredth time to make sure his wallet was still there, then checked the time on his phone again.

"Relax, Boo-Boo. You're going to ace this," Cameron said.

"I hope so. Otherwise I don't have a job on Monday."

"Don't be like that. Remember what we spoke about last night, you're going to be fine."

Dalcian finished his coffee just as the doors opened. The other students slowly filed inside.

"I guess I'm about to find out," Dalcian said wryly. "I'll come and see you when I finish at one."

"Ok. You've got this." Cameron gave him a quick kiss, then watched as he hurried inside. With a sigh, he turned and made his way to work.

Cameron's morning dragged on, as he checked his phone every five minutes to see what time it was. Each minute felt like an hour; it was torture. He was confident that Dalcian would pass, but the anticipation was killing him. Even Clarissa noticed his impatience, and approached him for a chat.

"What are you all antsy for?" she asked with a grin.

"What do you mean?" Cameron asked.

"You've been looking at your phone every few seconds ever since you started today."

"Just waiting on some news, that's all." Cameron

shrugged. "I need to go on my break at 12:50 to go and find out first-hand."

"Ooh, what news?" she asked.

"It's kind of personal," he said quickly.

"Aww, come on, tell me," she insisted.

"What, so you can tell my boss?" Cameron hit back. "I keep my work life and private life separate, and as such, Graham has no need to know what I do when I'm not on the clock."

"Oh my god, I'm so sorry, Cam!" Clarissa suddenly looked mortified. "I let slip that you've been hanging out with someone hot before and after work. I didn't tell him anything other than that, though. I hope I didn't get you into an awkward situation."

"Did you tell him the hot someone is a dude?" Cameron asked.

"No, not at all," she said.

Cameron breathed a sigh of relief.

"Thank God for that. I'm not out to Graham and the others, except for Sarah. I don't think I could cope with the amount of shit I'd cop."

"It only came up because he had some woman confront him and go psycho," she shrugged. "She found out that he'd been with both her sister and her best friend. Centre security had to escort her away."

"The bastard never told me that." Cameron cracked up laughing. "Mind you, he usually tells me all about his sexcapades in full detail."

"So, what news are you waiting on? I promise I won't say a word."

"Ok. Dalcian — the hot someone — is doing his barista course. He was so nervous last night he hardly slept. I'm going to drop down there at lunch when he finishes and surprise him."

"Aww, that's so sweet," Clarissa gushed. "I see him with you all the time. Do you live together?"

It was rare that Cameron opened up to anyone about anything, but he was grateful for the distraction. He had known Clarissa for around two years, and in that time, she had never given him a reason to dislike her. He was glad they had cleared the air about her stuff-up, and felt that he could somewhat trust her. He told her an abridged version of how he and Dalcian met, and she seemed genuinely happy for them.

"Clarissa to the service desk. Call on line three."

"Bloody hell," she sighed. "Nice talking to you, Cam. Catch you later." She started to walk off, then paused and looked back at Cameron. "If you want to tack your morning break onto your lunch break, I won't tell Graham." She winked.

"Thanks, mate."

Cameron looked at the time on his phone; they'd only been chatting for fifteen minutes. With a sigh, he stuffed his hands into his pockets and busied himself with a patrol.

By the time Cameron made it to the training centre, the frost had melted away, and the sky was a brilliant blue. It was a warm winter's day, too nice to be stuck inside all day. Cameron sat on a seat outside, enjoying the sunshine as he waited.

A few minutes after 13:00, a group of people poured out of the door, laughing and chattering amongst themselves. Cameron recognised a few of them from the morning. Dalcian was the last to leave, and pulled his phone from his pocket as he passed through the doors. He slowed down and held the phone to his ear, then froze when he saw Cameron.

Dalcian's face broke into the biggest smile Cameron had ever seen; before he realised what was happening, Dalcian rushed towards him and threw his arms around Cameron's neck. Cameron picked him up by the waist and spun him around dramatically.

"I PASSED!!" Dalcian yelled excitedly. "I DID IT!"

"I told you you would pass!" Cameron exclaimed. "I'm so fucking proud of you!"

Cameron pulled Dalcian's lips to his and kissed him so deeply, so passionately, that for a moment he forgot they were in the middle of one of the busiest streets of Parramatta. When he finally pulled away, Dalcian was flushed and a little short of breath.

"Maybe I'll make you proud of me more often if that's on offer," he said.

"You'll get the rest when I get home tonight," Cameron said as seductively as he could. "Are you hungry? I have around thirty minutes left before I have to get back to work."

"That's not very long," Dalcian said thoughtfully. "Do you like sushi?"

"Depends on the fillings. There are some I like," Cameron nodded.

"I've never tried it before. We could go to that place right next to the station?"

"Perfect. Let's go."

Once they'd scoffed down all the sushi they could eat, and Cameron had seen Dalcian to his train, Cameron spent the rest of his shift with a renewed pep in his step. Not long after he'd resumed his post, his phone dinged with a message.

```
DALCIAN: Jill's letting me practice
on the machine for a few hours.
I'm making the free coffees for the
homeless people, yay!
```

A picture came through of Dalcian standing next to the newer, yellow, coffee machine, wearing his black uniform, plus a barista apron. He had a pencil tucked behind his ear, and his hair was just long enough to pull into a tiny ponytail. He was the most beautiful man Cameron had ever laid eyes upon, and he stood staring at the photo for a moment, lost in his perfect smile. He saved the picture to his phone, then quickly tapped out a reply.

```
CAMERON: You are so beautiful. I
can't wait to get you home to give
you the rest of that kiss…and more ;)


DALCIAN: If that's the case…let's
ditch the toys. I think I'm ready for
you to top ;)
```

"How'd he go, Cam?"

Cameron jumped and fumbled with his phone; he looked up to see Clarissa staring at him.

"He passed," Cameron said excitedly. He quickly hid the messages and showed her the photo that Dalcian sent him.

"Oh, good on him! He's so cute. I can imagine him getting hit on all the time."

And there it was, like a slap in the face. Cameron wasn't an insecure or jealous person, but once again the thought of someone better coming along and sweeping Dalcian off his feet made Cameron's anxiety come flooding back with a vengeance.

Stop it Cameron, you're just feeding your anxiety. Your fears are irrational, and you know it. You're going to take him out tomorrow, have a great time, and tell him how you feel.

15

Cameron woke to the smell of fresh coffee wafting under his nose. He could hear the TV over the sound of something hissing. He stretched and yawned. The sun was streaming through the window, and sitting on his bedside table was a hot mug of coffee.

He reached over and checked the time on his phone; it was 08:50. Cameron sat up with a slight smile on his face, and leant against the wall, sipping his coffee. He was still naked from their lovemaking the night before, and as he replayed the night in his mind, he felt that warm feeling that had taken up residence in his belly, spread all the way down to his toes.

Dalcian had been amazing, of course. Cameron had always been a pleaser, but where Paul had never cared about reciprocating, Dalcian made up for it ten-fold. Cameron had topped for starters, but they soon flipped. Dalcian was getting better and better each time they made love, and Cameron loved feeling him buried deep inside him. *He's so perfect. I owe that boy my life. Tonight, I'll tell him how I feel...*

"Morning, Yogi," Dalcian said from the doorway.

Cameron looked up; he was leaning against the doorframe, still naked except for his smile.

"There's a sight I could get used to seeing every morning." He grinned.

Dalcian lowered himself to the mattress and crawled towards Cameron on his hands and knees.

"I could get used to last night, every night too," Dalcian said.

He stopped just inches from Cameron's face, and leant in for a kiss. Cameron leant forward, but instead of receiving his kiss, Dalcian pulled the doona back, exposing his naked body.

"Oi!"

Dalcian laughed and rolled off the mattress before Cameron could catch him.

"I made breakfast," he announced. "Get up!"

Cameron reluctantly dragged himself out of bed, and followed him to the lounge room. Two plates of bacon and scrambled eggs on toast were sitting on the coffee table.

"Where did you get the bacon and eggs from?" Cameron asked.

"There's a small shop just up the road. I went for a walk while you were asleep."

"You're so sweet." Cameron tucked into his breakfast, as *The Tom and Jerry Show* started on the Go! channel. "Wow. I haven't seen this since I was a kid. The original cartoon is almost as good as *Yogi Bear*."

"This version isn't nearly as good as the original," Dalcian said. "I like the older graphics better. Same with *Thomas the Tank*. It's all digital now instead of claymation."

"You would have liked *Top Cat* too," Cameron mused.

"Is breakfast ok?" Dalcian asked.

"Of course. It's the first home-cooked breakfast I've had for longer than I can remember," Cameron replied. "I didn't know you can cook."

"Not by choice." Dalcian's eyes grew distant for a moment, then he shook his head and blinked. "So, what are we doing today?"

"I got a big pay again, so I thought we might go over to Parramatta and see what movies are on. You know, just bum around and have some fun for once. Then we can head out for dinner."

"I've never been to the movies before," Dalcian admitted. "I wanted to see *Iron Man*, but of course I wasn't able to go."

"We'll just have to make up for lost time, then. After breakfast, we'll have a quick shower and get going."

Parramatta shopping centre was packed being a Saturday. Despite his hatred for crowds, Cameron was too happy and excited to be put off by the pushing and shoving of the savages around him. Their 'quick shower' had turned into hot couch sex, and Cameron was still glowing from the deed. They walked hand-in-hand through the throngs of people, slowly making their way up each level of the building.

Dalcian dragged Cameron into a comic book store, and spent almost an hour browsing and flipping through comics. Cameron bought him a book on drawing and writing techniques, and a few comics as a treat, then left with one happy boy jabbering about his favourite comics.

Cameron was as happy as a pig in shit, and listened to every word that Dalcian said with interest. He was so animated as he described the characters and personalities, and the plot lines of the few comics he had read.

"Do you see yourself publishing your comics some day?" Cameron asked as the cinemas came into their view.

"I don't think mine are good enough," he replied, his former excitement waning a little. "I mean, I like comics with the unlikely hero, the underdog, where I can relate to the characters. They kinda make me feel that I can be the hero, too, sometimes, if that makes sense?"

"I know what you mean. I used to enjoy reading fantasy books when I was at school, and I loved the ones where the simple farm boy ended up becoming a powerful king. I truly believe your comics are amazing."

"Maybe I should get another sketchbook and start working on something, then," he mused.

"Totally. We'll go and get one after the movie."

The lobby was packed with families, buying their snacks and tickets while their kids ran feral. Cameron shook his head and looked up at the large board with the movie times.

"Oh cool, *John Wick 3* is out already," he said.

"I haven't seen any of them," Dalcian said.

"I've seen the first one, it was great. Hmmm. Most of the new releases are sequels." He looked across at the special screenings of the older movies. "You get to pick, anyways."

"Oh look, they're showing *The Avengers*," Dalcian pointed. "Is that any good?"

"Yeah, I liked it. Getting to perve on Jeremy Renner is a bonus."

"Ok, let's watch that."

Cameron loaded up with an extra-large popcorn, a drink, and a choc top each, and led Dalcian up to the cinema on the top floor. Thankfully, most of the families all disappeared into cinema 2 to watch the new *Toy Story*; only a few other people went to watch *The Avengers*.

"Wow," Dalcian breathed as he eyed the size of the screen. "Oh look, they have recliners too!"

Cameron grinned and led him to seats towards the back, away from the other couples. He showed Dalcian how to put the seat back, then leant over and kissed him on the cheek.

"Don't forget to put your phone on silent," he said as the previews started.

Dalcian watched the movie wide-eyed, as though he were trying to take in every detail all at once. Somehow, they managed to devour the entire popcorn before the halfway mark. Cameron rested his free hand on Dalcian's crotch, and rubbed him gently through his jeans. He was sorely tempted to slip his hand into his underwear, but behaved himself.

Once the movie ended, and they'd caught the hidden scene in the credits, they walked out of the cinema hand-in-hand.

"What did you think?" Cameron asked.

"That was amazing! I see what you meant by Hawkeye, but oh my god, Tony Stark is cute too." Despite his excitement, there was a hint of sadness in his eyes.

"What's wrong, Boo-Boo?" Cameron asked.

"Sometimes I feel like I've missed out on a lot of things in life because of how I grew up. I mean, I'm not feeling sorry for myself or anything, but it makes me wonder what else I could have experienced had life been different."

"Well, things are different now. You have a safe home, and you start work on Monday. We can start doing all those things that you never got to do." Cameron slipped his arm around Dalcian's shoulder as they left the cinemas. "Are you hungry?"

"I ate too much popcorn," he groaned.

"It's only 16:00, we have plenty of time before we head to dinner. Too bad they don't have Timezone here, we could have played Laser Tag."

"Whatever that is, add it to the to-do list." Dalcian grinned.

They stepped onto the escalators and travelled up to level 5, and stood facing the supermarket where Cameron had been working. He pulled Dalcian in the opposite direction.

"I'm not going near work today," he declared.

"Why not?"

"I'll see more people stealing stuff in five minutes there than that guard has seen all day," Cameron sighed.

"That was Mr Singh. He's not very good. And besides, it's my day off."

"That's fair. You already work too much. How—" Dalcian broke off and stared open-mouthed at a large colourful store just down from Kmart. "Look! It's Yogi and Boo-Boo!"

Cameron followed his gaze, and sure enough, a large sign in the window depicted the two bears, and the slogan 'Build your own Bear!'.

"What is that place?" Dalcian asked, already hurrying towards it.

"It's The Bear Factory," Cameron replied. "I guess you get to build your own bear."

A small group of kids were sitting around a table, dressing up their colourful teddy bears and giggling amongst themselves, while their mothers chatted nearby. No one paid any attention to the two grown men rummaging through the un-stuffed bears, then standing excitedly next to the stuffing machine, waiting for their turn.

"Who gets who?" Cameron asked.

"Dibbs on Yogi," Dalcian said. "That way I can still snuggle while you're at work."

"That works." Cameron grinned.

The sales assistant eyed them with a smirk when she was finished with the little girl in front of them. Cameron couldn't care less; he was having too much fun to care what other people thought.

"G'day. Is this your first time here?" she asked.

"Yep, for both of us," Cameron replied.

"You can pick out one of those hearts there to add in for free, or those ones are $10 each and sound like a beating heart," she said, pointing.

"Do they need a heart?" Cameron asked.

"Of course they do," Dalcian said. He fished out a deep pink heart from the free dish, and Cameron picked out a red one.

"Ok. Now you have to kiss the heart to give it life."

"That's so cheesy." Dalcian grinned. He kissed the heart that Cameron picked, then held his out. Cameron kissed it, feeling silly but loving it anyway.

The lady half-stuffed Yogi, and paused so Dalcian could slip the heart inside. Once it was done, she tightened the fastenings and started on Boo-Boo.

"There you go. The official accessories are over there—" she pointed to a display stand, "—just ding the bell when you're ready to pay."

"Thanks," Cameron said.

Yogi and Boo-Boo were soon dressed in their classic outfits. Cameron paid, and they walked out with their bears in their arms like two happy kids.

"That was so cheesy, alright," Cameron said as they left. "Worth every cent. I would totally do that again."

"What bear would you make next time?" Dalcian asked.

"Dunno. Maybe one to represent Paul, so I can stick pins in him," Cameron laughed.

"Oh, that's mean!" Dalcian snorted. "What now?"

"I need coffee," Cameron said. "Let's try that café over there. I'll go and get a seat while you run into that art shop over there and get a new sketchbook."

The anxiety that had been ever-present in Cameron's gut had no room to move that day. As they sat in a booth in a tiny coffee shop, gazing into each other's eyes and chatting about nothing, Cameron was pretty sure his feelings were reciprocated. He fought the urge to blurt it out right there and then, determined to save it as the grand finale of their date. He had booked a table at the small restaurant near Old Government House, and planned to finish up with a romantic stroll through the nearby rose garden. Surely it would be perfect.

"I have something for you," Dalcian smiled, breaking Cameron's thoughts.

"Oh?"

"I was saving it for your birthday next week, but I didn't want to wait," he said.

He pulled something flat from his backpack, wrapped in a reusable plastic Woolies bag. He handed it over, and Cameron opened it slowly. Inside was a plain A5 photo frame with a black edge. Mounted neatly inside was a hand-drawn comic sketch of him and Dalcian. Cameron was depicted as a muscly security guard, and was holding Dalcian in his arms like he often did. Their two characters were locked together in a kiss. Unlike the comics in his sketchbook, this one had been inked, and took Cameron's breath away.

"Wow." Cameron sat staring at it, taking in the intricate pen strokes and tiny details.

"It's only something small. I hope you like it," Dalcian said.

"It's the most amazing gift I've ever received, and I'm not exaggerating," Cameron breathed. "I've said it before, and I'll say it again. You are so talented. This will be worth millions one day, and I will never part with it."

As they made their way from the coffee shop, hand-in-hand, each deep in their own thoughts, Dalcian suddenly stopped dead. Before Cameron knew what was happening, Dalcian yanked on his hand and pulled him into a service corridor.

"What's wrong?" Cameron blurted out.

Dalcian stood with his back against the wall, his hands over his face and shaking.

"I-I just saw him," he stammered. "*Him.*"

"Are you sure it was him?" Cameron asked.

Dalcian nodded.

"Do you think he saw you?"

"I-I don't think so. I don't know if he would even recognise me." Dalcian looked terrified.

"What does he look like?" Cameron asked.

"Like a taller, fatter version of me. He was wearing a dark blue shirt, no hat. Shaved head. It was definitely him."

Cameron carefully opened the door a crack and peeked out; Dalcian's father was nowhere in sight. A sense of unease started to gnaw at him.

"He's gone. Want me to call the security guys and ask them to watch him?"

"No." Dalcian shook his head.

"Do you want to skip dinner and head home?"

"No. I can't keep living my life in fear," Dalcian said fiercely. "I'm having too much fun to let him ruin this day. So long as I'm with you, I feel safe."

Cameron peeked through the door again.

"It's all clear. Let's just move with the crowd and head for the exit. Can you put Boo-Boo in my bag for me?"

Dalcian pulled off his beanie and shoved it in Cameron's bag along with the bear, and gripped his Yogi even tighter. He took a deep breath, and took Cameron's hand.

"Let's go."

16

Cameron led Dalcian across Argyle Street, and moved with a large group of people under the rail bridge. They walked swiftly and with purpose, until they reached Macquarie Street. Cameron stopped and pulled Dalcian aside.

"I don't think he saw us," Cameron said, looking around. "He's definitely not following us."

"Maybe I just imagined it." Dalcian shrugged, though he still looked spooked.

"Always trust your instinct, it will keep you alive," Cameron said.

The sun was starting to dip towards the horizon; it was only 17:10, but the air was getting cooler. In their haste to leave the centre, Cameron had forgotten to use the bathroom.

"Damn it, I'm busting for a pee," he sighed.

"Will you be able to make it?" Dalcian asked.

"No. I'll duck into the RSL club and use their loo." Cameron picked up his speed a little.

"I thought that's where we were going?"

"I have one more surprise up my sleeve. There's a little restaurant just up from the club that's part of Old Gov House. The building itself was built in 1887. They usually do high tea, but they've just started offering fine dining on the weekends. I was lucky to get us a table."

"You're really spoiling me today," Dalcian said.

"You're worth it. I wanted today to be special."

The RSL was just up the road, but Cameron was so busting it felt like it was miles away. He dashed across the road, then looked at Dalcian apologetically.

"I need to rush. I'll meet you out the front in a few mins. We're early, anyway." Cameron let go of his hand and hurried towards the entrance of the club. He looked back from the door in time to see Dalcian sit on the low brick fence with his phone in his hand.

Thankfully, the restrooms were just off the lobby, so Cameron didn't need to sign in first. He hurried into a cubicle and relieved himself just in time to prevent disaster. Once he was done, he washed his hands and looked at himself in the mirror. He looked better than he had in ages; he even looked happy, and smiled back at his reflection. He dried his hands on his jeans and strolled from the restroom.

He walked past the reception desk and nodded politely to the staff. Just as he was about to thank them, a bloodcurdling scream drew his and everyone's attention. Cameron's blood ran cold; he started running towards the exit before he even knew what he was doing.

A short distance away, a man was wrestling Dalcian into the boot of a car.

"CAMERON!!" Dalcian screamed.

The man forced the boot shut, and hurried around to the driver's seat.

"NOOO!! LET ME OUT!!" Dalcian's screams were muffled; Cameron could hear him banging his fists on the roof.

"DALCIAN!!" Cameron yelled, bolting towards the car. He leapt over the safety fence and dashed between the traffic, running as fast as his legs could take him. Just as he reached the car, the driver sped off, almost colliding with an oncoming car.

Cameron could feel himself panicking as the car disappeared from view. For a moment he wondered if he were having a bad dream; surely what he had just seen hadn't really happened? He looked around, not knowing what to do, tears streaming down his face.

Phone.

Cameron whipped his phone out of his pocket and dialled 000. His hands were shaking so much he could hardly dial. He couldn't think, he couldn't process what had just happened.

"Where is your emergency?" the operator asked.

"P-Parramatta, New South Wales."

"What is your emergency?"

"My-my partner has just been abducted," Cameron managed. "The guy is probably going to kill him! Please, you've got to—"

"Sir, please calm down. Are you or anyone in any immediate danger?"

Cameron couldn't calm down; he stood answering the questions as best as he could, as a horrible feeling started to grow in his gut. He managed to recall the description of the car and kidnapper, and gave the operator Dalcian's details. He was no stranger to calling 000 for work, but right now he was hysterical. In the distance he could hear police sirens.

"The police will be there in less than five minutes. You may hang up now."

Cameron hung up and dialled Sarah's number.

"How's it hanging?" she answered.

"Dalcian's been kidnapped!" Cameron burst into tears as the horrible feeling spread up to his throat like bile.

"What? What do you mean kidnapped?" Sarah demanded.

"He was just sitting there while I ducked inside to

pee. I came back out and he's gone."

"Are you sure he didn't follow you inside or go for a walk?" she asked.

"I saw him get thrown into the boot of a car," Cameron sobbed. "It happened."

"Jesus, Cam. Where are you?"

"Parramatta RSL," he managed.

"Have you called the cops yet?" she asked.

"Yeah. I can hear sirens all over the place, they're not far away."

"Hang tight. I'm going to call Graham and get someone to cover my site. I'm over at Rose Hill, I won't be long. Don't leave the RSL, ok?" Sarah instructed.

"Ok."

Cameron hung up just as two police cars sped around the corner, and screeched to a halt in the carpark next to the main entrance. A small crowd, including the club's security guard, had gathered outside, watching on with interest. He hurried across the road and approached the officers. Much to Cameron's relief, Senior Constable Saunders was there.

"Shit, Cam, are you alright?" he asked.

"No, I'm not alright. I just watched my partner get kidnapped," Cameron blubbered, a little harsher than intended.

"It'll be alright, mate," Saunders said. "Peters, take the probies and talk to the witnesses. Cam, let's go look at the club's footage."

"Shouldn't you be out there looking for him?" Cameron asked incredulously.

"The entire local area command is already scouring the area. If they don't find him in an hour, we'll escalate the job to the surrounding LACs. If all else fails, we'll apply to get Polair off the ground. Calm down mate, we've got your back." Saunders laid his hand on Cameron's shoulder, and pointed towards the entrance.

"Is this the victim's phone?" one of the officers called from beside the brick wall.

Cameron hurried over to him and picked it up.

"Yes, this is Dalcian's phone."

"What's the passcode? We'll need to examine it," the officer said.

Cameron unlocked it, and handed it to the officer. He flicked through the recent calls list, messages, then opened the photos app.

"Why are you looking at his photos?" Cameron demanded.

"How many selfies do you take each day?" Saunders asked.

"Me, personally? I don't. Dalcian takes a few, though."

"Let's see. He took six selfies in the last fifteen to twenty minutes."

Cameron looked over his shoulder as he examined each of the photos closely. Dalcian was smiling into the camera holding his Yogi bear, looking just as happy as Cameron had been twenty minutes ago. As the officer flicked to the fourth photo, they could see a person approaching him from behind. The final photo had a man's face, but it wasn't Dalcian's father.

"There you go. That's why we check the photos," the officer said. "Don't worry, we see dick pics on phones every day."

Cameron blushed. He had hoped they hadn't seen those.

"We're going to have to keep this phone for a more thorough investigation," he added.

"Can I get those photos first?" Cameron asked.

The officer nodded, and Cameron quickly Bluetoothed himself the photos.

"I've seen that face before," Cameron said. "I just can't think where."

"While the guys are talking to the security guard and

other witnesses, let's go look at the cameras," Saunders suggested.

"Since when do you allow members of the public to look at footage?" Cameron asked.

"We don't. But I've worked with you long enough to know that if I don't invite you, you'll just help yourself," Saunders replied. "Come on."

The RSL manager quickly obliged Saunders' request to view their CCTV streams. Cameron joined him in the small security office, and helped search through the footage.

"There — look." Cameron pointed as a white car pulled up, blocking the driveway to the main carpark across the road.

"Can't see the plates," Saunders said. "Whoever it was must be aware of the cameras. Oh, hang on."

A separate stream on a lone monitor was pointing towards the road. Cameron rewound the video, and there was a direct view of the number plates as the car drove around the corner and along the front of the club.

"*All units, abduction update. Vehicle registration is Charlie. Golf. Seven. Two. Delta. Lima. Repeat: Charlie. Golf. Seven. Two. Delta. Lima. White Holden Commodore. Over,*" Saunders said into his radio.

"*Yeah, roger that.*"

"Where's that camera hidden?" Cameron asked.

"It's in the light pole," the manager said from behind them. "We installed the hidden one because we had some vandals trying to ruin the memorial by the entrance."

Cameron wasn't listening; his eyes fell on the footage of Dalcian sitting on the wall, taking his photos. The car pulled in blocking the driveway, and the man opened the boot. He walked back up the road, avoiding the cameras, then snuck up behind Dalcian. A fresh wave of tears cascaded down Cameron's cheeks as his Dalcian was grabbed from behind, and wrestled towards the car.

"Now. Do you have any idea why Dalcian would be targeted in the abduction?" Saunders asked.

"He saw his father in Westfield before we left, and he got scared," Cameron said vaguely.

"Why would he be scared of his father? I need as much info as you can tell me that might help."

"Sorry. Dalcian ran away from home when he was sixteen because his father was beating him. He's been living on the streets until he moved in with me recently," Cameron explained. "He works at the Dirty Bean Café in Burwood."

"Does he have any aliases?" Saunders asked.

"Um. One time I had an incident at work. He said his name was Thomas. I can send you my report if you like?"

"Take a photo and text it to me. Right, I think I've got what we need. I have to get back to the station and start my investigation. You've got my mobile number, so if you hear from him or think of any other info that could help, call me personally," Saunders said, standing up.

"What am I supposed to do now?" Cameron asked blankly.

"Go home and stay there. If he escapes from his abductor, that's the first place he will go."

Cameron followed him back outside. The sun had almost disappeared; the streetlights had all turned on. The other police car had gone, leaving Saunders, Peters, and the other officer.

"Are you able to keep me updated?" Cameron asked.

"I'll do what I can, mate," Saunders replied. "Hang in there Cam, and stay positive. We'll do everything in our power to get him back for you." Saunders reached out and shook Cameron's hand.

Before he could even process anything, he was left standing outside the RSL building in the darkness.

Alone.

* * *

The darkness that squeezed Cameron's heart was darker than the night that surrounded him. He sat in the shadows, filled with a sense of helplessness. He wanted to jump to his feet and do something, but he knew there was nothing he could do. Dalcian was gone, and it was all his fault.

Cameron felt a wave of guilt wash over him, and a burning sensation crept into his throat. He turned and threw up the contents of his stomach into the garden as a car pulled up to the curb. He wiped his mouth on a napkin and tossed it onto the stinking puddle.

The sound of the car door slamming made him jump, and once again the image of the unknown man slamming the car boot on Dalcian replayed in his mind.

"Cam?"

Sarah's voice roused him from his flashback. He staggered to his feet and stood facing her. Before he could say anything, she swept him into a tight hug.

"He's gone," Cameron wept into her shoulder.

"Shhh." Sarah squeezed him tighter and gently rocked from side to side. "Tell me what happened."

Cameron backtracked to the moment Dalcian spotted his father, and told her everything from that moment.

"It's all my fault. I should never have run off like that. I should have pissed before we left, or waited til we got up the road," he finished.

"This is not your fault at all," Sarah said firmly. "It sounds like they were watching, waiting for the opportunity to snatch. This was all planned."

"I don't know. I can't think right now."

A white van with a large emblem of the local news station pulled into the club's carpark across the road. Sarah gripped Cameron's arm and pulled him towards her car.

"Come on, let's get you home. The media vultures are here already."

* * *

The drive home was all a blur. Cameron's emotions were all over the place, as his mind tried to process the trauma he'd just witnessed. It felt as though time itself had slowed to a crawl, leaving him with a strong sense of disbelief, shock that something so terrible could happen so suddenly while they were having the time of their lives.

"Is there another way into the apartment block?" Sarah asked, rousing him from his misery.

"What? Oh. Um, there's a walkway that leads to the next street over. Why?"

"All of those lights and cars are for you."

Cameron blinked and looked out the window as Sarah passed his driveway. A throng of reporters had already lined the street, scoping out his apartment building. Curious onlookers stood in groups, probably wondering who got stabbed or busted for drugs.

"How? How do they know?" Cameron asked.

"One of the cops would have tipped them off, or they were listening to the police radio. This is going to be big, Cam." She turned the car into the quiet back street and parked along the curb.

"I can't deal with this," Cameron sniffed.

"If they see us, just keep walking and don't say anything," she said. "They know the rules just like we do. At least I'm in uniform still."

Cameron slipped on his backpack and armed himself with his keys, then led Sarah along a dark path between two high fences. The path opened into the barbeque area towards the rear of the complex, somewhere below Cameron's balcony. They managed to sneak into the building without rousing the media's attention.

A few of Cameron's neighbours were standing in the hall, talking amongst themselves. Cameron tiptoed past and paused to unlock his door.

"There he is now!" someone said loudly.

Cameron froze as all eyes landed on him. A lone woman in a business suit broke away from the group and approached him, holding out her phone with a voice recording app rolling.

"Excuse me, Mr Greenwood? I was wondering if I could have a minute of your time?"

"Mr Greenwood is unavailable for any interviews right now," Sarah said in her most officious voice. "Please direct all questions to the police."

"Wait!"

Cameron slipped into the apartment and slammed the door once Sarah was safely inside.

"Fucking arseholes," she sighed. "Hopefully they get bored and leave by morning."

Cameron wasn't listening. He dropped his bag near the door, and drifted around the apartment, looking to see if Dalcian was there, even though he knew he was being silly. Everything sat exactly as they'd left it that morning. He wandered into the spare room and looked out the window; he could see the media down by the driveway. He pulled the blind down and backed out of the room.

Sarah busied herself with boiling the jug and making coffee. Cameron turned on the TV to the ABC, and immediately saw the breaking news headline: *Young man abducted in broad daylight outside club in Parramatta.*

"At approximately 5:15 this evening, a nineteen-year-old man was snatched from the front of the RSL club in Parramatta, New South Wales, while his partner had ducked inside. The man was thrown into the boot of a white Holden Commodore with the registration CG-72-DL. Anyone who has seen this vehicle should call Crime Stoppers immediately. The police have not yet released details. Let's go over to Cindy, who is reporting live from outside the victim's home."

The woman who had been in the hallway only moments before flashed onto the screen, standing next to the letterboxes with Cameron's apartment behind her.

"Thanks, Tom. I'm outside the victim's home right now. The police have not yet released any details, but I can confirm that the young man who was abducted was Dalcian Lang, who lives here with his partner, Cameron Greenwood. Mr Greenwood was approached, but was unavailable for comment this evening. It is believed that the police are still searching for the vehicle..."

"Oh, for fuck's sake!"

"I'd turn it off if I were you," Sarah advised. "It's only going to upset you. Saunders is a good guy, I'm sure he'll keep you updated when possible."

Cameron turned off the TV and accepted a mug of coffee from Sarah.

"How was your date before all of this?" she asked gently.

"Before all of this, I was having the best day of my entire life," Cameron said. "He was too. We watched *The Avengers* at the movies. It was his first time watching something on the big screen."

"Did you tell him how you feel?"

"No." Tears started streaming down his cheeks again. "I was saving it for over dinner. He's out there somewhere, scared, and he has no idea that...that I love him."

"Oh hon, I'm sure he knows it." Sarah patted his leg.

"I know, but he deserves to have been told to his face."

"Don't beat yourself up, Cam. I'm sure they'll find him in a day or two, you'll have your happy reunion, and you can declare your love to the world," she told him.

"What if...what if he's dead? What if I never get that chance?" Cameron wiped his tears.

"All you can do is take each day as it comes. You just need to hold onto hope that he's alive."

Dalcian's words came floating back to him. *"The only way to survive is to fight for the life you want. If you don't fight, you lose hope, and without hope, you have nothing to fight for."*

"I spoke to Graham, by the way. I told him you're having a crisis and need some time off work," she added. "I didn't go into details, but you will need to call him at some point. He deserves to know what's going on."

"You're right," Cameron sighed. "Do you have to rush off, or can you stay for a while?"

"Ron's working all night. How about I go and get a pizza, and hang out for a bit?"

"Please. I don't want to be alone right now."

Cameron couldn't stomach the pizza. He managed to eat one slice, before the churning of his anxiety made him feel like being sick again. Just as the weekend movie was about to start, Cameron heard an ominous sound outside. He pushed himself off the couch and went out to the balcony to investigate.

A heavy-sounding helicopter was flying overhead, circling the block. With a start, Cameron realised it was probably the police chopper, still looking for Dalcian.

"Polair 3," Sarah said from behind him. "Look at this."

She handed him her phone. A flight app showed that the aircraft had been circling Warrick Farm, Liverpool, Parramatta, and were now overhead.

"I guess they haven't found him yet," Cameron said, feeling sick.

"Give them time," she said. "Come inside out of the cold, *Fifth Element* is about to start."

Cameron was eternally grateful that Sarah was able to stay with him for a while that evening. Apart from Dalcian, she was the only true friend he had. As much as Graham was his mate, Cameron couldn't imagine hanging out with him outside of work, least of all while he was a sobbing mess.

Once the movie finished, Sarah made sure that Cameron had showered and brushed his teeth, and had dressed in his warm trackies and hoodie. She washed the breakfast dishes that were still in the sink, and fussed over him as though she was his mother.

"What's this script for on the fridge?" she asked from the kitchen.

"Antidepressants," Cameron admitted. "Don't ask."

"Do you need it filled?"

"Um."

Before Cameron could answer, she'd already put it in her handbag.

"I better head off I suppose. I'm back at work tomorrow," she sighed.

"Do you know if Graham's working tonight?" Cameron asked.

"He's staying at the office," she said. "He wasn't too happy when I called and ditched, but too bad."

"I'll walk you to your car," Cameron offered.

"No you won't," she said firmly. "You'll stay in here where it's warm. I'll drop in tomorrow and see you for a bit before work."

"This is a bad area and you're in uniform. Text me when you're safe in your car," Cameron insisted. The thought of losing another friend was too much to bear.

"Alright," she sighed. "Try and get some sleep. I'll see you tomorrow."

Cameron stood on the balcony and watched as Sarah walked towards the dark path. She turned and waved, then disappeared into the darkness. The night was eerily quiet except for the occasional dog barking in the distance. After a few minutes, he heard the sound of a car door slam, followed by a ding from his phone.

```
SARAH: I'm safe. Now go inside and
get some sleep xx

CAMERON: Thanks. Night, mate.
```

Cameron walked aimlessly around the apartment, feeling lost and alone. He picked up the throw rug that Dalcian liked to wrap himself in while drawing, and carried it back out to the living room. His eyes fell on his backpack, discarded by the door. Cameron retrieved his bag, and slid forlornly down the wall opposite the door.

Slowly, he unzipped his bag and unloaded the contents. He felt a fresh wave of tears threatening to spill as he cuddled his Boo-Boo bear, but he held himself back. He removed the framed comic print and sat it aside safely. He reached in one last time to search for his pack of Panadol, and instead he felt something soft.

Cameron pulled Dalcian's beanie from his bag. He studied it for a moment, then held it to his face, inhaling Dalcian's familiar scent. A wave of grief washed over him, and the ever-present tears spilled over once more. He pulled his Boo-Boo into his arms and sobbed uncontrollably. The pain in his stomach increased tenfold, as the feelings of his loss fully enveloped him. He curled up into a ball on the floor, and broke down completely.

17

The sound of someone banging on the door jolted Cameron awake. For a moment he was confused; the room was lit up by daylight, and he was lying on the floor covered in Dalcian's throw blanket, using his backpack as a pillow.

He heard voices outside his door, followed by another loud knock. Cameron dragged himself to his feet, and looked out the peephole. Two police officers stood outside, waiting expectantly. Slowly, Cameron unlocked the door and stared at them.

"Hi, Cam. Can we come in?"

Cameron blinked and realised it was Senior Constable Saunders. He stood aside wordlessly and let them in. He felt dazed, as though his brain was lagging.

"Um. I'm guessing you haven't found him, then?" Cameron asked.

"Not yet. There are some things we need to talk about," Saunders said.

Cameron gestured towards the couch.

"Coffee?" he asked.

"Sure."

Cameron filled the jug and fished out some clean mugs. Instead of moving to the couch, Saunders and the other officer pulled out a barstool each and sat along the kitchen bench.

"This is Detective Anders, he's assisting me with this investigation," Saunders said.

"Hi, mate," Cameron said. "So, what can I help you with?"

"First up, you may have noticed the media camped downstairs," Anders said. "We're going to address them at 10:00 this morning outside Police HQ in Parramatta. You don't need to attend, but if you would like to speak out, we can certainly accommodate you."

"Should I?" Cameron asked. "I mean, would it help?"

"It's up to you. I suggest you come along and talk to our media specialist before you decide. They will want a photo to release to the public to help identify him too."

"Ok." Cameron handed the officers their mugs, and pulled the third stool to the end of the bench.

"Now, about the case. In your statement, you mentioned that Dalcian was abused as a child by his father. Did he ever tell you more about it?" Saunders asked, turning serious.

"I've seen the scars on his back. I've seen the bruise that's in the photo in his school ID. I've seen how he reacts when he's threatened and has flashbacks," Cameron said. "It happened."

"Do you have any idea who his father is?" Anders asked.

"No," Cameron admitted. "He never spoke about his family."

"Dalcian's father is Sergeant Richard Lang, the duty sarge of Liverpool LAC. He is well respected in the force, so allegations such as these will require hard evidence." Saunders sat a folder on the bench and removed a few photos. "His mother, Gemma Lang, disappeared and was reported missing almost six years ago. The case was closed when Richard reported that he'd received a letter from her

185

saying she had run away with her lover to Queensland."

Cameron's mouth dropped open.

"So *that's* why he was so afraid of going to the police!" he gasped. "He was terrified of using his real name that night I got stabbed. He knew he would be found."

"We paid a visit to his residence in Warwick Farm last night," Saunders continued. "What we found was… disturbing."

He pulled a pile of photos from his folder and passed them to Cameron. The photos showed him and Dalcian hanging around Stanmore and Parramatta. Some of the photos were of Cameron at Strathfield and Granville, and another shot showed Dalcian entering and leaving the Dirty Bean Café.

"These were found hidden behind the fridge in the family home. It appears that Richard had engaged with a private investigation firm to locate his son," Saunders said.

Cameron was speechless. He flicked through the photos again, then stopped and stared at one of him at Parramatta, talking to Dalcian while on shift. With a start, he saw Dalcian's phone in his hand.

"This was taken on Thursday after I had given Dalcian his mobile," Cameron frowned.

And then it dawned on him.

"The pea man!" he blurted out. "The guy we saw in the CCTV, who snatched Dalcian, was in the frozen aisle on Thursday when we made our plans for Saturday. He was spying on us!"

"What time was this?" Anders asked.

Cameron quickly told him the time and details.

"Thanks. We'll review the security footage," Anders said, writing it down.

"Did you check to see if Richard was there on Saturday?" Cameron asked.

Saunders and Anders exchanged glances.

"Richard is also missing. We traced the abduction

vehicle to the Westfield carpark last night," Saunders said. "The car was abandoned and Dalcian was transferred into a different car. The white car was a rental, and we traced that back to the private investigator. This has all been pre-planned."

"Fuck me," Cameron muttered.

"We are one-up on them, though," Anders said. "They weren't expecting so many cameras in the carpark. We caught the footage of the transfer between vehicles."

"Since when do private investigators get involved like this?" Cameron demanded, suddenly feeling angry. "Dalcian was a missing person for a reason. Why didn't they approach him and ask him *why?* How many other missing people have been returned to their abusers like this?"

"This is unprecedented," Saunders said. "I have someone investigating the PI's office, so that we can determine if this was accessory or just a gross breach of ethics."

"I'll fucking sue them for this!" Cameron fumed.

"Mate, calm down." Saunders said. "I know you're feeling all sorts of things right now, but getting angry isn't going to bring him back."

"Sorry," Cameron sighed and held his hand over his eyes for a moment. "Where do we go from here?"

"We address the press at 10:00, then sit back and wait." Saunders pulled a card from the folder and handed it to Cameron. "This is the number of a trauma counsellor who can offer you some mental health support. I recommend you call them and have a chat."

"Ok. Thanks."

The detectives finished their coffees and stood up.

"Thanks, Cam. Rest assured we are doing all we can to find him. In the meantime, you know to contact me if you hear of anything."

"One more thing," Cameron said as they turned

towards the door. "Dalcian mentioned that he lied to his teachers about his bruises to hide what was happening. Maybe the teachers at Warwick Farm High School can help."

"We'll look into it," Anders said, scribbling in his notepad. "Thanks."

Cameron walked them to the door and pulled it open.

"Are you coming to the press release?" Saunders asked.

"I don't really want to have to pass through that mob down there," Cameron said. "I don't have a car."

"We'll send a car over to pick you up at 09:30. That's only an hour away."

"Alright. Thanks heaps."

* * *

Once Cameron was dressed, he sat on the couch in silence, staring at the wall. He still could not process anything except for the fact that Dalcian had been taken from him, and his sense of emptiness threatened to consume him. The worst feeling, though, was the confusion. He didn't know if he should be grieving or holding on to hope. The deaths of his parents were final, and he was able to grieve, but he had no idea whether Dalcian was dead or alive.

With a start, he realised he hadn't told Jill. Surely she would be expecting him at work the next day. Cameron fished out his phone and called the café.

"Dirty Bean Café, Ernie speaking."

"H-hi, it's Cameron. Could I speak to Jill please?"

"Oh, Dalcian's personal security guard," Ernie said with a chuckle. "Just a sec. It's Jill's day off, but she's out the back cooking for tonight's soup kitchen."

"Thanks." Cameron waited for a few minutes, and finally Jill came on the line.

"Hi, Cameron," she said.

"Hi, Jill. Um, have you heard about Dalcian?" he asked.

"No? What's wrong?" she asked.

"He was kidnapped last night," Cameron said. "It's all over the news. The police haven't been able to locate him. I guess he won't be in tomorrow."

"What the hell? Who would want to kidnap him?" she demanded.

"I-I think it was his dad." Cameron could feel his eyes starting to burn again.

"Oh my god, that poor boy." Jill's voice broke. "He is such a sweetheart."

"I know," Cameron sniffed. "He meant — means — the world to me."

"Is there anything I can do?" she asked.

"I don't know," Cameron sighed. "I wish I knew what to do."

"I'll make up some missing posters and circulate them amongst the homeless circles. If he finds his way back into the streets, we might be able to find him first," she offered.

"Thanks Jill, it means a lot."

Once he finished talking to Jill, Cameron brushed away his tears and hit Graham's number.

"Mate, what's going on?" Graham answered almost immediately.

"Dalcian's gone." Cameron broke down sobbing once more.

"Dalcian? The dude you brought to the office that day?" Graham asked, sounding confused.

Cameron blurted out everything, more than he ever would have had he been thinking straight. He told Graham about Paul, the hostel, and everything in between; it felt good to get it off his chest, as though he were honouring Dalcian by talking about him.

"Shit mate, why didn't you tell me about this stuff before?" Graham asked.

"I didn't want things to change," Cameron sniffed. "I was worried that word would get around, and the other guys would give me shit about it. You remember how everyone thought Sarah was a lesbian until they realised she was married to Ron."

"They wouldn't dare. And if Barry ever says one word, I'll punch him in the fucking face," Graham said. "You're my mate. I don't care who you shack up with."

Cameron sat sobbing into the phone for a moment, trying to get his emotions back under control.

"Do you need more time off?" Graham asked finally.

"Yeah. I can't afford to not work, though," Cameron replied. "My mind is all over the place at the moment."

"What if I send you to Marsden Park Council for a while?" Graham offered. "You're already inducted, so I can get you in for some afternoon shifts, 14:00 til 22:00. What do you think?"

"Alright. I'll just need another couple of days to get my shit together," Cameron said.

"I'll slot you in for Wednesday, and we'll see how you go," Graham said. "What are you doing today?"

"I'm going to the police press release soon," Cameron replied. "They're picking me up. Should be here soon."

"Alright mate, I'll let you go," Graham said. "If you need anything at all, call me, ok?"

"Okay. Thanks, mate."

* * *

The only way Cameron got through that day was by shutting down and withdrawing emotionally. The press release had been hard; the reporters down by his driveway had swarmed the police car, trying to get photos of him. A news helicopter trailed the car all the way to Police HQ in Parramatta.

He managed to read out his short statement, and was

bombarded with questions he wasn't prepared to answer. Luckily, the police media specialist had briefed him prior to the address, and was close-by to rescue him once the reporters turned savage.

The press release only lasted fifteen minutes, but for Cameron it felt much longer. Once it was finally over, a young constable escorted him from the press room back into the lobby. He had refused the offer of a ride home, and instead planned to go for a walk and clear his head. As he headed towards the exit, Sarah materialised through the doors.

"How's that for timing?" she asked, pulling him into a hug.

"How did you know I was here?" Cameron asked, hugging her back.

"Graham told me. He gave me tonight off and has put me back to day shift tomorrow, so I thought I'd pop over and check up on you," she said. "Have you had breakfast yet?"

Cameron shook his head. The thought of food was farthest from his mind.

"Let's go and have coffee. I'm starving."

Cameron managed to force himself to eat a toasted ham and cheese sandwich, and sat sipping his second coffee while Sarah ate her eggs. As they chatted about the press release, Cameron realised that Sarah had become his best friend over the last few weeks. Dalcian was so much more than a best friend, and once again Cameron felt the horrible taste of regret balling in his stomach that he had never told him so.

The obnoxious tune of his ringtone jolted him out of his thoughts, and he quickly fumbled to answer it. It was a private number, but he answered it anyway.

"Hello?"

"Hi Cam, it's Bill."

"Bill?" Cameron asked, confused.

"Detective Saunders," he said. "You got a moment?"

"Yeah, sure," Cameron said quickly.

"I just wanted to give you a quick update. Since we went live at ten, we've had several calls from the public in regards to the abduction vehicle. It's been located."

Cameron felt his anxiety soar, but fought to remain calm. *If they found a body, they wouldn't be telling me over the phone,* he thought to himself.

"The car was abandoned on the road leading to Point Pilcher Lookout, not far from Katoomba airstrip. The Katoomba police are on the way to secure the vehicle, and I'll be heading up there shortly."

"Um. Am I allowed to head up there?" Cameron asked.

"Not yet. I really don't know what we're looking at here," Saunders said. "As soon as I know more, I'll give you a call."

"Thanks, mate."

Cameron hung up and quickly filled Sarah in.

"Oh, hon. It's not sounding good," she said gently. "Do you want to head back to my place for a bit?"

"Alright," Cameron sighed.

Sarah's house was a modern double-storey home in a pleasant neighbourhood. The living area was separated from the kitchen and dining area by a long L-shaped couch that could easily seat twelve people. Cameron's eyes were drawn to a massive DVD collection in several bookcases next to the large TV.

"Make yourself comfy and pick something to watch. I'll go make popcorn."

Cameron picked *Scrubs,* and spent the next few hours munching on snacks and checking his phone. He was glad for the distraction, and even managed to laugh a few times. Each time he laughed, though, he felt guilty.

It wasn't until 16:00 that his phone finally rang. Sarah paused the DVD, and Cameron put his phone on loudspeaker.

"Hello?"

"Hi Cam, it's Bill again."

"How'd it go?" Cameron asked.

"We've confirmed that the vehicle is the car that was used to abduct Dalcian from the carpark," Bill said. "There was an attempt to torch the car, but the caretaker from the nearby airfield spotted it and extinguished the flames. We were able to gather some prints and DNA, which are being processed as we speak. The engine number matches the plates seen in the CCTV, so it's safe to say that this is the right car.

"We interviewed the caretaker. He's a retired police pilot, and was highly regarded by the force. He said there has been no out-of-the-ordinary flight activity. At this stage, we can rule out our kidnapper catching a plane."

"What are you saying?" Cameron asked.

"I've ordered a large-scale search of the bush surrounding the airfield. With no reported sightings of either Dalcian or the kidnapper, we need to start looking for evidence of on-foot travel. We're starting the search at 06:00 tomorrow. You won't be able to participate in the search, but I'll get you cleared to come up here."

"I'll be there," Cameron said quickly.

"I'm not supposed to, but I can pick you up in the morning if you like," Bill offered.

"Yes, please. What time?" Cameron asked.

"04:30. Dress warm, it's going to be freezing up there."

"Okay. See ya then, mate."

18

Set deep within the beautiful Blue Mountains, Katoomba was a small historical town loved by hippies and tourists alike. Cameron loved the small town, and thought of the mountains as Australia's version of the Grand Canyon. He thought back to when he was twenty-one; he and Paul had visited a popular tourist attraction nestled amongst the bushland. Paul had led him down a track that was obviously beyond the boundaries of the attraction, insisting it was the right way. It wasn't, and they found themselves at the base of the Giant Stairway.

Cameron grinned to himself as he remembered Paul's hissy fit, as he'd realised that Cameron was, in fact, right; they had just walked for almost two hours through giant orb weaver spiderwebs and puddles filled with leeches, only to face a wall of stairs. Paul complained and whined every single step of the 998 steps to the top.

Detective Bill Saunders slowed down the car, and turned onto a dirt road. It was still dark, and a thick fog hung over the tops of the trees. Neither of them had spoken about the search that would soon take place; they spoke about security and police work along the way, and Bill told Cameron about his wife and two young children.

A bright light ahead drew Cameron's attention. The

Katoomba airstrip's carpark was full of cars, and in a nearby clearing, a number of people were setting up marquees. As they arrived at the gates to the carpark, a lone uniformed officer held up his hand for them to stop. Bill flashed his badge, and they were waved through.

Cameron looked around the carpark; there were maybe twenty cars, and he wondered how the hell so few people would be able to search much of an area. He climbed out of the car and pulled on his work beanie and his thick jacket, then followed Bill towards the marquees.

"The superintendent is coordinating the search. We've got the SES and VRA teams coming, plus some of the volunteer firies to provide any extra numbers we may need," Bill said quietly. "You'll have to stay here, you're not cleared to join the search."

"Is there anything I can do to help?" Cameron asked.

"Yeah. Stay out of trouble. No one wants to have to search for you as well. The bush is dangerous, we don't want to have to call in a rescue chopper to dig you out of the gorge," Bill said firmly. Cameron could see he was in his serious work mode. "Head over to the drinks marquee and hang out there. If we find anything, you'll be the first to know."

Cameron sat on a camp chair and watched as SES minibuses, VRA support vehicles, and police rescue vans started rolling in. Soon, the area was teeming with people wearing their respective uniforms and hi-vis vests. Everyone was subdued, as though they knew a gruelling day was ahead of them. With a start, Cameron realised they were probably on the lookout for bodies, and the thought unsettled him.

"Ok everyone, listen up," the superintendent's voice called through a sound system. "We're looking for two people. Your squad leaders have photographs and will show you shortly. We're going to have teams Alpha and Bravo head towards the north. Teams Charlie and Delta, head towards the lookout, then follow the rim northwest to meet up with Alpha and Bravo. Finally, teams Echo and Foxtrot will spread out and fan the south. We'll be joined by Polair 5 at 09:00, and we'll also have some drones scouring the gorge. You've all done this before, you know what to do. We launch at 07:00. Be careful."

Cameron could feel himself becoming overwhelmed by the enormity of the situation. All of these people, the emergency services, untold expenses to launch such a massive search, all because he decided to piss at the wrong time. Deep down, he knew it wasn't his fault, but he still felt that he had let Dalcian down. He pulled Boo-Boo from his backpack, and sat squeezing the bear, retreating into his own thoughts. *Where are you, Boo-Boo? You've got to be somewhere. Wherever you are, I will find you and bring you home. I promise.*

Cameron didn't see Bill again until 16:00. As half of the exhausted search party slowly trickled back to base, some of the transport vehicles drove off to meet the other teams at their extraction points. Bill helped himself to a bottle of water and sat on a milk crate next to Cameron.

"Did you find anything?" Cameron asked hesitantly.

"Nothing conclusive," Bill said. "It's not looking good, mate. We found a shovel not far from here, but no one found any freshly dug holes anywhere, or any signs that they've passed through the bush. We found nothing that could give us any hints as to where they went. I'm so sorry, Cam."

"Are you sure they didn't fly out?" Cameron asked, feeling his stomach knot even tighter.

"We've inspected the logbook, nothing out of the ordinary. Like I said, the caretaker is an ex-cop, so we can trust his word too."

"Just like we can trust Richard Lang," Cameron muttered under his breath.

"It was decided to call off the search. We'll keep investigating of course, but it's clear that they are not in this area," Bill said wearily.

"Be honest with me. Do you think there's a chance he's alive?" Cameron asked.

"There's always a chance, mate. Until we find evidence that says otherwise, you just have to hope for the best. You never know, maybe they had another car waiting here. We'll brief the press again and put out a plea for anyone with information to step forward."

"Is there anything else I can do to try and find him?"

"Unless you're made of money and can hire a private investigator, not really. And without any clues to follow, it's really just another dead end." Bill paused and nodded towards another uniformed officer. "I just need to speak to someone. I'll meet you back at the car in five minutes."

"Okay."

By the time Wednesday rolled around, Cameron was almost glad to head back to work. He knew that lying around the apartment and wallowing in pity wasn't healthy, but he also knew that he wasn't coping well. He had the TV on constantly, hoping to maybe catch the breaking news that Dalcian had been found.

It was hard returning to work. His anxiety was through the roof, and he could feel the darkness of his depression growing thicker and deeper by the day. A few people around the council seemed to recognise him from the news; not only were the stations broadcasting Dalcian's photo, they were showing Cameron and Richard as well. No one said anything, though.

On Thursday night after the council was closed and he'd let the late-night stragglers out, Cameron ventured onto various social media sites and created his own accounts. He had never bothered with them before, but was determined to keep looking for Dalcian on his own.

There were a few news archives about the disappearance of Dalcian and his mother, but try though he might, he could find nothing that would bring him home.

* * *

Friday night's shift dragged on. It hadn't been a good shift; he had overheard a young blonde bimbo librarian talking about 'that big security guard that was on TV', and had made some horrible jokes about him and Dalcian. She hadn't noticed him patrolling the library, and when she did, she made no effort to apologise.

He was glad to finally knock off that night. Although it was only a twenty-minute walk home, Cameron caught a cab instead. The three days of work had been mentally taxing on him, and he was pleased that he had the weekend off to recover.

A part of him dreaded the next day. Not only was it one week since Dalcian was kidnapped, but it was also Cameron's twenty-eighth birthday. He had looked forward to sharing it with Dalcian and having a special day, but unless there was some miracle, he would be spending it alone.

With a yawn, Cameron let himself into the apartment, and kicked off his shoes at the door. He stripped off his uniform and threw it on the floor in the laundry, and pulled on his usual hoodie and trackies that he used for pyjamas. He walked around the apartment, staring blankly into the rooms, hoping to see Dalcian smiling at him, but as with every other night that week, Dalcian wasn't there.

With a sigh, Cameron turned on the TV, and drifted back into the kitchen. He hadn't bought any groceries that week, and the milk in the fridge was off. He fished out a packet of two-minute noodles, and turned on the jug.

As the water heated up, Cameron wandered into the spare room and sat at Dalcian's desk. The rest of the room was empty except for a few empty packaging boxes from the things they'd bought. Cameron had been meaning to take them downstairs to the recycle bin, but of course he had been too preoccupied to bother doing it.

He reached down and turned on the desk lamp. Dalcian's pencils and pens were all neatly arranged in the pen cup, and an eraser sat next to it as though it had just been used. A few random blank sheets of paper were neatly stacked on the other corner of the desk. Out of the corner of his eye, Cameron noticed a scrunched-up piece of paper wedged between the lamp and the wall. He reached out and unravelled it; it was a light sketch that had been scribbled over, as though he'd made an error.

Cameron noticed that the left side of the desk, behind the lamp, wasn't flush with the wall. He absentmindedly tried to shove the desk back so it was straight, but it wouldn't budge. He stood up and tried again, but the desk would not move. *That's weird. It was definitely flush when Ron and I put it here,* he thought.

Feeling frustrated, he pulled the desk away from the wall to see what was stopping it, and his breath caught in his throat when he saw what it was. The A5 visual diary that Dalcian had retrieved from the abandoned building sat wedged between the desk and the wall. He bent down and picked it up, then pushed the desk back to where it was supposed to be.

Dalcian had never showed him the book, nor mentioned it. As he thought about it, Cameron realised he hadn't seen it again since Dalcian had slipped it into his backpack at Darling Harbour. With trembling fingers, Cameron pulled back the elastic band fastener, and opened the book.

The drawings in this book were very different compared to the sketches Cameron had already seen. The images in this book were a lot rougher, and were much darker. The first page featured a boy cowering in the corner of a bedroom with his hands around his knees, a large bruise on his cheek, and tears in his eyes. With a start, he realised the figure was Dalcian.

As he flicked through the pages, Cameron felt a sick feeling growing inside his gut. The pictures showed a man, presumably his father, beating him, and administering all sorts of cruel punishments. He could feel the familiar palpitations of a panic attack brewing, but Cameron couldn't pull his eyes away from the grim scenes before him.

Just as he was about to close the book, Cameron noticed a third person in a scene on the next page. With a start, he realised it was Dalcian's mother, Gemma Lang. He flicked through, and scene by scene he saw Gemma and Richard arguing about something. Dalcian could be seen peeking out of his bedroom door; the door had three large locks on the outside for locking him up. On the next page, Richard stood over Gemma's body, wielding a large knife dripping with blood.

Cameron felt sick. The following pages showed Richard dragging her body into the backyard and digging a hole. Once her body was buried, another scene depicted Dalcian hiding in his bed, pretending to be asleep. Over the next few pages, Cameron could see that Richard poured a slab and built a large shed over the place where he buried her.

He couldn't bring himself to view any more of the book. Cameron stumbled from the spare room and headed straight to the bathroom, and threw up what little contents were in his stomach as the panic attack finally took over. *I'll fucking kill that bastard if I ever get my hands on him!* Cameron fumed. *I'll go see Saunders first thing in the morning and show him.*

Cameron hardly slept that night. Once he had calmed himself down and snuggled on the couch with Boo-Boo, he couldn't stop thinking about the images that Dalcian had drawn. He couldn't bring himself to sleep on the mattress; that had been his and Dalcian's safe spot, a place of happiness and love. He did not want to contaminate it with his misery; if Dalcian couldn't sleep there, nor would he. Finally around 03:00, he sat up on the couch and retrieved the book.

Being careful not to damage the pages in any way, Cameron sat the book on his lap and took a photo of each and every page. He knew the police would keep it as evidence, and despite the grim images, he didn't want to part with something that Dalcian had created. Once he was done, he settled back down and finally drifted into a restless sleep.

* * *

The sound of an incoming text message jolted Cameron awake. He fumbled for his phone and squinted at the screen; it was already 10:00. He hadn't slept that long for a while. Yawning, he unlocked his phone and read the message.

```
SARAH: Happy birthday to you!! Be
dressed and ready at 18:30, Ron will
pick you up and come meet me for
dinner.
```

```
CAMERON: Thanks, mate. I guess I'll
see you then.
```

There was another message from Graham.

```
GRAHAM: Happy birthday, mate. How's
work been treating you?
```

CAMERON: It was a hard few days tbh. Thanks for the weekend off, I needed it.

GRAHAM: No worries. Happy to stay at the council Mon - Fri next week?

CAMERON: Yeah, mate.

GRAHAM: Done. Try and have a good day.

CAMERON: Thanks.

Cameron dragged himself into the shower and stood resting his head on the wall. His brain felt clouded, as though there was a thick fog inside, and each time he started to feel miserable about Dalcian, it felt like an invisible hook dragged his mind back out of the pit of despair. After the failed search party, he had finally given in and started back on his tablets; it was all he could do to function properly and get his work done.

Once he'd showered, Cameron made himself a black coffee and called Saunders.

"Hi Cam, what's up?" he answered.

"Hi, Bill. I found something last night that you need to see. Are you working today?"

"I'm always working mate, you know a cop is never off duty. I'm at my daughter's dancing practice right now, but I can meet you at HQ around 12:30 if it's urgent."

"It is," Cameron said. "I'll see you there."

"Righto."

Cameron hung up and looked at the time; it was almost 11:00 already. He downed his coffee and got dressed, then hurried out the door.

* * *

The police building was busy for a Saturday. Members of the public roamed in and out, paying their fines and what not. Cameron sat on one of the seats in the lobby, waiting for Bill. He had downed a bacon and egg muffin on the way, and sat sipping a decent coffee. He was way early, but he didn't care.

After a thirty-minute wait, Cameron looked up to see Bill strolling into the lobby. He was wearing jeans and a leather jacket, and looked so different out of his usual uniform and suits. He caught sight of Cameron, and made his way across the lobby floor.

"Thanks for coming, mate." Cameron shook his hand. "I wouldn't have called if it wasn't important."

"It's all good," Bill said. "Let's head into one of the interview rooms. Follow me."

Cameron followed him down a hallway and into a small room, empty except for a desk with a computer, and two chairs. Bill tapped at the computer for a moment, then looked at Cameron expectantly.

"So, what have you got for me?" he asked.

"I found this hidden behind Dalcian's desk last night," Cameron explained, handing him the book. "It belongs to Dalcian, he drew the pictures. It implies that Gemma Lang was murdered by Richard."

Bill's face hardened, and he sat flicking through the images.

"This is huge, Cam," he said. "I've been to their house. I've seen that shed, and I've seen those locks on the outside of Dalcian's door, exactly as they've been drawn. The only way we can prove that Richard murdered her is to get a warrant and excavate the site. Did Dalcian ever talk about his mother?"

"Never," Cameron shook his head.

"Ok. I'm going to go and get started on this. I'll be in touch, mate."

"Thanks, Bill."

*

Cameron walked slowly through the lobby, lost in his own thoughts. *If Richard did murder Gemma, that means he is totally capable of murdering Dalcian too. But if he was going to kill Dalcian, why didn't he do it at the same time and say that Gemma took him to Queensland? Why did Richard keep him alive…does he know that Dalcian is an eyewitness? Or does he just want his own personal slave to cook and clean up after him? None of this makes any sense…*

Someone bumped into Cameron's shoulder, and caught him by surprise. A dull ache emanated from the healing knife wound.

"Sorry," he murmured, not turning around.

"Oh sorry, didn't see you there," an all too familiar voice said behind him.

Cameron felt a cold shiver run down his spine, and he slowly turned around. Paul was smirking at him with a terrible gleam in his eye. He still looked as handsome as always; wavy blond hair, a touch of makeup, and outrageous clothes, only this time Cameron could see him for what he really was: a nasty, despicable human being. He turned to walk away, but Paul dashed in front of him and blocked his path.

"Get out of my way, Paul. I'm not in the mood for your shit today," Cameron hissed.

"Don't be like that, Cammy. I see you've hit the news these days. Any news on loverboy yet?"

"I don't want to talk about it," Cameron growled.

"I bet the whole kidnapping ploy was just a way to get as far away from you as he could," Paul sneered. "It's pretty low if you're fucking homeless guys these days. You should get yourself tested for…"

Cameron balled his fist, ready to punch Paul in the face. He stopped himself, though; he was surrounded by police, now was not the time.

"What are you here for?" Cameron asked instead,

lowering his fist.

"Just paying a bill," Paul smirked. "None of your business, really."

"Whose car did you total this time?" Cameron shot back. "Whose house are you living in rent-free now?"

"You know what, you can go and get fucked," Paul snapped. "I'm done with you. Stay the fuck away from me."

"Likewise."

Cameron brushed past him and hurried down the stairs to the footpath. He was absolutely furious with what Paul had said, and could feel himself shaking in his anger. To hang shit on Cameron was one thing, but to attack his Dalcian meant war. With shaking fingers, he opened his wallet and fished out a small piece of paper with a phone number scribbled across it. Before he could change his mind, he dialled.

Human bones thought to belong to Dalcian Lang's mother found buried in backyard of family home.

Human remains believed to be those of Gemma Lang, mother of recently kidnapped Dalcian Lang, have been unearthed in the backyard of their family home in Warwick Farm in Sydney's south-west.

Friday, 20th June, 2019. Melissa Drake.

New evidence has been received by NSW Police, which implies that Gemma Lang, estranged wife of Sergeant Richard Lang of the Liverpool station, was indeed murdered.

Today, police demolished a shed in the backyard of the family's home, and found human remains buried beneath the concrete slab.

It is believed that the bones belong to Gemma Lang, who was reported missing in 2013 by her husband.

It was discovered that two weeks after the report was filed, Lang claimed to have received a letter from his wife, stating that she had fled to Queensland with her new lover. The report was subsequently dropped. The letter was never examined, nor was Gemma ever contacted to verify the story.

The remains have been sent for forensic testing to determine the identity, and cause and time of death.

Suspicion is mounting that the disappearance of Richard Lang is tied with the kidnapping of his only son.

It is alleged that Dalcian Lang was abused by his father, and ran away from home to escape the violence. For the next few years, Dalcian lived on the streets, homeless, out of fear of being found by his father.

Nineteen-year-old Dalcian Lang was kidnapped from outside the Parramatta RSL club on the 8th of June, by a private investigator who was hired by Richard Lang to locate his son. The investigator has been taken into police custody and will face charges of kidnapping.

Police are urging anyone who may have any information relating to the kidnapping or location of Mr Lang and his son to call Crime Stoppers immediately.

Part Three

October 5th, 2022

19

The sound of the Parramatta ferry horn jolted Cameron from his torpor. His head felt heavy and filled with fog; he tried to open his eyes, but he couldn't. The sound of voices floated through the wall, and for a moment he felt confused. *Where am I? What's going on?*

"Thanks for coming in so early for me," a woman was saying. "I know you don't open until nine today, but this couldn't wait. I'll happily pay extra for your troubles."

"It's no problem," another woman's voice said. "What can I help you with?"

"I'm convinced my husband is cheating on me," the first woman replied. "He's been showing all the signs. You know, hiding his phone, constantly texting someone but when I check, the messages are deleted. I confronted him, but he denies it. He didn't come home last night, and I'm pretty sure I know where he is."

"We can definitely look into this for you. I just need you to fill in this form… Oh crap, I've run out. I'll just duck into my partner's office and grab a copy, back in a sec."

Cameron slowly became aware that his head was resting in an awkward position, and as he heard his office door open, he finally managed to open his eyes.

"Jesus Cam, what are you still doing here?"

He sat up slowly, and through blurry eyes, realised that he'd faceplanted at his desk the night before. Sarah stood staring at him with her hands on her hips and a concerned look on her face.

"Um…er." Cameron rubbed his eyes and looked at the clock as his brain finally kicked in and started to work. "It's only 06:00, what are *you* doing here?" he rasped. His tongue was dry and felt like wood.

"Emergency call-in," she said. "I need a new client form."

Cameron's eyes swept across his desk and landed on his computer screen. He quickly closed his browser before Sarah could see what he had been searching the night before, then handed her a copy of the form.

"You don't look so good," she noted.

"I feel like shit," Cameron admitted. "Those new meds are kicking me around."

"Go and get some fresh air, and a coffee," she advised. "I'm sure Roger would love to have breakfast with you."

"Sounds good actually," Cameron agreed. "I'll be doing surveillance for that workers comp case for most of the day. The report is due Friday."

"Alright, hon. I'll go and get started with my new client."

Cameron watched as she left his office, then leant back in his chair and stretched. His office was nothing fancy; a medium sized room with several filing cabinets shoved against a wall, and his long desk overlooking George Street below. In the next room, he had a couch which he slept on most nights so that he didn't have to go home, and a small private bathroom. The building was once a group of four brick townhouses that had been converted into commercial businesses in the 80s.

He secretly dreaded going home. As much as his friends thought he'd gotten over what had happened three years ago, deep down, Cameron knew he could never get over it. As such, he still had the apartment in Western Sydney, which served as a time capsule for the day Cameron's life changed forever.

Three years on, after forensic evidence had proven that Richard Lang had indeed murdered his wife, it was widely speculated that Dalcian would be dead too, and given that there had been no sightings, many people assumed that Richard had probably killed them both in murder-suicide fashion.

Cameron refused to believe that, though. He couldn't. Holding on to the hope that Dalcian was alive was all that was keeping him going. Every decision he'd made since that day, was based on the belief that one day Dalcian would come home.

Once he'd gone over some paperwork from the day before, and had a quick shower, Cameron changed into his gym gear, then looked at Roger sleeping on the couch. His heart filled with love for the new man in his life.

"Come for walkies?" he asked.

Roger stirred and looked at Cameron for a second, then leapt off the couch and ran towards him as fast as his little legs could manage. Cameron swept him into his arms; Roger licked his face, his tail wagging with excitement.

"Who's a good boy?" Cameron gushed. "Where's your vest?"

He sat Roger back on the floor, and the excited pooch ran and fetched his lead and vest. Cameron strapped him in and headed downstairs.

It was a chilly for an October morning. Large puddles from the heavy rain the day before made the vacant block opposite the office building look like a dirty swimming pool. Cameron paused on the footpath so that Roger could pee on the power pole, and lit a cigarette. He turned and gazed back at his empire, reminiscing over the last few years.

He had taken Paul to court in an attempt to get back half of his house, in hopes to pay off the debt and get a fresh start. Instead, his lawyer had managed to get back 80% of the house's current value, 50% of all assets, and forced Paul to repay the debt, on grounds that he had technically stolen Cameron's car in the first place. He had walked away from court with over $1 million and debt free.

Cameron quit his job in security shortly after, and with Sarah's help, they started their own private investigation firm. Greenwood & Sullivan Private Investigations was growing by the day, as news of their work spread around Sydney. Cameron's specialty side-hustle was locating missing people who had become homeless. Unlike the idiot who was rotting in jail for fifteen years for kidnapping Dalcian, though, Cameron made contact with his missing persons first, and found out *why*. For those running from abusers, Cameron had built up an underground support network to either help them put their abusers behind bars, or help them to legally change their names so that their abusers couldn't find them.

It was a long process, but rewarding. His clients paid him a lot of money to track down their prey, which Cameron in turn used to help their victims. A few staged sightings far away from Sydney were usually enough to get the abuser to leave them alone.

In between his missing persons cases, Cameron was contracted with a large insurance firm to investigate suspicious claims. His years of doing covert security meant that he had a flair for blending in and getting the evidence he was required to obtain.

Sarah handled the non-contracted cases, usually the cheating wives and husbands, or staff theft claims. Between them, they made a respectable income each, which was much more than they earned in security for less working hours. Cameron was happy with his newfound career, but deep down, he was still missing his Dalcian with every fibre in his body.

Cameron took a deep drag on his cigarette and blew out a puff of smoke. A part of him felt ashamed every time he lit one up, but smoking helped keep the stress levels down. Three years on, his anxiety had only gotten worse; his therapist had linked it to PTSD, the trauma of witnessing Dalcian being abducted.

Once Roger finished spraying the pole and sniffed around the garden, Cameron tossed the butt into the makeshift ashtray, then made his way through the streets of Parramatta to a small café he'd been visiting every day for the last week.

The café was busy for a Wednesday morning. Cameron placed his usual order and sat at the table in the window, where he could clearly see the front of the store across the road. Roger sat by his feet as he had been trained, unperturbed by the noises and food smells around him. Cameron pulled out his video recorder and set it up discreetly to film the store, then picked up his fantasy book to read.

"Excuse me, may I sit here?"

Cameron looked up to see a man smiling down at him. His dark hair fell across his eyes, and it was obvious that he was on his way to the gym.

"Er, I guess." Cameron shrugged.

"Thanks. There's no other seats," the man said.

Cameron turned his attention back to his book. As much as the guy was a hornbag, Cameron wasn't interested. It was too soon.

"Oh. My. God. Your dog is the cutest!" the man exclaimed. "How do you get away with bringing him inside?"

Cameron groaned inwardly, and felt his anxiety soar.

"He's an assistance dog," he replied shortly.

"He's adorable. What breed is he? What's his name?"

"Cairn terrier cross," Cameron mumbled. "His name is Roger."

"Can I pet him?"

"No. He's working right now."

The man looked disappointed and was about to say something, but Cameron was saved by the arrival of his coffee and muffin. He busied himself with adding sweetener and tried to ignore his uninvited guest.

"You go to the gym on George Street, don't you?" the guy asked.

"Yep."

"I thought I'd seen you around. Are you one of the guys who were deadlifting last Friday night?"

"Yep."

"Oh nice. I'm Brayden by the way."

Cameron looked up to see a hand offered from across the table. He reluctantly shook it.

"Cameron."

Brayden's name was called above the noise.

"Oh, that's me. Nice to meet you finally." His smile was oddly enchanting. "If you ever need a training partner, hit me up."

"Ok. Bye."

Cameron watched as Brayden left the café with his coffee. He had a nice arse, and his calves were bulging. Had he any libido, Cameron *may* have tried to get him into bed. As soon as he realised he was checking out another man, though, a wave of guilt washed over him; it was still too soon. With a sigh, he turned his attention back to the store across the street.

As though by cue, the owner of the business and a staff member emerged from the building, pushing a heavy Coonara wood heater on a trolley. They stopped at the back of a ute, and proceeded to lift the heavy steel heater onto the back of the tray. Cameron whipped out his camera and took some extra photos, and made sure the video recorder was trained on them.

One of the staff members claimed that they hurt their back while installing a wood heater in a client's home. The boss had denied it, and insisted that they used proper safe lifting equipment. The client had also claimed that they lifted the heater manually. Cameron now had the final evidence he needed on his checklist to report back to the insurance company.

"Whatta ya think Rog, should we go to the gym now?" he asked, offering him a small piece of muffin under the table. Roger wagged his tail in approval and nommed it up. "Alright, let's go."

* * *

The gym was Cameron's temple; it was the one place where he could go to forget his troubles for a while, and focus on himself. At first, he had joined the gym as a way to punish himself, but over time he had come to appreciate how much better it made him feel. The gym was just across the road from the office, which made it perfect for Cameron's needs.

Everywhere he looked that day, though, Brayden was always nearby, casting furtive looks and innuendo in his direction. Cameron had never noticed the guy before, and soon wished that he had not allowed him to sit at the table in the café that morning.

He started off with a light jog on the treadmills, only to notice that Brayden was on the spin bike in front of him, wriggling his fine arse and eyeing Cameron suggestively in the mirrors.

Frustrated, Cameron cut his warm-up short and escaped to a squat rack. No sooner had he set up his music through his headphones and started pumping out his sets of speed squats with chains, there was Brayden curling in the opposite rack. *That fucking arsehole! Only wankers curl in the fucking squat racks!* Cameron snatched the weights off his bar and racked them, then stalked off to the back of the gym.

The back of the gym was reserved for the powerlifting and strongman teams. Cameron was so pissed off that his space was being invaded, he pulled out the heavy steel prowler and smashed out eight runs with only fifteen seconds rest between each one. The angrier he was, the harder he trained, and today was no exception, especially with Disturbed's *Meaning of Life* screaming in his ears.

He finished with his usual abs exercises, followed by three sets of reverse hypers; the hanging free-weight style designed by Louie Simmons. Once he was done, he stood next to the machine, wiping his sweat and catching his breath. *I really should quit smoking,* he thought.

Roger was watching Cameron, squirming as though he wanted to leave his designated spot. He looked agitated, and his tail was wagging a little nervously. Cameron knew him well enough to know what he was trying to communicate.

"Come here, then."

He patted his leg, and Roger scampered over. Straight away, he stood on his two back legs and placed his front paws on Cameron's knee. Anyone watching might think it was just cute puppy behaviour, but Roger was a trained dog with a job. He knew Cameron's anxiety was through the roof, and it was his job to alert Cameron in time to prevent a panic attack.

He sat down and leaned back against the hyper machine, and pulled Roger into his arms. The scruffy black terrier rested his face on Cameron's shoulder and snuggled in. Once again, anyone watching might think it was a cute exchange. The reality, though, was that Roger was helping to calm him down. Cameron hadn't even realised that he was so close to an attack.

"You're such a good boy," Cameron said softly, scratching him behind the ears. "Daddy's boy. I might even take you for a decent walk later."

Once Cameron cooled down, both from his session and his emotions, he headed back to his locker and mixed up a protein shake. As he shook the shaker, he pulled out his phone; it was only 12:30, but he was already swamped with messages. He slung his bag over his shoulder, and closed his locker.

As he turned to leave, he felt his mood drop again when he saw Brayden standing in the doorway. There was nowhere to hide, no other exit. He was trapped. He picked up Roger and held him protectively.

"That was some workout you just pulled." Brayden grinned, stepping closer. "I don't think I could push that big contraption let alone run laps with it."

"I don't work out, I train," Cameron said stiffly. "I don't mean to be rude, but I need to get going…"

Brayden moved forward until he was uncomfortably close, and rested his hand on one of the lockers.

"You're Cameron Greenwood, aren't you?" he asked. "I saw you on the news a few years ago."

"Yeah. Look, I really need to go…"

"How about we head back into the showers instead? There's no one in there right now." Brayden brushed his fingers along Cameron's forearm.

"No. I'm not interested," Cameron snapped.

"Oh, come on. It's been what, three years or something? Come and have a bit of fun, let off a bit of steam." Brayden ran his fingers farther up Cameron's arm.

"You sure have a lot of balls to be making assumptions about something you know fuck-all about," Cameron hissed. "No means no. Now *please* get out of my way."

As though to punctuate Cameron's sentence, Roger let out a low growl.

"Fine. Suit yourself. If you ever decide to stop pining

over a dead guy, look me up." Brayden turned and strolled out of the room before Cameron could even think about punching him in the face.

By the time Cameron made it back to the office, his chest felt tight and his belly was squirming from being anxious and overwhelmed. Every sound seemed to be amplified, putting him on edge.

"Morning, Cam," Candice, their receptionist, greeted with a smile.

"Hi, Candice. How are you, mate?"

"Not bad," she said. "I'll be glad for the weekend, to be honest."

"I hear ya," Cameron agreed. "I'm going to head upstairs and have a shower. If anyone calls, tell them I'll be back in an hour."

He unclipped Roger's vest and let him run ahead up the stairs. His legs already felt wrecked from the prowler sprints. *What is it with me and stairs? The next place I get will be on the ground floor or have an elevator installed.*

Once he'd calmed down, showered, and dressed in a clean suit, Cameron sat wearily at his desk and started checking the messages on his phone.

SARAH: That's got to be a record. I just busted a husband cheating and got the evidence his wife wanted in two hours. I'll be back there shortly.

CAMERON: Good work! Your shout for coffee.

SARAH: Prick. See you soon x

A message from Jill caught his attention, and he opened it next.

JILL: Hi, Cam. Just sending through
the soup kitchen schedule for the
month. I look forward to seeing you
there!

CAMERON: Thanks, Jill! Can't wait :)

He scrolled past a few progress reports from
subcontractors, and noticed one from an unknown
number.

UNKNOWN: Hi sexy. I just wanted to
say sorry for today. I was a rude
bastard and totally out of line. If
you could see it in your heart to
forgive me, I would love to meet
you for coffee sometime? Start over?
I've been eyeing you off for ages and
really wanted to get to know you.
— Brayden ;)

Cameron glared at the text message, his anger rising
once more. With shaking fingers, he tapped out his reply.

CAMERON: I already told you, I'm
not interested. If that's the level
you're willing to sink to just to get
laid, give my ex a call. Now please
leave me the duck alone!

CAMERON: Fuck*

BRAYDEN: Fine. Sorry. Bye. :(

Cameron tossed his phone on his desk and sighed. It
was going to be one of those days.

20

Cameron was glad for Friday. He had spent the day before working on his report and preparing his evidence for the insurance firm, and had planned to go to the gym that morning to reward himself for a job well done. As he looked out from his window, though, he had spied Brayden waltzing into the gym as though he owned the place, and decided not to go. Avoidance was his best strategy until he had a chance to speak to the gym's manager.

Friday morning was spent transmitting the report and all of the evidence Cameron had collated for his case. As he clicked send on his final email, his phone started buzzing with an incoming call. To his surprise, it was Graham.

"Hi, mate," Cameron answered.

"How's it going?"

"Busy. You?"

"Same shit as always," Graham sighed. "I swear Barry's lost the fucking plot."

"I told you. Quit security and do the PI course, come work with us. We're making more than you and I put together back in the day."

"Barry has me by the balls. With all the dodgy shit that goes on here, he's too scared to let me go in case I blow the whistle on the industry," Graham said wearily. "If he ever gets caught, he'll drag me down with him."

"Not good, mate," Cameron said.

"Yeah. I'll just wait til he has a fucking heart attack and then I'll walk. But anyways, enough about that. How have you been getting on?"

"Much like any other day, I guess." Cameron shrugged.

"I mean, have you started playing the field yet?" Graham asked.

"Nope. I'm not ready for that," Cameron said flatly.

"Mate, I know you suffered a big loss and all, but don't you think it's time?"

"Everyone thinks he's dead except for me," Cameron said irritably. "I refuse to believe that until I see his bones with my own two eyes. The only goddamned thing keeping me from ending things some days is the hope that I'll find him alive. So no, I don't think it's time, and no one has the right to tell me how long I'm allowed to grieve the love of my life."

"I didn't mean it like that…" Graham said quickly.

"Did you need something in particular?" Cameron cut him off abruptly.

"Oh. Er. I just wanted to pick your brains on a known POI," he said awkwardly. "She used to frequent Merrylands and Liverpool a lot, and steal shit from the kid's department. I seem to remember you nabbing her a few times."

"Yeah, I remember her," Cameron said shortly.

"The cops raided her house recently. Discovered she was a part of something much bigger and more sinister. They are requesting any information we have on her."

"Child smuggling?" Cameron guessed.

"Something like that, yeah."

"I'll go through my files and find the reports," Cameron said. "Same email as before?"

"New email. The company was liquidated and rebranded. I'll text it to you."

"That's illegal as fuck," Cameron sighed.

"I know."

"I'll see what I can find and send it through." Cameron said. "I need to get going."

"Righto. Thanks, mate."

"Bye."

Cameron hung up his phone and sighed deeply. Barry had been furious when Cameron put in his resignation, and had pushed Graham to pressure and threaten him to stay. It had not gone well, and Cameron's promise to do the odd shift to help them out was revoked. His relationship with Graham had been strained ever since.

Roger trotted out of the other room and sat at Cameron's feet. He picked him up and carried him to Sarah's office across the hall. Her door was open, and she waved him in.

"How'd your report go?" she asked.

"All done," Cameron replied. He helped himself to one of the client chairs and crossed his legs. "You'll never guess who I just spoke to."

"Graham?" she asked with a raised eyebrow.

"You did guess."

"I had a missed call from him earlier," she said. "I couldn't be fucked talking to him. What did he want?"

Cameron repeated their conversation, and her face turned into a frown.

"That arsehole. How dare he say that?" she fumed.

"No one has any right to tell me how I should be feeling," Cameron said. "I thought he of all people should know that since his own mum died last year."

"Oh hon, I wish I had words of comfort," she said sadly. "So, what are you going to do?"

"I'll get Candice to forward him all of my reports and intel on her," Cameron replied. "That way, maybe they'll realise that I'm a professional, and not corrupt like them."

"Graham's a good guy when Barry isn't forcing him

into shit situations," Sarah sighed. "If only he had the balls to take up our offer. He'd make a decent PI if he could keep his dick in his pants."

"I know. Anyways, I'm going to take Rog for a walk and have lunch. You got anything on this weekend?"

"I'm going nightclubbing in the city tonight," she grimaced. "Another cheating lover case. Covert surveillance. I'm leaving early this arvo so I can have a nap and get ready."

"You should take Ron and pretend you're reminiscing the old days," Cameron snorted.

"You don't think I look young and fuckable?" she retorted.

"Darling, you look fabulous," Cameron said in the most flippant accent he could manage. "But I could never fuck you. You don't have a cock."

Sarah cracked up laughing uncontrollably, and before he knew it, Cameron was laughing so hard, the delayed onset muscle soreness in his abs hurt.

"Oww!" he gasped.

"Serves you right," Sarah chortled.

"Right. I'm off. I'll see you later, mate."

* * *

Candice was tapping away at her computer when Cameron reached the bottom of the stairs.

"I'll be back in around an hour." Cameron shot her a smile. "If you need me, call me."

"No worries, Cam," she smiled back. "There's a parcel here that has been redirected from your home address, and some regular mail."

"Just chuck it on my desk if you don't mind," Cameron said. "I'll see you soon."

It was a glorious spring day, sunny with a chilly breeze. Cameron could see a few clouds forming, and knew the weather would probably turn to shit within an hour or two. Roger tugged eagerly against his lead, and pulled Cameron towards the footpath.

He was about to turn right and head to the small café next to his gym, but as he turned, he caught sight of Brayden once again infiltrating his space. He let out a soft gasp and quickly hurried in the opposite direction, and ducked into the office carpark, out of sight.

"That fucking arsehole," Cameron murmured to Roger. "Come on."

Roger said nothing, and pulled Cameron towards the hidden path through the trees that lined the rear of the carpark.

Directly behind the row of trees was a path that meandered along the Parramatta River. It was just a short walk to the ferry terminal, or a slightly longer stroll to the HMAS Parramatta memorial. Cameron unclipped Roger's lead and tossed his ball along the grassy area, and slowly made his way towards the historic site.

The words of Graham, Brayden, and everyone else who had something to say on the issue all came flooding back. Cameron sat on a seat by the memorial, and pondered over their words, while Roger sat at his feet, grooming himself.

"Grieving is ok, but you can't grieve forever. You need to move on." "You know it as much as we all know it. He's not coming back." "You only knew him for a month. Move on, you'll find someone else." "What was so great about a homeless guy? Did he have a big dick or something?"

Cameron had heard it all. Sarah and Ron were the only ones who hadn't pushed him to 'get over it', but instead supported him through his ups and downs. He owed his life to them, his only family. *Should I give up? Will I ever find him, or is he gone forever? I just wish I had appreciated him so much more when he was here. I should have told him how I felt sooner and made him feel loved. I'm such an arsehole.*

With a despaired sigh, Cameron picked up Roger and walked slowly back towards the office. The wind had picked up, and it was getting colder. He had left his suit jacket draped over his chair, and the wind cut through his slacks and business shirt.

Maybe I should apologise to Brayden. I was pretty rude to him the other day. Maybe we could be friends, he thought, though he knew that friendship was farthest from Brayden's mind. *No. Brayden has already shown how low he can go. I already got rid of one toxic arsehole from my life, I don't need another one.*

By the time he'd made it back to the office, Cameron wasn't hungry. He trudged upstairs and locked his door, and sat staring out of the window, his mind miles away. He felt conflicted; should he move on? Or should he hold onto hope?

He spun back around in his chair and faced his computer. The mail sat in a neat pile next to his keyboard; he ignored it and opened up his emails instead.

One of the emails was a confirmation that the insurance firm had received his report. Another one caught his eye, and he clicked it.

The email was an offer for a new case; he had two days to accept or decline. He opened the PDF file and set it up to print on the printer downstairs, then finally turned his attention to the other mail on his desk.

The envelopes were mostly bills that had been redirected from his apartment. Cameron tossed them into his to-do tray, then turned his attention to the parcel. It was a small white book-sized padded mailer, only it was grubby and had a few scratches in it. The black pen on the front was smudged, and it had several redirection stickers on it, indicating that it had been sent to at least two wrong addresses before finally reaching him.

He could make out that the parcel had been sent from Western Australia, but there were no other identifying features. With a shrug, he opened it with scissors and pulled out a small sketchbook. There was no note inside, but once he studied the front of the book, his hands started shaking and a fresh wave of guilt washed over him.

The book had become worn and dog-eared since he'd seen it last. With tears streaming down his face, and his mind too numb to fully comprehend the moment, he opened the sketchbook and flicked slowly through the pages.

Where it had once been only half-full, the book was now filled with comics and drawings. As he flicked through the pages, he stopped on the page that Dalcian had drawn when they first met. Cameron burst into tears. He had no idea who sent the book or what it meant, but it could mean one thing: that Dalcian was still alive.

After a few pages of random doodles and pictures, Cameron came across a title page with Yogi and Boo-Boo bear holding up a sign, *The Adventures of Yogi and Boo-Boo*. At first Cameron thought it would be a cartoon about the bears, but instead it was his and Dalcian's story, as though his memories had been drawn onto the pages before him. Cameron jammed his fist into his mouth to try and stop his hiccuppy sobs.

And there it was. The kidnapping, only the comic didn't end with Cameron watching the car disappear. The comic showed Dalcian in the boot of the car, clutching his Yogi and trying to escape. Once the car stopped, the boot opened, and someone dragged Dalcian out by his arm. It was his father, Richard Lang, and Cameron flinched as Dalcian's character was slapped in the face with a *THWACK!*. Richard handcuffed Dalcian to the Jesus strap in the back seat of a different car, and drove off.

The next scene showed them abandoning the burning car. A third man greeted them, and with a start Cameron realised it was the retired police pilot who was the caretaker of the airfield. The pilot led them to a small airplane, and

Dalcian was dragged inside. Richard raised his hand, and the scene went black.

The final page was a lighter sketch of a property with a long driveway that led to a house atop a small rise. A single shed stood just inside the gate, and a large tree with a branch that curved down to touch the ground marked the corner of the property's boundary. A lone figure sat on the branch with his sketchbook.

In the bottom left corner of the page, a part of the tree looked out of place. Cameron studied it through his teary eyes, and noticed that it looked like an E. Intrigued, he flicked back to the previous page, and looked closer. There in the black shaded scene, Cameron's eyes made out an S, slightly darker in the middle of the page.

Cameron started back at the beginning of the story, and scanned the pages one by one, and scribbled down the hidden letters.

HELP ME. PLEASE.

* * *

It took Detective Saunders around fifteen minutes to arrive out the front of the office. He screeched to a halt in an unmarked black car with the covert lights flashing, and hurried to meet Cameron on the footpath.

"Hi, Cam. What did you find?" Bill asked.

"I got this in the post today. Dalcian's alive!" Cameron handed him the sketchbook, opened at the start of the kidnapping scene. "Just like I suspected, they flew from the airstrip in a light plane. Your pilot friend was in on it."

"Fuck me!" Bill swore. "I'll send some guys to go and pick him up. How did you get the book?"

"It was posted here from Western Australia."

"I seem to recall that Richard has a brother over that way. Go get the packaging, we'll head straight over to my office and see if we can trace it."

Cameron ran back inside and bolted up the stairs three at a time. He snatched his backpack and packed a few essentials, his secret file on Dalcian, his meds, and Boo-Boo, and quickly fastened Roger into his vest. He picked him up and hurried back down the stairs.

"What's going on?" Candice asked from the reception desk.

"I found a lead on Dalcian. He's alive!"

"Oh my god!" she gasped. "Where is he?"

"I don't know. Possibly in WA. I'm heading over to HQ with Bill to track him down."

"Go go go! Let me know what happens," she said. "I'll call Sarah."

"Thanks. Catch ya later."

Cameron rushed back outside and noticed a small group of people had gathered by the café and were watching on curiously. Cameron ignored them and slid into the front passenger seat with his bag between his legs and Roger on his lap.

"How's work been?" Bill asked as he did a U-turn and sped off back along George Street.

"Getting busier. I just completed a big contract for a dodgy work compo claim," Cameron replied. "If we keep going like this, we might land a whopper of a contract soon."

"That's great, mate. You'll be pleased to hear that the stepdad of your last case was sentenced today. Twenty years, no parole."

"Oh, excellent. Another abuser behind bars."

Cameron should have felt excited, but his emotions were so overwhelmed that he shut them down completely. His therapist had referred to it as a subconscious coping mechanism, and they had been working on it. A part of him felt safer being able to switch off his emotions, but she insisted that it was unhealthy long-term. He knew Bill was attempting to distract him by talking about work, and deep down he appreciated his efforts.

Bill pulled the car into the HQ carpark and rolled to a stop. Cameron held the end of Roger's leash and let him jump out of the car first, then slid out after him. They walked with Bill towards the staff entrance that Cameron had used many times since becoming a PI, and headed through the rabbit warren of passageways to the office in silence.

Bill's office was spacious and neat, except for his desk. Cameron helped himself to a seat and waited for Bill to log into his computer. After a moment, he put out his hand, and Cameron passed him the padded bag.

"Let's see. Hmm." He typed in one of the codes on the label and tapped his fingers on the desk for a moment. "It's regular untracked post."

Cameron watched as he pulled a magnifying glass from his drawer and studied it closer.

"Can you make out the postcode on this stamp?" he asked.

Cameron took the items and looked closely.

"653, I can't make out the last number," he replied.

"Hmmm. There are six postcodes starting with 653, and eighty-four places that slip into those codes," Bill mused, staring at his screen.

"Where does Richard's brother live?" Cameron asked. He shifted his chair next to Bill so he could see the screen.

"Let me see. Hmm. The address just says Port Gregory Rd. No number or area."

"Didn't you interview him at some stage?" Cameron asked.

"Yeah, via video link with the local coppers. He hadn't been in touch with Richard since they had a falling out a few years ago."

"Open Google Maps and go street view," Cameron suggested.

Bill obliged, and soon found the road in question,

north of Geraldton.

"That's a long road. We don't even know what we're looking for." Bill said.

"Yes we do." Cameron flicked open the sketchbook. "Switch it into satellite mode. Start at Northampton and follow the road along. It'll look something like this."

Cameron sat nervously, holding his breath every time they slipped into street view to look at the front of a dwelling. He was starting to think it was another dead end, when he saw the ominous icon of a house a fair distance from the road.

"There! Check that one," he said.

Bill clicked on the map, and Cameron held the sketch up next to the screen. There was no mistaking the shed, tree, and house farther up the drive.

"That's it! That's where he is!" Cameron let out a deep breath.

"Right. I'll get on the blower and see what I can organise with the Geraldton crew."

Cameron whipped out his phone and opened his flight app.

"What are you doing?" Bill asked.

"Booking a flight," Cameron replied. "Oh. The next flight is 17:35. I'll land at 20:40 local time, which is after the final flight to Geraldton. I'll have to catch the night bus at 22:00, which means I'll get there around 04:30."

"You're serious, aren't you?"

"I've never been more serious in my life," Cameron said, standing up. "Dalcian needs our help. This parcel was sent weeks ago, we can't risk taking our time."

"Alright. Want a lift to the airport?" Bill asked.

"I'll catch the train. I need you to organise everything so that I receive a happy welcome."

"Ok. I'll keep you posted. Good luck."

21

Cameron had flown to Melbourne a few times since commencing his career as a private investigator, but never before had he felt so nervous about flying. Travelling with Roger had its challenges, but Cameron had gotten used to it, and always made sure he had his handler's ID, and Roger's ID with him. Luckily, the airline rules that required fourteen days' notice of travelling with a service dog had changed, so Cameron was able to book a flight at a moment's notice and still take Roger with him.

Travelling with Roger also meant that Cameron got to board the plane first, which he was eternally grateful for. He wasn't scared of flying; he was more concerned about his companion's comfort and well-being during the flight, and being able to board without people pushing and shoving him was less stressful for both of them.

Once Roger was lying calmly at Cameron's feet on his mat, Cameron sat tapping his fingers on his knee nervously, his mind full of anxious negativity. *What if I'm too late? What if he isn't there? Oh my god, he probably doesn't even like me anymore! What if…what if he's happy where he is, and doesn't want to come with me? Oh stop it Cameron, he wouldn't have sent his sketchbook and hidden the message in it had he not wanted your help.*

The sound of the other passengers boarding the plane in a rush interrupted his thoughts, and he distracted himself by looking out of his tiny window. In the distance, beyond the runways, sat a dark grey military plane. Cameron squinted, and recognised it as a C-17 Globemaster, his favourite aircraft. In the lonely nights at the library after Dalcian disappeared, he had spent many hours poring over books on aircraft of all types and learning as much as he could about them. His interest had been fuelled by his theory that Dalcian and Richard had been flown out of Katoomba via the airstrip.

The plane finally took off, and once they reached cruising altitude and the seatbelt sign was turned off, Cameron pulled out his folder and sat it on his lap table. It was full of newspaper clippings, website articles, and anything that mentioned Dalcian or his family.

His theory was that a small aircraft, likely the Gippsland Airvan GA-8 that was a regular at the airstrip, had been flown by the ex-police pilot to either Tamworth or Orange, where they would have transferred onto a different plane and flown elsewhere. Cameron had investigated the flight logs and aircraft at Katoomba, but had hit a dead end.

He pulled a map of Australia from one of the pockets, and unfolded it, doing his best not to elbow the person next to him. He gingerly circled Geraldton and Dalcian's rough location, then sat pondering his options. *This isn't going to be easy. I hope Bill can sort something out.*

Cameron's nerves didn't ease during the flight. The woman sitting next to him was complaining loudly about everything to her partner, from the flight assistants to the taste of the in-flight meal, the turbulence, and she even complained about the free airline magazine. The woman reminded him of the classic Karen memes, and once she noticed Roger, it was on.

"Cute dog. Can I pet her?" she asked.

"No. Roger is working right now." Cameron looked out the window and rolled his eyes.

"Oh, it won't hurt him," she scoffed.

She reached out her hand and started to reach down.

"No, but he might hurt you." Cameron grasped her wrist angrily. "Never touch an assistance dog while he's on duty."

"Assistance dog? What's he assisting you with? You don't look disabled."

"When was your last pap smear?" Cameron snapped back.

"I beg your pardon?!" she gasped.

"I'm sorry, I thought you wanted to share private medical information." Cameron glared at her.

Karen glanced around the cabin as though looking for someone to complain to, but there were no flight attendants close enough. She shot Cameron a death look, then turned in her seat and said something to her partner. Cameron couldn't hear what he mumbled, but Karen became even more pissed off. She snatched her Sudoku book and kept to herself for the rest of the flight.

Cameron was exhausted by the time the plane landed in Perth. As soon as he disembarked with Roger in his arms, he ducked to the loo for a quick pee. He studied his appearance in the mirror as he washed his hands; his eyes were tired and grey, and his suit had become wrinkled from the long flight. He dried his hands, then headed straight for the pet relief area. He knew Roger would be busting, and they still had a long trip ahead of them.

Once Roger had relieved himself, Cameron gave him a small treat and drink, just enough that he wouldn't be caught short on the bus, and headed for the exit. Apart from his backpack, he had no luggage. He'd worry about clothes later.

As soon as he was outside, Cameron reached into his

bag for his pack of smokes. When he flipped open the box, though, he stopped, and with a sigh, threw them back in his bag. *Dalcian thinks smoking is gross. I don't want to disappoint him, I've already let him down enough,* he thought. With another sigh, he ignored his nicotine craving, and made his way to the taxi rank.

* * *

It was 21:00 by the time Cameron was dropped off at the bus terminal. Armed with a large coffee and a dozen chicken nuggets from Maccas, Cameron found his bus bay and made himself comfortable on one of the bench seats. A digital display was showing the current temperature as 13°c, though it felt much warmer. Compared to Sydney, the air felt drier and less soupy.

He poured some water into a small travel cup that he always carried for Roger, and blew on a nugget until it was cool enough for him to eat.

"Here you go, Rog. Eat 'em up." Cameron sat half of the nugget on the ground and nodded to let him know it was ok to eat. Roger scoffed it down hungrily, then sat looking up at Cameron and wagging his tail. "You're such a good boy. Here you go."

Cameron finished his snack, then pulled out his phone and switched flight mode off. A number of text messages came through almost instantly.

```
SARAH: Been trying to call. Where are
you?
```

```
CAMERON: Just landed in Perth.
Waiting for a bus to Geraldton.
```

Within seconds of hitting send, Sarah's name flashed up on his screen with an incoming call.

"What the fuck are you doing over in Perth?" she demanded as soon as he swiped to answer.

"Didn't Candice call you?" Cameron asked.

"No. I've been sleeping. I'm about to head to the nightclub," she said.

"Oh my god. Remind me to fire her when I get back," Cameron said, though he didn't mean it. "I—" He broke off as the reality of it all suddenly hit him all at once. His numbed emotions all kicked into overdrive, and he sat staring into space as he realised he was about to either fulfil his promise, or get the closure he so desperately needed.

"Cam? You there? What's going on?" Sarah sounded concerned.

"I…found him," Cameron said slowly, disbelievingly. "I'm sorry. It's just hit me all at once."

"Dalcian? I thought you'd stopped looking for him?" Sarah sounded confused.

"I never stopped," Cameron confessed. "I have an entire folder dedicated just to him."

"Jesus, Cam."

The obnoxious beep of another incoming call caused him to frown and check his screen. His heart skipped a beat.

"I have to go, Bill's calling. I'll call you back," he said quickly.

"I have to go now, anyway. I'll call you tomorrow. Night, hon."

Cameron hung up and accepted Bill's call.

"Hi, mate," he said.

"Hi, Cam. I've been trying to call," Bill said. "Get there alright?"

"Yeah. I landed around forty mins ago, only just turned my phone on," Cameron replied. "Please tell me you have good news?"

"You could say that. You're to rendezvous with the Geraldton crew by 06:00 for a briefing. They will fill you

235

in there," Bill replied.

"I should get there around 04:30," Cameron mused. "So they're going to help?"

"They are. Remember, Perth is two hours behind Sydney, so they've had extra time to sort shit out. I've been in video conferences ever since you left this arvo."

"Shit. Thanks mate, it means a lot." Cameron said.

"I just wish I could be there in person. I'll be joining the briefing via video."

"Has any of this been leaked to the media?" Cameron asked. He shuddered at the memory of the vultures when Dalcian disappeared, and again when Gemma's remains were exhumed.

"Absolutely not. This is all on a need-to-know basis. We can't afford the media to interfere and jeopardise the mission," Bill replied. "If this makes the news, Richard could panic. We don't want him to kill Dalcian before we get there."

Cameron's blood ran cold.

"Anyway, I need to get going. It's 23:30 here. Just head to the station as soon as you get to Geraldton." Bill said. "Oh, and one more thing. Keep your relationship with Dalcian to yourself. I've told them this is your case, and promised that your personal feelings won't get in the way of the operation. I've managed to convince them to allow you into the briefing and to tag along, despite the massive conflict of interest. Even cops don't get to work on cases involving family, so happy birthday and Merry Christmas for the next ten years. You're welcome."

The night coach to Geraldton was warm and built for comfort. There were only around five other passengers, and no one paid him any attention. Cameron found a seat towards the middle of the bus, and snuck Roger onto his lap. The driver seemed a nice bloke, and had welcomed the little dog onboard without any issues.

Using his suit jacket as a pillow, and with Roger in his arms, Cameron was soon lulled into a deep exhausted sleep.

* * *

Cameron felt his shoulder being shaken gently. For a moment he thought he was on the train home after a long security shift, and Dalcian was waking him up for their stop. When he opened his eyes, though, he realised he had been dreaming. He turned to see the bus driver looking at him.

"Sorry to wake you up. We're here, mate," he said.

"Already?" Cameron sat up and rubbed his eyes.

"It was only an almost seven-hour trip," the driver chuckled. "It's almost 5am, we had a few delays."

Cameron shimmied across the seat and stood up in the aisle, with Roger still in his arms. His body was stiff, and he felt his bladder about to burst.

"Thanks, mate. Are there loos out there?" Cameron asked as he slipped his bag over his shoulder.

"Nah, not around here. There's one down near the water, but I'm not sure if it'll be open," he replied.

Cameron made his way down the front of the bus, and stopped at the bottom of the steps.

"Would you happen to know where the police station is?" he asked.

"Oh, that's easy. Just walk back down Chapman to the lights and turn right, then left at the roundabout. You can't miss it." The driver smiled.

"Thanks again, mate." Cameron managed a smile, then turned and headed in the direction he was told. The bus took off behind him, and soon Cameron was alone in the darkness, with only Roger and the streetlights for company.

He sat the sleepy pooch on the ground and led him

across to some bushes shrouded in darkness.

"Go wee wees," he said quietly.

Roger lifted his leg and watered the bush; Cameron was pretty sure he could see a look of relief on his face.

"Good boy. Do your business."

He looked around and made sure no one was watching, then dropped Roger's lead and unbuttoned his pants. He watered the other bush as Roger found a nice patch of grass to decorate with a turd. Once he was done, Cameron tucked himself away and picked up Roger's lead. Usually he would pick up his turds and bin them, but he realised he left the doggy bags in his office.

"Feel better?" Cameron asked softly as they stepped back onto the footpath. "I sure as hell do."

Roger's happy prance indicated a strong "yes".

On the corner of the intersection, a lone bakery was lit up and open. Cameron walked towards it, drawn by his empty stomach. It had been well over a year since he had last indulged in a pie; he much preferred his healthier lifestyle and diet over the fast food that he lived off while doing security.

A lone truck driver was seated inside, eating his breakfast and staring at his phone. Cameron made his way to the counter, and was greeted by a bubbly lady.

"Morning, darl. What can I getcha?" she asked.

"Morning. I'll have a plain pie and sausage roll, and a large coffee thanks," he replied.

"Having here?" she asked.

Cameron nodded.

"Take a seat and I'll bring it out for ya."

Cameron headed back outside, and sat his backpack on one of the small tables. He fetched Roger's travel cup, and filled it at a tap in the garden.

"Good boy. Drink up," he said, and quickly washed his hands in the cold water.

Roger took a deep drink while wagging his tail.

"Here ya go, darl," the lady said.

Cameron turned to see her sit his coffee and breakfast on the table.

"Thanks, mate," he said.

He wiped his hands on his pants, then broke up half of the sausage roll and left it to cool down for Roger. As he sat sipping his coffee, he felt his familiar nervousness and anxiety rising a little. He had no idea what was awaiting him at the station, but he was determined not to let the police see his emotions. He sent Sarah a text message to let her know he was safe in Geraldton, then quickly scoffed his breakfast and took his morning meds.

As he took a deep swig of his coffee, he heard the sound of a chopper flying overhead, and flashed back to the night of Dalcian's kidnapping. He felt his hand start shaking slightly. *Keep it together, man. You've waited three years for this day, don't fuck it up. Keep those emotions bottled up; you can let them out later once today is over and done with. You've got this.*

22

The Geraldton Police Station was much like any station Cameron had ever been in. The lobby was lined with hard plastic seats, and felt sterile, cold, and intimidating. Cameron forced himself into his professional work mode, and walked up to the counter. After a few minutes, a door opened, and a lone officer sauntered up to the counter.

"What can I do for ya?" he asked through the clear safety screen.

"I'm Cameron Greenwood from Sydney. I'm here for the briefing at 06:00."

"Oh, g'day, mate. I'm Adam. Come on through."

The officer opened a door at the end of the counter and ushered Cameron through the door he had entered from.

"You're a bit early," Adam noted. "I'll take you to the meeting room. You can wait in there for the others. They shouldn't be far off."

They walked down a plain dreary corridor that connected the interview and processing rooms behind the scenes, then turned a corner into a large open office. Six rows of long desks, which had the space to accommodate three officers each, filled most of the room. In each space, a large computer screen emblazoned with the Western

Australia Police logo sat atop the desk, surrounded by personal items and papers. Two uniformed officers were kicking back watching videos on their phones, and looked up as Adam and Cameron entered the room.

Adam ignored them, and led Cameron past the rows of desks, and into a hallway. A short way down the hall, Adam opened a door and let Cameron into a conference room.

"Take a seat. It's 05:33, the others should be here soon," he said.

"Thanks, mate."

Adam left the door open, and Cameron walked slowly around the room, taking everything in. A large table filled most of the room, surrounded by comfy leather seats in a U-shape setup. At the head of the table, a podium stood in front of a map of the Geraldton area and surrounds, and a large smart screen covered the rest of the wall. He found a seat in the back corner of the U, and stretched.

Cameron grimaced as a faint whiff of BO caught his attention. He rummaged around in his bag and quickly applied some roll-on deodorant, then fished out his intel folder on Dalcian. He slipped off his suit jacket and draped it neatly over the back of his chair, straightened his tie, then sat down with Roger and his bag down by his feet.

As he waited, Cameron counted twenty-four seats around the table. *I wonder why they need such a big meeting room. It's not like this is going to be something big…*

The sound of many pairs of boots stomping down the hall drew Cameron's attention to the doorway. Twelve elite Tactical Response Group officers dressed in black tactical gear, automatic rifles slung over their shoulders and helmets tucked under their arms, filed into the room. Cameron ogled them in surprise; he knew the TRG team were experts in anti-terrorism, hostage situations, and all sorts of high-risk missions, but certainly wasn't expecting them to be involved. He watched in awe as they wordlessly took their seats along the far side of the table.

Shortly after, a number of uniformed officials bustled into the room, an air of seriousness on their faces. Cameron had been in briefings and meetings before, but never with such high-ranking officials, or the elite anti-terrorism team. He sat in awed silence, wondering if he was in the right room.

Everyone took their seats; no one chatted, no one paid any attention to Cameron. A Senior Sergeant fiddled on a laptop for a moment and fired up the smart screen. The screen split into three sections: the Western Australia Police logo on the left half, and two squares on the right. After a moment, Bill appeared in the top square, and another man appeared in the bottom.

"Everything is ready to go, sir," the Senior said to another officer.

The officer nodded and took his place at the podium.

"Morning, all. We have quite a bit to get through, so I'll just briefly introduce you all. I'm Commander Stise of WA Police. Going around the room, we are joined by Captain Briggs of the Royal Australian Navy, and his helicopter squadron leader, Lieutenant Commander Brown. Director of Ambulance Operations and acting Royal Flying Doctors liaison, Lucy Phelps. Senior Sergeant Bo Williams, head of this station. Officer Stevens, team leader of the surveillance team. Officer Greenway, police media specialist. We have the Tactical Response Group and team leader. We are also joined via video link by Detective Bill Saunders from Sydney, and Senior Sergeant Dayle Hicks from Northampton station. Finally, we are joined by Mr Cameron Greenwood, private investigator who has been handling this case for the last three years."

Cameron was overwhelmed by the number of high-ranking people in the room; they were all there just to help rescue Dalcian. He sat listening as Bill gave a brief background of the case, and a photo of Richard, his brother, and Dalcian flashed up on the left side of the screen.

"We believe that Richard — the suspect — could be armed and dangerous. He did not return to his station after his last shift, and instead went missing with his son. We believe that he has his sidearm and taser. His brother Travis has a rifle registered in his name, and possibly a shotgun," Bill said. "Given the suspect's experience in NSW Police, he knows the tactics and procedures we would employ in a standard operation. Therefore, it is imperative that we move with caution."

"Thank you, Detective," Commander Stise nodded towards the camera. He moved the photos to the bottom of the screen, and opened a satellite image of the property. "It is believed that the victim is being held at this property in Sandy Gully. As you can see, it's remote, which will make the extraction high risk. The plan is to station two units from Northampton station at the northern point of the road, and two units from Geraldton at the southern end, along with the comms bus, an ambulance, and Mr Greenwood. These units will provide a roadblock during the operation. I'll now hand over to Captain Briggs to go over the details."

"Thanks, Commander. Two Navy Taipan helicopters are standing by for stealth insertion; a team will secure the shed on the property, another team will secure the house, and the remaining two teams will secure the perimeter of the complex. The goal is to apprehend the suspect, accomplice, and victim.

"Once the TRG have rappelled into position, the Taipans will return to GET to refuel and standby for team extraction. Obviously, surprise is the key element here, so the Taipans will use whisper strategy to avoid detection," Captain Briggs nodded and sat back in his seat. He was replaced by Lucy Phelps from the ambulance.

"Given that this is a high risk operation, we will send

an ambulance crew attached to the southern roadblock team. We have a doctor and a PC-12 aircraft on standby at Meekatharra base. There are adequate landing areas for the aircraft along Port Gregory Road if needed, between the roadblocks."

Lucy sat back in her seat, and Officer Stevens took her place.

"Yesterday, we did some preliminary surveillance on the property. We can confirm that persons matching the description of the suspect and accomplice were spotted moving about the property. I have a covert team with a drone in place who will alert us if they try to leave the property."

For the next thirty minutes, Cameron tried to keep up as they discussed strategy, safety, contingencies, all sorts of operational elements. He was shocked to learn that Richard was probably armed; Bill had never mentioned that before. The thought of Dalcian being shot terrified him, but he pushed it out of his mind.

"We will launch at 08:00. This will give the northern and southern teams time to get into position. Time is of the essence. Any more questions?" Commander Stise looked around the room. "Alright. Move out."

Everyone stood, and the TRG team shuffled out of the room. Cameron hovered by his seat until the big wigs left, and the Senior Sergeant beckoned him over.

"Welcome, Mr Greenwood," he said, his hand outstretched.

"Thanks, Senior," Cameron replied, shaking his hand.

"Please, call me Bo. You'll be riding with me. Are you good to go?"

"I've been ready for three years," Cameron replied.

"Good. Let's go."

* * *

The Great Australian Outback, while mostly barren desert land, had a sheer beauty that Cameron instantly fell in love with. He loved the laid-back country towns, a stark contrast from the hustle and bustle of metropolitan Sydney. The small town of Northampton was dotted with historical buildings, and the houses all boasted large yards that could easily fit three or four Sydney homes. Tourist buses and four-wheel drives towing caravans were the main traffic that Cameron saw along the roads.

Bo pulled up at a service station and ducked inside, and shortly after returned with some bottles of water. He handed one to Cameron as he slid back into the car, and tossed the rest into the back seat.

"Drink up. It's easy to get dehydrated out here in this sun," he said as he clipped in his seatbelt.

"Thanks, mate," Cameron said.

"So many people drive these roads every day and don't have basic essentials like water. It's ridiculous. If you break down and don't have phone service or a radio, you could be stranded for days before someone happens to drive past," he said.

"If you don't mind me asking, how are the Indigenous people able to survive off the land out here?" Cameron asked as Bo turned the car onto Port Gregory Road.

"My people are one with the land. We respect Mother Nature, and pass down our stories and skills to each generation," Bo explained. "We are taught how to find water and hunt, amongst other things. I remember being on country with the elders, learning the ways of my people. I look forward to when I can do the same with my grandkids, keep our traditions alive, you know?"

"Yeah. I used to do security in the Marsden Park library. They have a massive collection of Indigenous oral histories and artefacts," Cameron said. "Western Sydney is home of the Darug people. I've met one of the elders, he's such a great man."

"Yeah. I think it's good that white Australians are finally working towards embracing Indigenous culture and protecting it. It would be a shame to lose any more of our history."

Cameron's attention turned back to his surroundings. The land was open and golden, except for an occasional row of trees in the distance, indicating a dry creek that seemed to meander at will across the countryside. Every now and then, they drove past green shrubs on the side of the road, usually accompanied by dead bushes.

After around ten minutes of driving, Bo stopped the car, and pulled a 'Police Roadblock Ahead' sign out of the boot. He cable-tied it to a speed sign, then hopped back in the car and drove off.

Cameron tried not to think about the mission that would commence in just over forty minutes; the mission that he had dreamt about and imagined nearly every night for the last three years. He petted Roger's head and cuddled him protectively, as his belly churned unceremoniously.

Bo slowed down, and turned onto a dirt road. He pulled the car to a stop next to a police mobile communication van, nicknamed a comms bus, another squad car, and an ambulance.

"I'll just go and check in with the others," Bo said. "Once the north team are in place, we'll head back down and block the road."

"Righto," Cameron nodded.

He looked around and spotted a dead tree just up the road; Cameron climbed out of the car and stretched, then led Roger to the tree. Once they had both relieved themselves, Cameron headed back and poured Roger a small drink.

"North team are ready and standing by. It's time," Bo said, walking back to the car.

Cameron felt his stomach jump into his mouth; he quickly hopped back inside and slammed his door shut.

Followed by the squad car and ambulance, they drove slowly back to the main road and parked lengthways across the road.

"*Southern roadblock is in place. Over,*" Bo said into the radio.

"*Roger that. Northern roadblock is in place. You've got one minibus of tourists heading your way. Over.*"

"*Roger that. Standing by. Over.*" Bo climbed out of the car and helped the other officers set up the roadblocks.

Cameron leant against the car with his door open, sipping at his bottle of water. It was hot already, and he had ditched his jacket and tie long ago. Even though it was only 07:35, the sun was already harsh. Roger sat on the floor of the car in the shade, panting softly.

The wait seemed to stretch out forever. Cameron had already chewed off all of his nails by the time the tourist bus passed through the block.

"*All units stand by for insertion. Taipans inbound. Over,*" a crackly voice called through the radio.

Cameron had raised his concerns about radio eavesdropping during the long drive from Geraldton, but Bo had assured him that they were using FHSS hopping to avoid detection. Cameron wasn't a praying man, but that day, he prayed that Bo was right and that everything would go smoothly.

An ominous shadow moving swiftly across the ground drew his attention, and he looked up to see two Navy choppers flying silently overhead. He quickly pulled out his phone and took a photo, then watched as they separated and flew into the distance.

"Not long now," Bo said, joining Cameron at the car.

Cameron tapped his fingers on his leg nervously. He wished he could just jump in the car and speed off to the house, and barge in himself to rescue Dalcian, but deep down he knew how risky that would be. Having the TRG elites made him feel better about the rescue, but there was still so much that could go wrong. A burning sensation filled his throat, followed by the horrid taste of bile. He took a few steps and spat it onto the ground.

Two cars had pulled up at the roadblock already. The driver in the first vehicle had turned his engine off, and looked pissed at having to wait. Cameron took another swig of water; he felt eager to get going, but was nervous as fuck. Finally, a message sounded from the radio.

"Team Alpha is in position. Suspect down. Shed cleared and secure. Over."

"Team Bravo is in position. House is secure. Hostile captured and neutralised. No sign of package. Over."

"Team Charlie is in position. Zone one is clear and secure. Over."

"Team Delta in is position. Zone two is clear and secure. Officers, you are cleared to move in. Over."

"That's us. Let's move."

23

The front of the property looked exactly as Dalcian had drawn it; there was no mistaking the tree with the curving branch that Dalcian had clearly climbed and sat on to do his drawing. It was eerie driving up the long driveway towards the house at the top of the rise. As they drove past the front shed, Cameron could see one of the TRG troops guarding the entrance. He knew there was someone lying dead in there, and shuddered at the thought. He was more worried about one of the other calls, though: *No sign of package.*

A rusted old farm truck and pale green Toyota Corolla were parked under a big gumtree opposite the entrance to the house. A lone TRG officer was perched atop a tall windmill, watching the ground below like a hawk. Bo followed the driveway around the house in a loop, and finally came to a stop in the shade. Cameron scrambled out of the car with Roger, and looked around nervously.

Someone was lying on the ground in the shade under the gumtree, his hands and feet bound by zip ties, guarded by two TRG officers. As he walked closer, Cameron recognised Richard Lang's portly shape. A bitter taste grew in his mouth; there was Dalcian's abuser, the sack of shit who scarred him both physically and mentally for life. The thought of knocking his teeth out was certainly appealing, but Cameron knew better.

Another police car and the ambulance were slowly making their way up the driveway. One of the TRG officers caught sight of Cameron and Bo, and waved them over.

"How'd it go?" Bo asked as they approached.

"We have captured the suspect and located a body, believed to be the accomplice," the officer replied. "No sign of the victim I'm afraid."

"May I take a look around?" Cameron asked tentatively.

"Go ahead. Don't touch anything, though," Bo nodded and handed Cameron a pair of disposable gloves. "I'll go and call for forensics."

Cameron walked towards the house, a feeling of dread rising inside him. He should have felt happy that Dalcian's abuser had been captured, but the only thing he could think about was finding his boy. As he walked closer, he noticed a number of solar panels on the roof of the house. Although there were powerlines passing through the property, the house didn't seem to be connected.

The house was old, and the grimy white paint was peeling from the weatherboards. Cameron slipped on the gloves and led Roger through the already open door. They stepped into the kitchen, which was painted a horrible green colour. A cold fireplace was embedded in the far wall, accented by a dusty mantelpiece. A number of ornaments and a broken mug sat on top of the shelf, covered in a thick layer of dust. Between the fireplace and kitchen bench, was a small dining table with four chairs around it.

An archway next to the fireplace led into the lounge room. There was no TV, just two armchairs in front of another fireplace. This room was painted pink, broken up by a few bookcases along the right wall. A large window let in some natural light, which fell across the dingy brown carpet. A few photos hung on the walls, most of them crooked.

Cameron could hear his heart pounding in his ears; he was afraid at what he might find, but he had to see it all with his own eyes. He walked through another arch, and found himself in a long dark hallway. Ugly brown dado boards lined the grimy pink walls. To his right were the back door, bathroom, and laundry.

With Roger by his side, Cameron drifted from room to room, scrutinising everything in his hunt for clues. The first bedroom was obviously Richard's, and the next one was more than likely his brother's. Cameron felt strange being in someone's house uninvited.

Although it was cooler inside, the house was still uncomfortably warm. Cameron noticed a large air conditioner vent in the ceiling of the hallway, and wished he could turn it on. He nervously made his way to the final bedroom.

There were a number of locks on the outside of the door, but they were all unlocked. Cameron's belly churned uneasily, and he felt a little nauseous as he carefully swung open the door and stepped inside.

There was no doubting that this was Dalcian's bedroom. Cameron could almost feel him in the air, even though he wasn't there. The room was the hottest of the three, and was the least furnished of them all. It had a single bed and a desk, nothing else. The window was boarded up from the outside with corrugated iron, and there was no glass in the window frame.

The bed was unmade, the covers pushed roughly to one side. A small stain that looked like dried blood marked the sheets. Cameron knelt down and looked under the bed, but Dalcian wasn't there. A few pens lay on the desk, and under it was a lone backpack, but there was nothing else in the room. He could feel a sense of despair rapidly growing inside him, but he fought to control it. He reached up and wiped the sweat from his brow, and retreated from the room.

He walked slowly back up the hall, and once again his eyes fell on the air conditioner vents. He walked back into the lounge room, then froze as a sudden realisation dawned on him.

This house runs off solar power and probably a generator. There is no way an air con can run on those systems! What the fuck? Cameron spun around and walked back into the hallway, and examined the vents closer.

There were six square vents installed together in a 3 x 2 format; they looked clean and modern compared to the rest of the house and contents. He had seen the square vents before in Sarah's house, but there was only ever one vent per room. He found the light switch, and turned on the hallway lights.

Upon closer inspection, Cameron could see a small loop protruding from between two of the vents. He felt his heart start beating even faster, and looked around for a something to help him reach the vents. A broom leaning in the corner next to the back door caught his eye, and Cameron quickly fetched it. Sure enough, on the end of the broom was a moulded plastic hook, meant for hanging. With trembling hands, he reached up and slotted the hook into the loop, and pulled.

The vents separated from the ceiling with ease, revealing a set of folded-up attic stairs. He sat Roger's lead on the floor and told him to stay, then unfurled the stairs and climbed warily into the roof.

A lone window to his left cast just enough light for Cameron to see. He climbed the stairs one after another, allowing his eyes to adjust as he went. The roof space was small and dusty, though he could make out a few footprints. He followed them with his eyes, and felt himself flinch as they landed on something dark towards the back of the roof.

He could almost feel his blood pumping through his body. A horrible smell hung in the air, almost making him gag. He switched on the light on his phone, and shone it at the dark lump.

It was a body.

Cameron gasped and shuffled closer. He was lying on his side, facing the wall, wearing only a pair of shorts. His hair was matted, and his frame was so emaciated that Cameron was pretty sure that he was dead. He fell to his knees, and hesitantly reached out his shaking hand to touch Dalcian's shoulder.

Dalcian flinched, and raised his hand weakly to protect himself. Cameron jumped and almost had a heart attack. *HE'S ALIVE!!*

"Dalcian?" Cameron whispered, his voice hoarse.

Dalcian cowered, but didn't say anything. He was clutching his Yogi bear to his chest. Cameron touched him again gently.

"It's ok, baby, I'm not going to hurt you. It's me, Cameron. I've found you," he blubbered.

He gently rolled Dalcian onto his back, and their eyes locked for a split second; the untold horrors, fear, and pain reflected in his eyes.

Dalcian fainted. Cameron scooped him up gently from the floor and hugged him for a moment, then carefully carried him back downstairs. He hurried back through the lounge and kitchen to the front door with Roger following, and back into the sunshine.

"HELP!" he yelled as loud as he could. "I FOUND HIM!"

Two ambulance officers sprang into action and pulled a gurney from the back of the ambulance, and hurried towards Cameron. He met them halfway across the driveway, and laid Dalcian down gently. Everything became a blur as Cameron focused all of his attention on Dalcian and the ambos, and shut out everything else around him.

"Bloody hell, this guy doesn't look so good," one of the ambos announced. "Corey, go and call Meek for help, he needs urgent care."

"Righto, Gaz." Corey disappeared around the side of the ambulance.

"Can you give him food and drink?" Cameron asked.

"Not until he sees a doctor," Gaz said firmly. "I just need you to step back from the patient for me. Thanks, mate."

Cameron picked up Roger and Yogi, and hovered around anxiously as the ambo hooked Dalcian up to a heart rate monitor and did what he had to do.

"They're sending the Flying Doctors," Corey said as he reappeared. "They will fly the patient to hospital in Perth. We need to transport him down the road and wait for them. We've got just under an hour."

"I'm coming with him," Cameron declared.

"We only allow family to travel with the patient," Corey said.

"I am family," Cameron said. He looked around to ensure he wasn't overheard. "I have spent three years of my life searching for him since he was abducted. I'm not losing him again."

He pulled out his phone and showed them one of the few photos he had of him and Dalcian together, looking happy, without any cares in the world.

"In that case, you're welcome to come along," Corey nodded. "You can help us clear the runway."

"Thanks. I'll just go and get my bag."

Cameron made his way back towards Bo's car to fetch his bag and jacket. He hadn't noticed the arrival of a divisional van; he vaguely registered two TRG officers escorting Richard towards it. As Cameron started to reach for the door handle, a loud shout followed by a gunshot made him freeze. The rear passenger window of the police car shattered into a thousand pieces not far from his head; Cameron recoiled and covered his face with his hands instinctively. A volley of gunshots fired, and when Cameron finally dared to look, he saw Richard collapse onto the ground.

Dead.

* * *

Cameron was more than shaken up by Richard's final attempt to torture Dalcian's existence; a suicidal attempt to snatch an assault rifle from one of the TRG troops and shoot Cameron led to him being pumped full of bullets. The anger and resentment coursed through Cameron's veins; not only had that man robbed Dalcian of his childhood, three years of his life, and his mother's life, but he had probably robbed him of ever receiving closure and seeing him sentenced by justice.

The flight to Perth was surreal. Cameron sat in a seat towards the front of the aircraft, holding Roger as his emotions finally escaped their prison. Tears, strong nicotine cravings and a panic attack later, he felt drained and overwhelmed, and promised himself to call his therapist once he had a chance. Thankfully, Roger kept him grounded and had helped to pull him out of the darkness that was hovering.

From his seat, all he could see was Dalcian's feet as the doctor and nurses worked on stabilising him. Cameron overheard the doctor talking to a dietary specialist on the satellite phone, talking about refeeding syndrome and IV dosages. Cameron had no idea what it all meant.

It wasn't until just before the plane started its decent that the doctor took a seat opposite Cameron with a serious look on his face.

"How is he?" Cameron asked quickly.

"He's stable for the moment," the doctor replied. "He

is severely malnourished and dehydrated, so I have started him on a very low dose of fluids intravenously which will gradually be increased. We've placed him in an induced coma for a little while to keep him calm while his body heals. We also suspect his right hip is fractured. We did an ultrasound, but he'll need an x-ray to confirm, and possibly surgery when we reach the hospital."

"Is he going to be ok?" Cameron managed.

"That will depend on a number of things, but the specialists should be able to give you more information when he's at the hospital. I've already called ahead, we've secured a bed in Intensive Care so he'll be monitored around the clock." The doctor paused for a second, then smiled. "When we land, you'll be transported with him straight to the hospital. Once you arrive, the patient will be taken for tests and prepped for ICU. You won't be allowed in with him until he is settled in, which may take a few hours at least."

"What am I supposed to do, then?" Cameron asked.

"I always recommend family to use this time to organise a hotel room, get a bite to eat, have a shower or whatever, so that you're fresh and rested when you're allowed in. There are several hotels a short walk away. The ICU nurse will call you when you can go in."

"Alright. Thanks so much, Doc."

The small aircraft landed smoothly on the runway and finally screeched to a halt. Cameron was deeply impressed by not only the PC-12 aircraft, but how the Royal Flying Doctor Service had handled the flight and Dalcian's care. The aircraft really was a flying ICU ward, and he knew had they not come when they did, Dalcian's health would have deteriorated quickly in the harsh outback.

Dalcian was lowered to the tarmac by a special lift in the side of the plane, and loaded into the back of a waiting ambulance. One of the ambos turned and eyed Cameron with a smile.

"Hi darl, I'm Louise. What's your name?" she asked.

"I'm Cameron, and this little guy is Roger," he replied.

"Aww, hello Roger! Ok, that's your seat there. Make sure you strap yourself in, and keep your seatbelt on at all times." She pointed at a fixed seat next to the stretcher.

Cameron wordlessly climbed in and buckled up. Louise pulled the door shut and sat up near Dalcian's head.

"Let's roll."

The hospital was a hive of activity as the ambulance pulled into the driveway of the emergency department. Cameron stood to one side and watched as Dalcian was whisked away inside. He desperately wanted to go with him, but Louise had echoed the doctor's instructions, and told him to go and find a hotel instead. A loud rumble escaped from his belly, bringing him back to the present. He looked at his phone; it was almost 13:00.

"Are you hungry?" Cameron asked.

Roger looked up at him and wagged his tail as though to say 'yes'.

"Come on, let's go and get some lunch. You deserve a special dinner today."

24

The Intensive Care waiting area was a small open room lined by banks of hard plastic seats, joined together in lots of four. A low coffee table sat in the middle, loaded with all sorts of magazines, and a few children's picture books. A small TV was mounted in the corner, though it was on mute with captions enabled. The beige walls and echoey halls made the place feel more like a morgue than a place of treatment.

Next to the waiting area, opposite the large double-doors of the ward, was a small room with a recliner, TV, and a private toilet. Cameron figured it was for those who didn't want to leave their loved ones while they were in ICU.

Cameron sat against the wall that allowed him to see the entrance to the ward, tapping his fingers on the plastic arm of the seat. Roger was curled up on his lap, asleep. His fur was still damp from his bath in the hotel room, but it was much softer to touch, and he no longer smelt like a farm dog.

Cameron had changed his dirty business shirt and tie for a basic navy tee with 'I ❤ Perth', and a matching hoodie that lay on top of his backpack. A tacky souvenir store near the hospital had saved him from needing to venture too far away.

He pulled out his phone and dialled Sarah's number. After a dozen rings, though, Cameron sighed and hung up. *That's odd. I guess she must be busy.* He tapped out a message instead.

```
CAMERON: Hi, mate. Just letting
you know I've been trying to call.
Everything went as well as it could,
I'm at the Perth Hospital waiting see
him in ICU. I won't know much until
I get in there, been waiting for the
call for almost 5 hours. I'll try and
call you later. Love you x
```

He hit send on the message, and as he was about to pocket the phone, it started vibrating in his hand. It was an unknown number; with shaking fingers, he answered the call.

"Hello?"

"Hello. This is Mary, the ICU nurse. Am I speaking with Cameron Greenwood?"

"Yes, that's me," Cameron replied. His heart started beating faster.

"Oh, good. I have you listed as spouse and contact for Dalcian Lang…"

"How is he?" Cameron interrupted.

"Oh, he's been stabilised and has been settled into the ward. I was calling to say that you're welcome to come and visit him," Mary replied.

"Oh, good. I'm already here in the waiting room," Cameron breathed.

"Ok. Go to the double-doors, and you'll see an intercom on the wall. Press the button, and I'll buzz you in. See you in a moment."

Cameron hung up and switched his phone into flight

mode. He placed Roger on the floor and stretched, then snatched his bag and hoodie and hurried to the intercom. As soon as he pressed the buzzer, he heard the door click, and he pushed it open.

He was in a short hallway, much the same as the hall outside. A nurse was walking towards him, and fixed him with a smile when their eyes locked.

"Hi Cameron, I'm Mary."

"Hi," Cameron replied.

"Er, we don't allow dogs in here," she said, eyeing Roger.

"He's a registered assistance dog," Cameron said quickly. He pulled his wallet from his pocket and fished out his ID card.

Mary glanced at the card, then smiled and handed it back.

"Sorry about that. I'm not familiar with MindDog, but the codes are right so you can bring him in. So long as he's clean and well behaved."

"He's the best dog you'll ever meet," Cameron assured her.

"Good. This way."

At the end of the hall, the walls gave way to curtains which shielded the patients from view. Mary led Cameron to the right, and stopped at a desk facing the first bed. He glanced along the row of cubicles; there were four that he could see, and on the other side of the hall, just the one bed. In the middle of the ward were an admin area and patient restrooms, and more beds on the other side of the room. It reminded him of a rectangular donut.

Mary pulled a clipboard off her desk, then gestured to a comfy looking armchair next to the bed. Cameron felt the all-too-familiar churn of his stomach, and swallowed as he tiptoed along the side of the bed. He hadn't been able to get a good look at Dalcian since he placed him on the gurney all those hours ago.

Dalcian's face was pale, and he looked peaceful, except for the breathing tube coming from his mouth. He was hooked up to all sorts of machines and drips. Cameron stood staring at him, hardly believing his eyes. Without a word, he pulled the chair closer to the bed and sat awkwardly, his eyes not leaving Dalcian.

"We are currently reintroducing him to fluids intravenously, and feeding him TPN via a PICC line. The quantities are being closely monitored as his body adjusts and learns how to process the nutrients again," she explained, pointing at some of the equipment. "His body has already been reacting positively to the TPN which is what we want."

"When will he wake up?" Cameron asked.

"We're keeping him in the induced coma for a few days while his body absorbs the nutrients and gets stronger. If he was awake right now, the tubes and pain would have him very stressed and uncomfortable, so we want to make sure he can breathe by himself before we remove the tube and wake him up."

"Ok."

"Now, we found a fracture in his right hip, which has undergone surgery. He will have daily physio to help with the recovery process," Mary explained.

"How could he have broken it?" Cameron asked. His head felt clouded, and he shook it to try and clear his brain.

"Any number of ways. Given his frail and malnourished state, a simple fall is all it could take. With regular physio, he should heal up fine. The physiotherapist will be here early tomorrow morning for his first session."

"How can they do physio if he's in a coma?" Cameron asked.

"The patient doesn't need to be awake for it. The physios move his limbs and do the exercises for him." Mary fluffed up Dalcian's pillow and checked a few of the lines protruding from his body.

"Can — can he hear us?" Cameron asked.

"It's possible," she replied. "Some patients have woken up and recall things that were said around them. Go ahead and talk to him, give him some encouragement and let him know that you care about him. Don't be afraid."

Cameron reached out and nervously took Dalcian's hand. It was cold and bony; he gave it a soft squeeze, then reached up with his other hand and gently brushed the hair away from his eyes. He looked much cleaner than when Cameron found him, and smelt cleaner too; he could have smelt like an open sewer and Cameron still wouldn't have cared.

"I've missed you so much," he said softly. A stray tear escaped from the corner of his eye and ran down his cheek. He stood up and kissed his forehead gently. "I need you to get better. These three years have been a nightmare, and I can't go on any longer without you by my side."

Cameron had no idea how long he sat there, holding Dalcian's hand and watching him breathe in and out with help from the ventilator. He paid no attention to the rest of the ward; all he cared about was his boy. He thought back over the last twenty-four hours, astounded by everything that had happened since the sketchbook landed in his hands.

He knew he should feel some sort of happiness or emotion, but the great emotional strain he had been under since he opened the parcel had seemed to take its toll. He yawned deeply and massaged his throbbing temples; as though his body were trying to punish him, a strong nicotine craving reared its ugly head, making him groan.

A gentle hand on his shoulder made him jump; he looked up to see Mary smiling at him.

"Sorry to disturb you. Dalcian's sister is here to see him."

"His sister?" Cameron asked, confused.

"Yeah, she just called via the intercom. Would you like me to let her in?" Mary asked.

"Er — ok."

Since when does he have a sister?! I can't cope with much more today, I haven't even processed everything yet, he thought.

The sound of footsteps walking along the hall on the other side of the curtain drew his attention away from Dalcian, and he looked up to see who was claiming to be his sister. With a soft gasp, Cameron sprang out of his chair and hurled himself into her arms.

"I got here as soon as I could, hon." Sarah squeezed Cameron tightly. "How's things?"

"He's alive and will heal," Cameron said. "Come and have a seat."

Sarah approached Dalcian on the other side of the bed, and planted a big kiss on his forehead.

"We've all been worried about you, hon," she said. "We've missed you. Don't worry, we're all here by your side."

Cameron stretched and sat back in his chair. Sarah helped herself to a spare seat and sat next to Cameron.

"Where's Roger?" she asked.

"He's right here." Cameron reached down and picked him up, then held him out so Sarah could pet him. She was the only person he permitted to interact with him while wearing his work vest.

"Aww, hello Roger. Did you miss me?" Sarah shoved her face into Roger's and let him lick her nose.

"I think he did. He's been on one hell of an adventure," Cameron said. "He's been such a great travelling companion."

"I'm glad you didn't come over here all alone," she said. "Has he looked after you?"

"He has. I couldn't have made it through these years,

let alone today, had it not been for Roger. I love him so much." Cameron kissed Roger's head and sat him back on the floor where he was supposed to stay.

"And he loves you too. Now, you need to fill me in on what happened today, and why there is a crowd of media camped downstairs at the entrance to the hospital."

"They're not, are they?" Cameron groaned.

"They are. This is much bigger than when he was abducted. Worry about that later, though. I want to know how he was found and rescued."

* * *

Over the next few days, Cameron didn't leave Dalcian's side, except when asked to during treatment, or to take Roger for a walk to relieve himself. He spent the first few nights in the small room across from the ward with Roger, while Sarah stayed in the hotel. Thankfully, she brought Cameron some spare clothes to change into.

By Wednesday, Cameron was so exhausted he headed back to the hotel, and crashed into bed by 20:30. It wasn't until Sarah shook him roughly the next morning that he woke with a start.

"What time is it?" he grumbled.

"It's 09:00. Get up get up, they're going to start waking him up today."

Sarah pulled back the covers, making Cameron flinch. He was sprawled across the single bed in nothing but his jocks.

"Gee, thanks," he grumbled. He rolled onto his back and rubbed his eyes. "What time are we allowed in?"

"10:00. He has physio first, then they're removing the breathing tube. They're changing him from IV feeding to enteral or something like that." Sarah sat on the other single bed with Roger's ball.

"I'll just have a quick shower first," Cameron yawned.

*

Cameron's quick shower turned into a full body cleanse; the sudden realisation that he might get to see Dalcian awake sent his anxiety in overdrive, and he scrubbed every part of his body. Once he was finally done, he pulled on fresh tight jeans and a clean white business shirt that Sarah brought, brushed his hair, and looked at himself in the mirror. He had to admit, his body looked amazing compared to the last time Dalcian had seen it.

Getting into the hospital was a challenge. Cameron had forgotten all about the media, and by the time they realised their mistake, it was too late. A swarm of journalists surrounded him and Sarah, taking photos and shoving microphones in his face. Cameron swooped down and picked up Roger before he got trampled.

"Mr Greenwood! Can you tell us what happened?" "Mr Greenwood — Cameron! Is Dalcian alive?" "Can you comment on Dalcian Lang's condition?" "Are you and Dalcian going to get back together?"

Cameron and Sarah walked slowly through the crowd, not saying a word, until they reached the entrance. As the sliding doors opened, Cameron paused, then turned around and faced the crowd. The journalists all focused on him, as though waiting for him to speak.

"I just want to take a moment to thank New South Wales and Western Australia police, the Royal Flying Doctor Service, the Australian Navy, the ICU nurses, doctors, and surgeons. These people have all banded together and done an amazing job.

"I also wish to thank the few people around me who never gave up hope of finding him alive. He would not be alive and recovering today, had it not been for everyone involved in his search and rescue. So thank you, from the bottom of my heart.

"I will not comment on Dalcian's private medical information, or the methods the police used to rescue him. But I will say that the emergency services went above and beyond when it came to his care. The Royal Flying Doctor Service saves countless lives all over Australia every year, and the only way they are able to fund their services is through generous donations. Were it not for them, Dalcian probably wouldn't have made it. So if you have a spare $5 or $10, please dig deep and send them a donation, and help them to keep helping others.

"I will ask that you respect our privacy going forward. It has been three years of emotional torment for the both of us, and we will need lots of time to heal and reunite. Thank you."

As Cameron turned to go inside the hospital, the sound of clapping made him pause and turn. A group of curious onlookers had gathered nearby, and were applauding his speech. A few of the journalists were clapping too. Cameron waved and wiped a tear from the corner of his eye, and hurried inside.

"That was some speech," Sarah smirked.

"Hopefully they got what they needed and will piss off now." Cameron shrugged. "It may be the only way to thank all those people involved, so why not use the media for something positive for once?"

25

The ICU ward was its usual buzz of activity that morning. Mary was seated at her desk, and stood up with a smile when Cameron and Sarah approached.

"Morning! Sleep well?" she asked.

"I slept for just over twelve hours," Cameron confessed. "I'd still be asleep now if someone hadn't woke me up."

"I thought you'd want to be here for when Dalcian comes to," Sarah said defensively.

"I know. Thanks." Cameron grinned. "So, how long until he's awake? How does all of this work?"

"The anaesthetist dropped by after you left last night, and started the reversal process. Being that he was only under for a few days, he should come out of it sometime today or tomorrow, there's no telling how long it will take," Mary explained. "Usually as they're coming out, they hallucinate or have vivid dreams, so they may not make sense for a few hours or days. Everyone is different, so we'll just have to wait and see."

Cameron sat in his usual seat, and Sarah sat on the opposite side of the bed. As Cameron took Dalcian's hand, he squirmed in the bed for a moment, then went still again. The breathing tube had been removed, replaced by a simple oxygen mask, and his face looked a little pinker than it had in days.

"Morning, beautiful," Cameron said, squeezing his hand gently. To his surprise, Dalcian squeezed his hand back, just enough for Cameron to register. He stared at Dalcian in astonishment. "Can you hear me?"

Dalcian squeezed his hand again. Cameron felt the first burst of happiness that he'd felt in a long time. He looked at Sarah and nodded; she took his other hand, and he squirmed again.

"It's ok hon, It's me, Sarah, and Cameron. You're safe, we've got you."

Dalcian seemed to sigh, and he settled back down. After around forty-five minutes, his eyes shot open and darted around the room, and he started mumbling something. At first Cameron was afraid, but Mary calmly approached the bed and took Dalcian's hand from Sarah.

"Hello, Dalcian. Can you hear me?" she asked. "Squeeze my hand if you do — good boy. I'm going to ask you some questions, and I want you to squeeze my hand once for yes, twice for no. Understand?"

Cameron watched as she asked a series of questions: "Can you breathe ok?" "Are you in any pain?" "Do you know where you are?" She seemed satisfied with his responses.

"He's doing well," she said quietly to Cameron. "He'll be in and out all day, but he'll become more alert each time."

It was a long exhausting day watching Dalcian float in and out of consciousness. Cameron only left his side to take Roger for walks, and use the loo himself. Around 16:00, Mary's phone rang on her desk. She spoke quietly for a moment, then hung up.

"I need to ask you to leave for an hour. We've got a few tests to run," she said.

"Alright," Cameron said reluctantly.

"It's only an hour. He'll be fine." Mary smiled.

"We'll go and get coffee. See you soon." Sarah stood up and gestured to Cameron.

He stood up and kissed Dalcian on the forehead. His eyes flickered open, and locked onto Cameron's.

"Hello, you," Cameron said softly. "We're just popping downstairs to get a coffee while the doctors take you for tests. We'll be here when you get back, ok?"

Dalcian looked like his mind was miles away. Cameron kissed him again.

"See you soon, baby."

The cafeteria was a wide room with large windows that let in copious amounts of natural light. It was more like a food court; there were four different restaurants offering Asian cuisine, a salad bar, a rotisserie, and a sushi place. Cameron picked out two sushi rolls and ordered a coffee, then sat at a table waiting for Sarah.

As he took a bite of his sushi, he flicked off flight mode and sat his phone on the table. He hadn't switched it off flight mode for a few days, and got a surprise as his phone started buzzing on the table with an influx of messages.

"Is someone calling you?" Sarah asked from behind.

"No, they're messages," Cameron replied.

"That's a lot of messages. I wonder what's going on back home?" She sat down at the table with her coffee and a baked potato.

Once his phone settled down, he picked it up and started scrolling through the messages. It wasn't long before he'd teared up from all the messages of love and support.

```
BILL: You owe me a scotch lol. Nah,
just kidding. So glad he's ok, I'll
drop by when you're back on the job.
Take care, mate.
```

KRISTY: Oh my god, I just saw you on
the news! I had no idea that you were
in Perth, but I'm so glad you found
him! When you two feel up to it, come
over for dinner. Be it a month or
year away, whenever you're ready. I'm
here if you want to talk. <3

CANDICE: I'm so happy for you Cam!
Don't worry about work, I've declined
a few assignments already and have
sent a few subbies on some easy
cases. I'm holding the fort down,
take as long as you need.

BRUCE: Hey mate! Glad to see you
found your man! Let's catch up soon
for some beers at the pub, my shout.

GRAHAM: Holy shit mate, you found
him! I'm so happy for you. I have big
news, but it can wait until you're
ready to hear it. I hope you're still
hiring…

JAKE: Jesus fuck, he's alive!!
Sending you both kisses and hugs from
the both of us. Can't wait to see you
two and finally meet him! Xx

BRAYDEN: I just saw you on the news.
I'm so sorry for being a jerk. I just
wanted to say that I'm so happy for
you. Maybe when you guys get back to
Sydney, we can all catch up? And no,
I don't have an ulterior motive.

SOPHIA: Mama Mia Cameron darling! You
are looking so handsome now! You had
better come and see us sometime soon.
Much love to you both darling xox

JILL: OH MY GOD YOU FOUND HIM!!
You're forgiven for not showing for
soup kitchen on Sunday. I expect
Dalcian to be back at work next
Monday! (Just kidding) Give him my
love please!

There were so many more, and the thought of replying to each and every message was overwhelming. The outpouring of messages made him feel loved and supported; the friends he had made over the last few years had all been amazing, and he could not have made it without them.

"Are you ok, hon?" Sarah asked.

"Yeah. Just overwhelmed, that's all. Take a look at these."

He handed her his phone, and sat eating his sushi in silence.

"How nice. I wonder what Graham's up to now," Sarah mused.

"I don't think I'll call him just yet," Cameron said. "Let's let him squirm for a few days. I've got more important things to think about."

"Are you sure you're ok?" Sarah pressed.

"No. I'm dying for a smoke, and want to get back upstairs to Dalcian," Cameron admitted. "It's also kind of hit me just how far I've come. When I left Paul, I had nothing except for a few clothes and my uniforms. Had I not met Dalcian, my life would have been so different today; who knows, I probably would have crashed and burned. But I didn't. I now have more money than I can spend, I have friends, a business, and absolute control of my life. Not to mention my adopted family. You and Ron are like my brother and sister. I guess I just have a lot to process, that's all."

"You've been through a huge ordeal, especially with the scale of the rescue mission and being shot at," Sarah nodded.

"I know. I'll call my therapist and book some sessions when I can. But first, I'm going back upstairs to see how the centre of my universe is going, because like I said, without him, I wouldn't be here right now."

* * *

Dalcian was sitting more upright when they were let back in, and the mask had been removed from his face. Apart from the thin tubes in his nose, his face was unobstructed. His eyes were closed when Cameron took his seat, but as soon as he touched his hand, Dalcian woke up and looked slowly around the room.

"Where's your boyfriend?" Dalcian slurred. His voice was raspy, no louder than a whisper.

"Huh?" Cameron was caught off-guard.

"You have a new boyfriend now. I heard you talking about how much you love him."

Cameron and Sarah exchanged glances; this was not how he had expected their first conversation to go.

"I haven't so much as looked at another man since you left," Cameron said.

"Bullshit."

A feeling of dread crept from Cameron's throat and made its way to his gut. He had never heard Dalcian swear before either.

"Are you talking about Roger?" Sarah interrupted.

"Yeah, that's him." Dalcian managed a frown.

Cameron breathed a sigh of relief.

"Yes, I love Roger, but he's not my boyfriend," he said. "I think you'll love him too."

"The only way I made it through *hell* was by believing that you loved me. When I sent my sketchbook and you didn't come, I figured you'd just given up on me and moved on. I should have just shot myself years ago." Dalcian scrunched his eyes closed. "You can go and get back to your lives now."

Cameron couldn't believe his ears, and his heart gave a lurch when he realised the extra torture Dalcian must have gone through. He reached down and picked up Roger; after a quick glance to ensure Mary wasn't looking, he placed the pooch on the bed.

Roger licked Dalcian's hand, making him flinch. His eyes shot open again, and landed on the dog. As though guided by his special abilities, Roger took a few steps up the bed and started licking Dalcian's face. Cameron quickly pulled him back to the vicinity of Dalcian's hand.

"Meet Roger," Cameron said pointedly.

"*That's* Roger?" Dalcian seemed unsure.

"Yes."

"Why didn't you come?" Dalcian asked. A lone tear made its way down his cheek. "Uncle Trevor sent it weeks ago. I thought the clues would be easy for you to figure out."

"The parcel was sent to two other houses before it got to me. The package was hard to trace, but we got there. The day it came, I was on a plane that afternoon."

Dalcian still looked dubious. He was looking at Roger and petting him gently. Cameron slipped his hand into his bag and pulled out his folder.

"I never stopped searching. Here's an entire folder dedicated to finding you. Different theories, different leads, but they all led to dead ends." He flicked through the pages, holding it up for him to see.

Dalcian looked confused, but lost for words.

"I'm just popping out to the loo," Sarah said. She winked at Cameron. "Back soon."

Once she was gone, Cameron looked back at Dalcian. He was still looking at Roger, though his anger seemed to be replaced by sadness.

"I never got the opportunity to say it before our lives were turned upside down, but I sure as hell am not going to miss the opportunity again. You need to know that I loved you then, and I have never stopped loving you. I have not lived a day of my life since you were taken from me."

When Dalcian looked up, there were tears in his eyes. He tried to wipe them away, but the catheter got in the way. Cameron reached out and tenderly wiped them for him.

"Every day of that nightmare, I wondered if you were thinking about me. I wondered if you'd look for me, or if you had just moved on. Then I thought back to the time we had together, and was pretty sure that you loved me too. I held on to that hope. It's all that kept me alive."

Cameron unbuttoned his shirt and pulled the left side open, revealing half of his muscly chest. Tattooed on his left pec was the comic that Dalcian had drawn for his birthday. Dalcian's eyes widened, then swept over the rest of his body.

"You've been going to the gym," he noted. "You look amazing."

"I had to make myself look like the way you'd been drawing me." Cameron shrugged and buttoned his shirt back up.

Dalcian lifted his arm weakly and beckoned Cameron closer.

"Come here," he said.

Cameron obeyed and moved closer, unsure what Dalcian wanted from him. Dalcian hooked his finger into the gap between two buttons, and tugged him closer, until their faces were just millimetres apart. Before he knew it, their lips were pressed together in a kiss.

"I love you Yogi Bear, and I never stopped loving you."

"I love you too, Boo-Boo. Now that I have you back, can I keep you officially? I can't live another day without you being mine."

Dalcian kissed him again, this time deeper and with more tongue. Cameron felt his knees turning to jelly, and the butterflies that he thought were dead sprang to life. It had been so long, too long. For the first time in years, he finally saw a happy future ahead of him, not one clouded in doubt and darkness. It would take time for them both to heal, but together, they could do anything.

Part Four

March 23rd, 2025

26

Cameron stood watching the stage, fiddling with the folds of his suit and readjusting the elastic band on his arm that held his security license in place. He couldn't believe that after six years, he was back in a security uniform. The sound of the crowd was deafening; thousands of nerds, geeks and cosplayers all packed into the exhibition hall in Melbourne, to see their favourite artists.

"I can't believe I'm finally at a Comic'Spo," Dalcian said.

He seemed a little nervous, but excited at the same time.

"I can't believe I'm back in this uniform," Cameron sighed. "Oh look, the lights are dimming. It's almost time."

"Where are the others?" Dalcian asked.

"Sarah's down there, and Graham's just over there," Cameron replied calmly.

A hush fell across the crowd, and a loud voice boomed from the speakers.

"Welcome to Comic'Spo Melbourne 2025! We have three amazing artists here to answer your questions. Introducing Miko-Chan, author and illustrator of the *Little Lulu* anime comic series."

The crowd clapped and a few cheered as Miko-Chan

glided onto the stage and sat on one of three seats. She was dressed like an anime character from her comics.

"Next, please welcome Benjamin Smith, one of the artists from—"

"I like his work, but that guy is an arsehole," Dalcian whispered. "I will never buy any of the comics he's associated with."

Cameron eyed the second person; he walked with an air of arrogance, though he received a slightly louder round of applause than the previous person.

"All clear here, Cam," Sarah's voice said in his ear.

"All clear here too," Graham echoed. *"Let's do this."*

"Roger that. Stand by." Cameron gave a signal, and the announcer started to call the final artist.

"And finally, the one you've all waited two hot days for. The author and illustrator of the award-winning series, *Beneath the Grandstand,* I bring you Mister Dalcian Lang!"

The crowd erupted into a deafening round of cheers and applause. Dalcian hobbled onto the stage, using his cane for support, and paused to wave and blow kisses at his fans. As he took his seat, he looked back at Cameron and smiled, then turned to face the crowd.

Cameron stood on the edge of the stage, scanning the wings and steps for any idiots who wanted their moment of fame. He crossed his arms and listened to the Q&A panel; most of the questions were aimed at Dalcian, which he answered honestly and full of confidence. He was beaming, living his dream.

During the years that Dalcian had spent in captivity with his father, he had written and drawn a series of comics in the new sketchbook that they'd bought on that fateful day. Cameron had helped him to find an agent, and given his exposure in the media, his comics were published and an immediate success.

The road to recovery hadn't been easy. Months of rehabilitation and physio, dietician appointments, and therapy sessions left Dalcian exhausted and moody for a while. The nature of his hip injury left him with a permanent limp that often caused him pain.

Dalcian never went back to work for Jill. After a few months of catching up with friends and reintegrating into the world, it became apparent that the painful memories in Sydney were too much for Dalcian to cope with, and instead, they settled in country Victoria.

Cameron opened a new branch of Greenwood & Sullivan in Melbourne, and spent his days picking and choosing his cases. With Graham managing the Sydney branch, Sarah was able to travel between the two and visit regularly. Cameron's favourite job, though, was acting as Dalcian's private bodyguard during events.

When Dalcian wasn't drawing and busy being famous, he spent his time helping homeless people connect to various support services. He was in the process of starting his own charity to help fund self-sustainable microhomes. Cameron was so proud of how far he had come, from the shy boy who lived on the streets, to the confident, successful, young man.

"Did the events in the comics really happen?" someone asked, drawing Cameron's attention back to the event.

"They are all 100% real," Dalcian replied. "Some names were changed, of course, and I did use creative license to make them a bit more fun and interesting, but the core story really did happen."

A mumble went through the crowd.

"I have a question for Dalcian," another fan from the audience stood up and pointed. "Is that the security guard from your comics?"

Dalcian turned and looked at Cameron, then back at his fan.

"After what I've been through, do you really think I would entrust my safety to anyone else?" Dalcian asked. "That's him, the love of my life."

Cameron stood rooted to the spot, well aware that hundreds of pairs of eyes were looking him up and down. He wished that he had stayed inside the wings, out of sight.

"What's the colour of red?" Sarah laughed.

"I can see it from over here," Graham chortled.

"Oh, fuck you two. You're just jealous you don't have a famous hot boyfriend who's incredibly rich now." Cameron's face broke into a grin.

He looked back at Dalcian; he was beckoning to Cameron to walk out to him. Cameron shook his head, and attempted to retreat into the shadows.

"Come and say hi, Cameron," Dalcian said into the microphone.

Cameron sighed and walked stiffly onto the stage. Dalcian stood up and limped next to him.

"This is Cameron, the inspiration behind all of my comics so far. He has saved my life more than once, and yes, he is the security guard from the comics. All of those stories were pretty much our story so far."

The crowd started clapping and cheering. Cameron turned and started to walk off stage, but a collective gasp rippled through the audience. Cameron spun back around to see Dalcian on the ground.

"Are you alright?" Cameron demanded, rushing to his aid and forgetting the crowd.

Dalcian grinned and held the microphone to his lips.

"If it weren't for you, I wouldn't be here today, and none of these amazing people would have derived so much pleasure from reading about our adventures. You are my world, my superhero. Will you marry me?"

Cameron brought his hands to his mouth. Dalcian was holding up a small box with a ring in it. He looked out at the crowd, then back at Dalcian.

"I guess you just saved me from having to ask you the same question tonight." Cameron pulled a small box from his pocket and held it up so the crowd could see. "Of course I'll marry you."

The crowd went absolutely wild. Cameron helped Dalcian to his feet, and they shared an epic public display of affection. The cheers were deafening. Cameron didn't care if the event was over or not; he scooped Dalcian into his arms, and carried him off stage.

"Oh my god, you two! Get a room!" Sarah chortled.

Cameron reached up and plucked the earpiece from his ear.

"I am so going to get you for that," he said as they made it into the privacy of a small change room backstage.

"Are you going to lock me up and throw away the key?" Dalcian smirked.

"No, there has been enough of that in your life. I'm going to get you for real."

Cameron grabbed his arm and started tickling him in all of his most sensitive spots. Dalcian squealed, until Cameron finally stopped.

"Ok ok, now we're even," Dalcian gasped. "Now, come here and kiss me."

Everything they had been through together had only brought them even closer together. As Cameron kissed him with everything he had, he knew one thing for certain. Whether they lived in a fancy two-storey house, or beneath the grandstand, nothing could ever destroy the love that had grown between them.

Remember, you are not alone. Mental health is just as important, real, and valid, as your physical health. If you need to talk to someone in that moment of darkness, reach out to family or a friend, or call Lifeline. Lifeline was there for me in my darkest hour.

Lifeline: 13 11 14

To make a donation to the Royal Flying Doctor Service, please visit:
https://www.flyingdoctor.org.au/donate/

Also by Amy-Alex Campbell

The Miscreant
#1 The Lowest Realm
#2 The Darkest Realm (forthcoming)

The Marsden Park Series
A Catalogue of Disaster
Beneath the Grandstand

For additional content, visit amyalexcampbell.com

Acknowledgments

I would like to take a moment to thank everyone who has helped me along this publishing journey. My beta readers, editor, proofreader, and my amazing support network of friends and family.
And most of all, I want to thank you, my dear readers.